AN INNOCENT BYSTANDER

AN INNOCENT BYSTANDER

H. R. PERCY

MACMILLAN OF CANADA
A DIVISION OF CANADA PUBLISHING CORPORATION
TORONTO, ONTARIO, CANADA

The author wishes to thank the Canada Council for making possible the time and the travel required for the writing of this book. Thanks are also due to Ants Reigo, who sowed the seed, and to Carlos Barba, maestro bueno y paciente.

Canadian Cataloguing in Publication Data
Percy, H. R. (Herbert Roland), date.
    An innocent bystander

ISBN 0-7715-9464-X

I. Title.

PS8581.E64155   1989   C813'.54   C89-094322-2
PR9199.3.P47155   1989

Design: David Montle
Jacket illustration by: Sarah Jane English

Macmillan of Canada
A Division of Canada Publishing Corporation
Toronto, Ontatio, Canada

Printed in Canada

For Jon and Roger

There is no such thing as an innocent bystander.

Johann Most, nineteenth-century German terrorist

AN INNOCENT BYSTANDER

PART ONE

I

I saw myself as such: an idler who chanced to see things happen. Not that there was anything in the aspect of that afternoon to engender thoughts of guilt or innocence. All that came afterwards. If there was guilt at all, it had another cause and was of a different nature. Guilt of an innocent sort, I venture to say. There I was but six months married and with a roving eye already. Pure coincidence that the leg my idle glance caressed was that of the General's English nanny. I hardly knew the woman. Not well enough, at any rate, to account for the feeling—a mere inkling at most—as I stood leaning on the little stone bridge and feeling otherwise deeply content, that my marriage might have been a mistake.

Only in long, sour retrospect is there anything arresting or portentous about the scene, as in a movie, calling for premonitory music. Beethoven's Fifth, perhaps, or a few repeated bars of the Warsaw Concerto. As it is, memory remains mute, as though deafened by anticipation of the noise to come. Imagination must conjure the sounds I know, from many earlier visits, must have been there. I could always ask Paulo, who has a prodigious memory for detail, but he is too deaf to hear the question, let alone the medley of small sounds woven into the fabric of that fateful afternoon. The raucous entreaty of the ducks, for example, swimming in the shadow I cast upon the water. Or the dulcimer drip of water falling from rocks of different heights and at different intervals, so that they play a melody that endures for forty-five seconds before repeating itself. Nina timed it the day we were married, when we went there for the pictures.

What I remember most clearly, apart from the legs and the heat—one never forgets the heat—is the manifest peace of the place. Perhaps it is this above all that imbues the scene with significance: the unwitting apprehension, the sense of ill omen one always has when things are too peaceful in this cursed country. Even the plaza seems subdued, the beggars less aggressive, the pedlars less strident. I could see them beyond the park fence, caged behind the tall railings with gold tips glinting in the sun like the spears of some superbly drilled army. I can see them, but memory cannot hear them. I can see the cruelly disfigured one-legged man by the bake shop, holding up a big red handkerchief like a signal of distress. And the skinny brown arms of the sandal-maker waving, antennae of some predatory insect, as he offers to measure the feet, and to pay for the privilege by cutting the corns, of the less beggarly passers-by. If he once latches onto your foot you are lost. Snared, you look down upon his snooker-ball scalp with its garland of curly grey hair. He looks up at you with big, brimming eyes from where he squats on the sidewalk. It is a wonder he can see with such eyes to carry on his intricate trade. They swim in their gummy sockets, drowning, crying for help. They look up at you with harrowing entreaty as his hands explore and flatter your foot. His whole being becomes centred in this reverent appraisal. You feel like making him a gift of it, his hands are so covetous. He merely wants your money, but you feel he wants your feet, your most eligible, most desirable feet. You feel privileged to be in the presence of this connoisseur of feet. You yearn for his favour, this dried-up cricket of a man who has no feet of his own. He lost his feet—but that is another story, for another time. This day he is catechizing the foot of a tall, scholarly man with long hair—a poet *manqué*, perhaps, sunk in the slough of academe—who is turned in my direction and is perhaps idly watching me, as I am watching him. I am feeding the ducks and he is being fitted for a pair of sandals he does not need, which will be ready for fitting in two hours, or would be in the normal course of things. CHULETAS! Around his

2

leonine head the light of the chop-house sign throbs feebly against the sultry glare of the afternoon.

Beyond, perched cross-legged on the lip of the fountain, which has dried up because of the drought, plump Clementina offers her body for hire. There are no takers. It would be too much like an *auto-da-fé*, frying there upon that quenchless pyre of flesh. An immense straw hat floats a foot or so above her shoulders, deep shadow filling the space between the saucy dip of the hat brim and the dazzle of sun on her sweat-bedewed bosom. You cannot tell which way she is looking, or at what. One leg is crossed upon the other, her white shoe arching up and down. Her cinnamon thighs pout with promise. Her legs are impressive, but less so than those of Eliza, the English nanny.

Eliza comes slowly, lingering in the shade of the moss-draped oak trees, delaying, since she is a little early, the moment when she must wheel the carriage into the cruel sunshine. She passes, perhaps exchanges some small pleasantry with, a bundle of feminine apparel—a veritable rag-bag—on a bench beside the playground. Eliza likes to share her happiness, even with such a one as this, who seems not so much to wear as to be enmeshed in swathes and flounces of grimy calico, from which blooms improbably, as if drawing sustenance from that fertile corruption, a lacy yellow parasol. Too well brought up to stare is our Eliza. (She has become ours as a work of art passes into the public domain, not because we possess it but because it possesses us. Not ours, alas, in any other sense.)

Not so the man who saunters some thirty paces behind. He is not good at sauntering, it seems to me; at feigning interest, for example, in the big hibiscus flowers that smother the bush he passes. Perhaps it is just that he does not seem the flower-fancying sort. It is hard to believe, too, that he is truly fascinated by the antics of the kindergarten set: the two small boys who leap in long parabolas from the swings to attack a would-be interloper; or the little girl whose dental brace explodes with sunlight as she swoops, her frilly dress opening like a parachute to show her tiny pink pudendum. But when he slows to stare at the sunshade-toting person on

3

the bench his interest is unmistakably genuine. Downright unmannerly, in fact. He takes the dowdy apparition in from the soles of the once-white shoes to the tip of the jaunty parasol; over the thick ankles and the long unseasonable skirt, which even from my remoteness I can tell is none too clean; over the small protuberant stomach and the heavy bosom sagging upon it in a blouse festooned with black and mangy-looking lace; up to the dowager-duchess hat from which impends a tattered mantilla pressed into service as a veil.

The object of this shameless scrutiny, embarrassed or incensed, snatches up an overstuffed handbag, stands, puts down the parasol, shakes like a wet dog to dispose the many folds of drapery, and goes across the path to the door marked DAMAS: a progress less than elegant. The man watches the door for some moments with the solicitude of a waiting lover, then with evident reluctance turns to follow the nanny. I have seen him before, this jackal, no doubt because I watch Eliza a lot. I resent him. Perhaps I am a little jealous, although I suppose he is only there to ensure her safety.

I often wonder what became of him. He deserved, at any rate, a fate no less harsh than mine.

He could not have had a memorable face. Eyes that darted about a lot in the band of shadow under the brim of his beat-up sombrero, which he wore tilted forward in a comical fashion. In fact he comes back to me now as a somewhat comical figure. Inept. A sort of pantaloon in that farcical situation.

Of course in truth it wasn't that way at all. But in my memory (or is it my dream?) there he always is, darting eyes and droopy moustache, mooching along behind Eliza, a necessary adjunct, assiduously pretending he is not. He wants to be mistaken for one like me, an innocent looker-on, but he lacks the one essential quality: innocence. He lacks another: inconspicuousness. (Although even I, apparently, was not inconspicuous enough.) Why, I remember asking myself, does he wear tight pants like a toreador with—I could swear—a sizeable codpiece, which must embarrass the ladies walking their poodles, and a ruffled and embroidered shirt—blouse—that embarrasses the men?

Eliza stops at the second bench along, surprising her shadow, who stops also. He bends as if to tie his shoe, but

4

in those pants it is not easy. Instead, he straightens up and looks about him, feigning enjoyment of the day, swivelling slowly on his tall heels, as though in a sudden access of *joie de vivre*, taking in the flowers, the birds, the trees, the children. And me.

I fiddle with my small pocket radio to dispel the sense of furtiveness one always has when idle under scrutiny; the feeling that prompts one to smile at policemen and take an urgent interest in out-of-date bus schedules. The very feeling, in fact, with which Codpiece himself must be painfully familiar.

Eliza bends over the baby carriage, peering in at the General's son and heir, debating, perhaps, whether to pick him up. She is facing away from me. Her bending distracts me from the ducks. I light a cigarette.

Ah, a cigarette!

Eliza looks at her watch and decides to sit down. She reaches out to the carriage and rocks it gently as though to quiet the child, but the cry, if there is one, is silenced, like all the other memories of that day. All the other sounds, except one. Codpiece looks at me and I look at Eliza. She wears a short, pale-blue dress that in some indefinable way suggests a uniform. Not too well filled out aloft, I am reminded, seeing her thus, side on. Indeed, she is decidedly skinny. But Eliza is lovely. Not beautiful, lovely, in the sense of inspiring love. Her loveliness is an incurable ache within me. Her lack of *embonpoint* merely adds poignancy to my remembrance, as it added piquancy to my illicit ardour. All the women of my life have been ample, to use an expression of my father's: big-boned and bountifully fleshed out. Beguiling as feather beds.

Leaning on the parapet, unable to tune in the station on which, according to Juan Moreno, the winner of the Nobel prize is to be announced today, watching the ducks disperse now that my largesse is exhausted, I find myself analysing the attraction Eliza has for me, almost as though I must justify myself to her jackal, who has wandered a little off the path, watching me still. Her eyes, for one thing. Brown. Large. At once gentle and compelling. Shy but not fugitive. Brown, of course, gives no idea. There are hints of gold, a tawny lambency. If you hold her gaze long enough, you feel the start

5

of a melting at your heart's core. And yet they are not beautiful, those eyes. Nothing is beautiful about Eliza except her legs. And, I suppose, her soul, which seems to open to you when she offers her face. An odd way of putting it, perhaps, but that's exactly what appears to happen. Nina, with a menaced woman's prescience, calls it ogling, but it's nothing like that, nothing forward or immodest. Eliza visibly fights, in fact, a painful shyness. It is part of her appeal. For in this shy offering of her face to be looked upon there is a great trusting. One is touched, complimented, instantly protective of such vulnerability. All this is in some strange way related to the way her face is framed by her hair, which plunges straight down and then curves a little inward under her chin. The hair is lustrous but its styling is severe; its colour is neither blonde nor brown, but it contains her face lovingly, like a calyx. This day she is wearing a white straw hat, and there is something about the tilt of it, about the way its curve converges upon the long, pale line of her throat, that deeply moves and is destined to haunt me.

And her hands. Lace-gloved and at this distance no more than two tiny white moths, one of which leaves the handle of the carriage and wings down to join the other in her lap. They evoke for me the image of themselves as I saw them first when I was waiting for Nina one lunch-time in the Café del Rey.

I should mention here, lest these pages should ever be produced in evidence (of what?), that we did not patronize the Café del Rey, Nina and I, because its name had made it a symbol and gathering-place for those critics of the regime who were too cowardly to declare themselves with bombs and bullets. The decadent and self-serving dictator of the earlier regime, who became known satirically as "The King", may have been in some sense the antithesis of what we have now, but I for one did not hanker for the return of *that* sort of freedom. No, we used the Café del Rey because José makes the best tortillas in town, and in any case it is only a short stroll from the university. It had also a certain sentimental attraction. Nina and I first met there.

And then, Eliza.

We did not actually meet there, but I was sitting by José's revolting plastic palm tree when I first saw her, first looked all-unsuspecting into her eyes and had that fearful sense of destiny. Perhaps José's espresso has aphrodisiac properties. Anyway, I am sipping my coffee and studying the picture of the General's young wife and her new baby, enlarged, perhaps intentionally, until it has become a little fuzzy at the edges, taking on a certain spectral quality, an unearthly fragility reminiscent of the age-dimmed Madonna above the altar in the Cathedral of San Pedro. The selfsame pose. My eye runs along the headline and keeps going, responsive to some subtle compulsion; and there, amputated by the paper's edge, are Eliza's hands. Even her hands, although arresting, are not beautiful. Their movement is, though. And, in some strange way, their stillness. In any case, with time—so very little time—her hands, like all the other aspects of her person, begin to impose their own criteria of beauty. When I see them first they are breaking bread. A symbolic act, it is true, but why this instant fascination? All around me other hands are breaking bread and I do not spare them a glance. Their pallor, perhaps? She always wears gloves when she is out. They lie beside her now on the table, tiny white exuviae of lace. The hands are small, slender, and—shy?

Eliza prompted so many of these small surprising epithets.

Exposed, the hands look. I've not yet seen them gloved, but my first impression is of their shy nakedness. And as if they are aware of my attention they become suddenly still, alert, as though about to scuttle away somewhere, into hiding. Even before I lower the paper I know she is watching me, like a wild creature sensing a strangeness on the wind.

The eyes are narrowed at first, then they flare wide. Apprehensive? Defiant? Impossible to tell. I know only that I feel clumsy, menacing. I sometimes imagine now that that look of hers signalled dread, but of course that is foolish. I hold her gaze and smile, wanting her to smile back. But perhaps what I think is a smile on my own face is to her a frightening grimace. Before I can read an answer in her eyes they are eclipsed by the ample body of Nina, my bride-to-be.

II

"Room-mates again, my Gaspar."

He was only a smell to me at first, coming into this dark hole from the blinding sunshine. The place itself stank. Since then I have had more than enough time to disentwine the many odours that roost in this place, haunt it like the spirits of those who have gone before. Piss predominates, except when the bucket and its vicinity have been lately sanctified with Lysol. Yes, the wall as well. My room-mate's legendary marksmanship seems to abandon him at such close range.

Let me catalogue the smells, pick them out from the pot-pourri (how apt the phrase, in its literal sense!) like the instruments in a symphony.

The ghosts of bygone bowel movements, clearly distinguishable in density and bouquet from Paulo's frequent farts. But who can blame him, on a diet of half-baked beans?

Damp. The stone walls glisten with it, sometimes audibly drip. No discernible rhythm, however, comparable to that of the droplets in the park, which maybe Nina at this very moment listens to as she weeps and wonders where I am. Here, only the excruciating suspense in the long night's silence, waiting for the next thunderous "plop!". The walls glisten. One wonders where they find the light.

Mildew. My shoes grow fuzzy as peaches overnight.

Rot. What there can be in this stone sarcophagus to rot, except perhaps our own foul bodies, remains a mystery. Maybe a rat has crawled in through the window and died in a corner somewhere.

The dissimilar musty stench of our blankets, Paulo's and mine, unwashed ever since I came here. How long, in God's name, is that?

The waft of decaying vegetation from outside, very strong when the wind is southerly or thereabouts but faintly lingering always, as poor Eliza's perfume lingered, maybe only in my imagination.

But distinct from all that, as the lout helped me in with his government-issue boot and slammed the door, was the intrinsic smell of Paulo himself, his own substantive stink, a pong with personality, tangible, mobile in the midst of what I have since mapped out as a navigable landscape of odours.

The only source of occasional fresh air is the window. We call it "the window", but in truth it is only a roughly rectangular hole where one small block of stone was left out by the builder, not much above the level of the ground outside, I judge, because at times I can just see the tips of tall brown grass waving when there is a breeze, which is not often in the daytime. Some nights the wind off the mountains thrusts into the cell like an icy lance. Inside, this hole is more than a foot above my head, and I can see out of it only by balancing precariously on the bucket when it is returned, empty and briefly overcome, by the halfwit. The view is not worth the effort. A few feet from the hole there rises a slope of rocks, but whether it is the start of a mountain or merely a cartload dumped there for some forgotten building project there is no way of knowing. Nevertheless, I like to look out every day, to breathe something faintly resembling fresh air and to imagine that I have still some tenuous link with the world beyond.

What is more important about the window is that it lets in a little light; not much, most of the time, but each day at a certain hour a beam of sunlight spears our gloom, very narrow at first, for the wall is thick and the hole not big enough to pass anything larger than a cat. Which it did a few days ago. A poor wet, bedraggled creature seeking shelter from a passing shower. I fed it a few of my beans.

As the sun aligns itself with the hole, the beam fattens and changes shape, sweeping slowly across the wall from Paulo's side to mine. Ah, yes, we have defined our territories, Paulo and I. The window marks the boundary on one side, the bucket on the other, so that we may share equally its convenience and its fragrance. When the sunbeam waxes fat, the bucket stands enshrined in its radiance like a chalice. But by the time it reaches Tit Rock, about three feet above my bed, the beam has shrunk down to a tiny triangle. Then it becomes a mere thread and vanishes. The gloom that returns to the cell is more than physical. A daily death.

On the day of my arrival the sunbeam had reached its diminishing-triangle phase. Afterwards I could recall it slanting across the stinking cesspit of Erebus I found myself cast into, but to my sun-blind eyes it offered no illumination. It had almost vanished before my dilating pupils began to distinguish shapes. One of which was Paulo. Curiosity, at that moment, was not uppermost among my emotions. I was full of a sick fear. In fact, if anything has come out of all my days and nights of vertiginous thought it is the conviction that I have been such a reasonable man all my life only because I am a coward. But even in the midst of my cowardly confusion and self-pity I was aware of the contrast between the figure I faintly discerned and the image conjured up by the words "my Gaspar".

He always called me that. Not, however, in such a voice. It was the words I recognized, not the voice. The words and a certain satirical way of bringing them out, as one might say "my lord" to one of anything but lordly pretension. The voice that came out of the darkness was gravelly and uncouth; the sort of voice you might hear insulting the lower-town whores as the men coming off shift at the copper mine head for the bars.

The voice that went with the image, on the other hand, was urbane, some even said effeminate: upper-crust *latino-americano* with a Cambridge veneer. The image was—or had seemed—tall, well-muscled from much tennis, but slight. I recalled an aristocratic cut of the jib with a certain disquieting hauteur, offset to some extent by a mop of curly hair in calculated disarray. Whereas the shape that now spoke, no more at first than a piece of the dark that moved, seemed squat, immensely broad, neckless. Had he not spoken, I was distraught enough to imagine that I had been thrown into the den of some untamed ape or gorilla. Except that he was hairless. All that differentiated him from the surrounding darkness was the faintest imaginable sheen of sweaty roundnesses where the last vestige of departing light found a bald expanse of scalp, a shoulder, a beefy thigh. Hairless, that is, except for the chin.

But it was not until the window vouchsafed the next day's ration of light that I saw with any clarity the details of his person. That daily beam of light, of hope, a blessing in so many ways, can also be a curse, a revealer of things best left unseen. Like Paulo's beard. Imagine it if you can. I could look up and see it now, as I write, with the sunbeam already on the wane, but I am more than content just to imagine it with you. Even that is enough to turn one's stomach.

The beans were especially bad today—the halfwit's turn to do the cooking. Several of the beans are still in Paulo's beard. So are the beans of yesteryear, along with liberal droolings of their juice. The beard reaches halfway to his navel, which winks above the waistband of his cut-off canvas trousers like a dark lascivious eye. The beard, with its petrified amalgam of bean juice and saliva, is as solid as the beard of our national hero Mateo Cannas de Utrera on his pedestal in the plaza. Lacking only the pigeon shit.

But that first day I only smelt it when he hugged me. I know its distinctive smell now because sometimes he bends over me as I write, but that first day it was only a smell among many: caries-tainted breath, chronic flatulence, polecat armpits, to name the more obvious.

He hugged me and said, "Within a week, my Gaspar, we shall want to kill each other, but now, this moment, only a woman could be more welcome."

I could have killed him right then. Him or anybody.

Even so, I was fool enough to think his hugging me was something that arose out of the ashes of that ancient friendship; some phoenix of affection, of nostalgia at least. I know better now. Sentiment of any sort is anathema to Paulo. Why he did hug me is something to wonder about, to be deduced perhaps only from intimate knowledge of his Satanic character, and I am fast acquiring that.

I try to find some inkling of this present odious Paulo in the young man who was once my superior in just about everything. All through the intervening years I remembered those first undergraduate days with the keenest pleasure. Or with despicable sentimentality, as Paulo would doubtless have it. We were not, of course, *compañeros de cuarto* in the strictest sense, as Paulo in his welcoming words suggested with such relish, but we faced each other across the narrow landing and our doors were always open. We seemed then to exist on a more exalted plane, to see everything more clearly, in a heightened hue. Our capacity for pleasure was infinite, our sensibilities sharp beyond belief. Our ambitions knew no bounds, but they demanded no immediate commitment. It was as though they awaited us somewhere already achieved, ready to be put on like graduation gowns when our shared voracity for learning and experience was satisfied and we "went down" like Olympians into the mortal world. All of which was intensified for me because Paulo was there to admire, to emulate, to rely on.

And now all that enchantment comes into question. Did Paulo cultivate me merely because we were two dagos together in a snobbish crowd of gringos? Did he play tennis with me in preference to more worthy opponents only to gloat over my discomfiture at my inevitable defeat? Did he wangle invitations for me to the estates of his "county" friends—the friends, that is, of his father the former ambassador—so that I would make a fool of myself for his secret pleasure, fumbling among the daunting array of cutlery, behaving with deference towards lackeys better dressed than I had ever been? If that sadistic streak was truly present in him then, many indeed must have been the opportunities I afforded him to gloat. How callow and uncouth I must have appeared beside Paulo, who spoke English as well as our public school companions. I, who had excelled at the language at school, won prizes and scholarships for my proficiency, now seldom came out with the appropriate word, and mispronounced it when I did. Not until I met Paulo did I become aware that I spoke my own language like a *campesino*.

Sometimes, writhing wakeful in an agony of discomfort, yet caught in the mesh of nightmare, I am borne back to those early Cambridge days, borne back with the same dread that possessed me when, under the muscular arm of my father, I was carried back to be beaten at the scene of some childhood crime. And then, through the sardonic eyes of my contemporaries, I see myself as a freakish appendage to the aristocratic Paulo, an exotic but slightly repulsive pet: "my Gaspar", as one might say "my chimpanzee" or "my bandicoot". In these half-waking dreams the cruel cynicism of my cell-mate is reflected back upon his youthful self, perceived and relished by everyone but me.

Yet surely it was not that way. I felt all too keenly the scathe of snobbery, but not from Paulo. He was all I could love and admire in a man, my exemplar in just about everything. Even when he stole my girl I accepted it with grace; with resignation at least, as one must accept such manifest acts of God. After all, how could anyone, even—especially— an *ingénue* like Martha, choose a lout like me in preference to Paulo? (His word for her, of course, *ingénue*.) Perhaps it was the same sort of innocence he found in her that attracted him to me, perceived in my case, however, as crass naïveté.

But for a time—all too short a time—she was my secret, sweet Martha.

III

Light comes. Barely enough to write by as yet, but I dare not miss a moment. Who know how many moments there may be? Paulo is sleeping, for which I am thankful. Although his drainpipe snore would break the concentration of a yogi, it is preferable to his waking presence. Awake, he can keep neither still nor silent. He prowls, he sits, he stands. If the bucket happens to be empty he upturns it and looks out of the window, cutting off my light; if it is not, he squats upon it in the attitude of Rodin's *Thinker* and holds forth from both ends. And he talks. He talks but he does not listen. Cannot. He lost his hearing in a "little bit of business" with a bomb, badly bungled. Not, of course, by him. To make him hear, I must shout so loud that the lout comes running and tells me to shut up or else. I shut up because I am by nature a submissive person (coward), even though reason tells me there are no teeth in that "or else". The lout is not entrusted with the key except at feeding and clean-out times, and, short of physical violence, how could he make my life more wretched?

If I wish to converse with Paulo, as opposed to being talked at by him, I must use my precious paper. This restricts my side of the dialogue to the times when there is enough light for his failing eyes to read what I write. But this is a recourse I use less and less. Paulo talks so much and with so little apparent regard for consequences—for surely these mouldering walls have ears?—that I have only to wait and he will tell me all I could possibly wish to know. And more. Ah, Martha!

And how, in this hell-hole, do I come by paper? And pencils? Well, short, almost unmanageable stubs which I sharpen laboriously on the wall. Long pencils are potential weapons. Indeed, it is something to ponder, this rare indulgence. It may well be that they (ah, the elusive, ubiquitous "they", who make cravens of us all!) indulge me in my scribbling as I tolerate Paulo's unceasing chatter, in the belief that, given enough time (pray God!), everything will out. Whatever, from their unimaginable point of view, "everything" may be. And of course it will. What do I have to hide? As for Paulo, I may add to their knowledge of his despicable deeds and his twisted personality, but nothing I write can alter his fate.

Who can fathom their motives in so readily furnishing me with these primitive tools of my trade? It suggests a subtlety such as our rulers seldom exhibit. They believe in the harpoon rather than the trout-fly. No, someone must have known the right words and the right ear to whisper them into. Who cares enough? Nina? Nina cares too much. Does she not? I have thought and dreamed and disoriented myself to the point at which there are no longer any such certainties. There I was, tripping through life in my egregious innocence like a child at play in a garden, only to find that the garden was a jungle of ravening beasts. Tigers do not discriminate between guilt and innocence. But Nina? I have gone over and over the recent past with the burning-glass of my suspicion until no person, no word, no silence or trivial gesture, is beyond doubt.

I say that Nina cares too much because her last concern would be for my need to write. My liberation she would fight for: is, presumably, fighting for at this very moment. Fighting shadows, however. First she must find among all those insouciant eyes one that betrays knowledge of my existence, one that does not become opaque at mention of us *ningunos*, this phantom army of nobodies. If Nina ever penetrates *that* smoke-screen, her first concern will be for my physical well-being. After that she will worry about an abstraction called justice, that delusion of the powerless. But pencil and paper to save my sanity? True, she was drawn to me by the lure of my all-too-modest celebrity, but she secretly despises my books because they make no money. She resents the time I devote to them. She could not resent it more if I spent those hours in the arms of a mistress. Which makes me think of Eliza. But that, alas, is pure fantasy.

But if not Nina, who? My colleagues at the university? Those who might have the right connections care nothing. Less than nothing. Those who do care, and who know what writing means to me, are more innocent than I am. Innocent, I mean, in the sense that they have no idea of the webs of intrigue they move among. As in one of those science fiction stories in which two worlds coexist in space, each unaware of the other, communication is given to but a special few: commutation to fewer yet. Not, for example, to such as Juan Moreno, who when drunk proclaims me more worthy of the Nobel prize than the great García. So loyal, so admirable, so naïve. Such plaudits, however, are less than flattering from one who after another drink or two will declare that draconianism is a threat only to the guilty. How could such a one suspect the presence of that coextensive world, much less know how to break into it? Or Rob Roy McAvity, that Caledonian anachronism washed up here by God knows what tides and cross-currents of inscrutable destiny, three or four centuries out of phase with his own history, let alone ours. Flaming red hair, shot-putter's shoulders, bagpiper's jowls, and arms that cry out for a claymore. He would tear this dungeon rock from mouldy rock. But first he would have to find it; a search that would take more subtlety than Rob could muster.

Ergo, I must have unknown friends. Or, I should say, "friends". Friends, enemies, it's all a matter of motives, is it not?

A sudden darkening of the cell shocks me out of my reverie. My heart for an instant quails, for in this place change is always for the worse. I wouldn't put it past them to seal off our only source of air and light. But it is only the cat. A young tabby with a white patch over one eye, very handsome, or would be if better fed. It stands looking in upon us doubtfully. I pick up my plate from the floor, empty save for the unsavoury bean-juice already congealing in the bottom. The cat leaps

15

down and approaches suspiciously. Treachery and mistrust are in the very air of this place. While it licks the plate I make bold to stroke it, but it draws away, obviously unaccustomed to any display of affection. When the plate is clean, it stands watching me for a few moments with yellow, dispassionate eyes, gives a faint cry to which I reply, "De nada," leaps for the window, and vanishes.

My cell-mate snores, stretched out like an effigy of himself upon a tomb. And there I catch my inkling of that other, younger Paulo. Some cruel parody. A tenuous, paradoxical likeness lies embalmed in that gross, near-naked body lying sunk in merciful sleep. Or is it mere antithesis that calls up the shade of Paulo as I saw him first? Coincidence of pose is surely not enough, so extreme the contrast: Adonis versus Caliban.

Yet there he lies in my remembrance, a locker full of life-buoys his catafalque. He is sunning himself on the first-class deck of the *Esmeralda*. The masts comb the cloudless sky in gentle arcs. The surly North Atlantic smiles for once, sparkling, almost Bahama blue. A tide of shadow from the starboard lifeboat creeps slowly up to Paulo and recedes, barely touching at first the spread fan of his hair, but soon its sharp edge rests across his neck, as if in fell omen. He lies there headless. Soon, I assume with satisfaction, the shadow will make him move. The only reason I notice him at all from my second-class exile is that he spoils my view of the shapely occupant of a deck-chair just beyond. She is daringly dressed (if "dressed" is the word for such provocative exposure), but Paulo's recumbent form truncates her in the most interesting places. I am about to turn and survey the talent on my own deck, where, unfortunately, the women have bourgeois inhibitions, when the girl gets up, stretches sleepily in a way that makes my swim trunks suddenly too tight, rounds up her paraphernalia, and walks away. I watch her out of sight. When I look back at Paulo, he is sitting up, watching me.

As if activated by that ancient image in my mind, this other Paulo wakes and sits up also, cursing quietly to himself and making loud smacking noises with his mouth to dispel the evil aftertaste of sleep. He, too, watches me. Surprisingly, he says nothing, but sits there mulling over some sleep-spawned memory of his own. I ignore him and escape back into my own dream.

I was quite prepared to hate him. In our world, affluence was power. Power was oppression. My own parents had struggled up laboriously from the slough of poverty, but had not yet forgotten how to curse the rich, and I had indigent cousins enough, God knows. But this well-heeled stranger gives me a polite and airy wave. Next day, a smile. Then a conspirator's wink the morning after, as he strolls the deck with the heavenly sunbather clinging to his arm.

Suddenly, after that, rain and chill misery, so that I see him no more until, burdened down with luggage and bemused by the jostling crowds at Liverpool Street Station, I hear a voice shout:

"Hello! You're Jesus, aren't you?"

He is leaning out of the first-class carriage window beckoning to me and shouting.

I stare up at him nonplussed, ready to be resentful. *More* resentful, that is. The lofty demeanour, the peremptory crook of his finger that had brought me scurrying over with the alacrity of a *peón*. And now this crazy question. Some tasteless esoteric joke? A trick to humiliate me in front of the idlers on the platform? It leaves me, at any rate, abashed to the point of speechlessness. The oft-swallowed bile of class hatred begins to rise.

Then he gives a great bellowing laugh.

"Aren't you for Jesus College?"

"Oh. Oh, yes."

"Well, better wriggle your arse, man. You'll get left behind."

To bear him out, the guard blows a piercing blast not four feet from my ear and shouts, "Orl abawd!"

"Here, hop in here with me. Glad of the company." He climbs down and grabs my luggage (having, I discover later, paid a porter handsomely to carry his own).

How often he told the story in the months to come, each time with a little more embellishment. "Colossal ego, our Gaspar. First time we met, he thought I had mistaken him for the Messiah." And always that loud, infectious laughter.

17

(He no longer laughs, Paulo. His lack of mirth is like an amputation. I cannot look at him without seeing the raw stump of his jocularity.)

So there I sit, on the edge of my seat, surveying the opulence of the first-class carriage, a hand in my pocket clenching my third-class ticket. The train moves jerkily out of its sooty, cavernous lair and gathers speed, rattling past endless rows of grimy back kitchens, acres of sooty yellow brick roofed with slate, bristling with blackened chimneys. Minuscule backyards walled like fortresses, harbouring beaten-up motor-bikes, shiny prams, tipped-over tricycles. Curled-up cats on the roofs of rickety sheds and obsolescent outdoor privies. Sagging lines of limp washing, leprous-grey with railway grime, reminiscent of the rows of pelts outside the shacks of Indians back home, as if whole families had been skinned and salted down. Rows of windows blinded by the sun, with lace-curtain cataracts. Except that in one, shaded by an iron stairway, I see a woman singing, holding a book in one hand and conducting with the other. She is naked but for a tasselled mortar-board and a giant cross that dangles down her belly. She has long hair and her breasts hang down like wineskins almost empty.

All this is somehow intrinsic to my earliest impressions of Paulo, to my memory of the way he won me over, filled as I was with apprehension about the future, uneasy and suspicious in his presence, depressed by the passing scene outside.

"So *this* is London!"

"Ah, no, my friend. This is just London's arsehole."

We plunge into a tunnel. Paulo raises his voice above the clatter. "Every city has one. Haven't you noticed Montevideo's? Rio's? Bogotá's?"

Knowing none of these places, I stare at my sullen reflection, hating his wealth, his urbanity, his airy cosmopolitanism. Cambridge, I tell myself, is not going to be easy for this bumpkin, this *palurdo*.

"What better place, after all, to run a railway?"

We erupt into sunshine. I glance at Paulo. He is staring down into a weedy backyard where a man in a yellowing undershirt squats among the parts of a rusty dismembered bicycle. In a deck-chair behind him a fat woman lies asleep in open-mouthed abandon. There is something unutterably depressing in this fleeting tableau.

"Art thou poor, yet hast thou golden slumbers?" Paulo intones, striking a histrionic pose.

Long after these people have been snatched into the past, I find myself pondering their squalid lives, the rancorous cohabitation proclaimed by the pathetic, profitless industry of the man and the sluttish insouciance of the woman. Slaves of circumstance, enduring their life of futility because there is no other. A malaise only too common in my own country but somehow shocking and obscene here, where I had anticipated some degree of old-world opulence, however faded.

Pondering, too, Paulo's strange words, which I take to be purely sardonic. It will be a long time before I encounter them in context, listen for the echo of their intonation against the background of the train's steady rhythm, and wonder if they hold a clue to some seething chasm underlying the surface of Paulo's easy gentility, some key to his subsequent behaviour and his outrageous destiny.

> *Art thou poor, yet hast thou golden slumbers?*
> *Oh sweet content!*
> *Art thou rich, yet is thy mind perplexed?*
> *Oh, punishment!*

First class. I note how smoothly the carriage rides compared to the bone-shaker that brought me from Southampton. How innocent the floor of chocolate wrappers, cigarette butts, and chewing-gum. How transparent the windows, inviting no puerile art or lewd graffiti. How voluptuous the plump green cushions after the jazzy red and black of the third class, biscuit-thin and threadbare from the boots of the unmoneyed multitude. I steal a shy glance at Paulo. First class personified. He starts from a reverie, smiles, and offers a cigarette from a silver case. Only then, after I have accepted the cigarette and offered a light from my penny book of matches, does it occur to me to say, "My name is Gaspar. Gaspar Sánchez Caramés."

He shows strong teeth through a trickle of smoke.

"I know."

Now that, in these latter days, would make a man uneasy, some stranger professing prior knowledge of his name. Especially when said with eyebrow-hints of knowing more. But those were less phrenetic days, and Paulo's smile belies his haughty countenance and sets me quickly at my ease. No hint, there, of any lurking danger.

Several seconds pass before he thinks to say, offhandedly, "I'm Paulo Martínez Alcina, of course."

IV

Tit Rock is all aglow. Paulo's eyes are upon it. Mine also. Still Paulo says nothing. He lies back, head pillowed in hands, elbows spread, so that in the deepening shadows at his end of the cell I catch eye-corner glimpses of a great black moth or monstrous bird. My own mind is full of aimless, fragmented thoughts. I wonder what images parade in Paulo's as he stares unblinking at the granite boob. Fond memories of Martha?

I imagine some horny apprentice mason sculpting out in secret the lineaments of that seductive roundness, tapping with his finicking fine-honed pecker at the saucy sauceless nipple that measures out my daylight, sundial fashion. Once when Paulo was asleep I succumbed to the fascination of that suggestive swell, imagining the stone Amazon immured within the wall; caressed it, flinched a little from its clammy hardness. It yielded a little in its socket of ancient adobe, prompting extravagant fantasies of escape.

Paulo, realist that he is, or, rather, anti-romantic, contends the rock simply split that way. God the sly pornographer. One wonders then what greater lecheries lurk in every wayside boulder, awaiting only the emancipation of the splitting wedge.

Martha's were somewhat bigger. Nina's, much. I'd sit on the bed and she would rest them on my shoulders until I sank and smothered in her fleshy fragrance. Eliza's? Never known. Only with difficulty and contrition imagined. I ache with reverence for her deficiency, fancying shyness even there, in the diffident thrust, the coy burgeoning. Modesty made flesh.

As a boy I used to dote with pious lust upon the peekaboo bosom of the Madonna in the plaster Nativity scene set up in the *plazoleta* between the boys' and girls' schools; the cleavage, so to speak, between the sexes.

Briefly I am back on that little stone bridge in the park, watching Eliza rise from the bench and saunter on, stroked by the dapples of shadow, out into the glare where her white straw hat is a pleasant pain upon the eye. The carriage wheels, one wobbling a little despite the recent repair, launch dazzling spears of brilliance as they turn.

This gives me pause. Did I really notice that slight flutter of the buckled wheel? Did it, indeed, even exist? Or is it merely a figment of my retrospective fancy, a sycophantic eagerness of the memory to accord with subsequent knowledge? A trivial question, but one with dread implications for a man in my predicament. If memory can play such involuntary tricks, can for the simple sport of it colour and shape the past to conform to present notions, what might it not do under compulsion? Or, as Paulo with all solemnity calls it, "catechism". If our recollection of events alters to accommodate a self-induced idea, is it such a great step to the acceptance of ideas posited by others? Godlike others, possessed of potent means of persuasion.

Godlike? Well, take it on the impassioned say-so of Paulo himself.

"A man (or a woman, they are the worst) who has had a pair of pliers on your toenails for a few minutes, or has done a little prospecting around your prostate with a hundred-volt electrode, takes on all the attributes of God. Wrath. Jealousy. Vengefulness. And grandeur. Let's not forget the grandeur, the omnipotence. To him, anything is possible. Anything your mind can encompass, shrunken as it is down to the ultimate shrivelled kernel of self. But, beyond all else, he is the fount of all mercy. From him, up there in the glory of his untortured heaven, all blessings flow. He is the only bestower of peace."

"Love?" I interrupted. He has a way of going on, Paulo. He read my lips. Or perhaps my mind.

"Ah, love above all. You are infinitely dear to him. Your abject helplessness is alone the source of his power. Without you he is nothing. He does not exist. No believers, no God." And much more along the same lines. I have yet to find a way of turning Paulo off. Your would-be redeemer, he thundered on, loves a cheerful giver, is no respecter of persons, first makes mad whom he would destroy, et cetera, *ad nauseam*.

I shut him out and groped back first to my gloomy train of speculation and then to the flow of memory that triggered it.

When a man breaks under interrogation, I was thinking, he exhibits at best weakness, at worst, cowardice. Such tends to be one's simplistic belief. But surely if you slip enough ideas and images into the mind while the body is otherwise engaged—ideas, moreover, which the beleaguered body devoutly wishes were true, however staunchly the mind at first rejects them—then, surely, the brain might be purged of mere actuality and made ready to receive a new perception of the past. To see the light. To be born again. The torturer's lie after long catechism becomes the victim's truth. By what canon shall such a man be condemned? I begin to sound like Paulo.

Whatever I may have noticed at the time, my mind's eye will insist on seeing that wheel, running the merest scintilla out of true, shooting its arrows of brilliance awry. Arrows of desire. Eliza leans a little to her work as the path slopes upward. The dress is short. The legs are long. The blue fabric, taut, ripples with the crescent shadows of her exertion. Beautiful to the point of pain is her motion in my beholder's eye. I have her there in slow motion, no motion, on the path up to the great iron gates of the *palacio*, to the dark tunnel of trees beyond. Above the trees, the painful éclat of the westering sun upon the bullet-proof windows. The flag on the central rotunda, proud emblem of the General's power, hangs dishrag-limp in the sultry air.

The jackal relinquishes me. I am not the killing or the kidnapping kind. My cowardice is so obvious on the outside, then? The jackal, I imagine, is disappointed. He glances back as the door marked DAMAS opens and the dowd comes forth, still fussing with arcane fastenings, squirming to find comfort within the unimaginable substrata of lingerie. The parasol blossoms. In its saffron shadow, the veil is twitched properly into place and the figure shuffles back to the bench to sit scratching voluptuously beneath the folds of drapery.

As if triggered by my thought, Paulo sits up and sets to clawing furiously at his incessant itch. He must have every parasite known to man, and a few known only to the devil. Nights, I hear him at it like a flea-demented—

Dog. The jackal, walking away from me, very much aware, I can tell, of his vulnerable back, is suddenly tense, gun hand at the hover as a big black Labrador comes bounding up to Eliza. Its owner is some yards off, heading her way. Eliza strokes the dog, but unaware of its blessedness it cocks its leg against the carriage wheel and circles away. The owner, a monkish-looking man, spreads deprecating hands that seem to say this is not a political statement, shouts "Lo siento" or some such thing. Eliza raises a dog-loving white lace hand in absolution.

Again I have that fleeting sense, not of *déjà vu*, exactly, but of a disturbing nostalgic apperception. You doubtless know the sensation. All your remote yesterdays spinning by in a blur like the drums of a one-armed bandit. Sudden stop, not so random as it seems. What comes up is woman, dog, white hand.

The woman is Martha, the dog, Rover, Pluto, Spot, whatever. The white hand, fresh from the flour bin, is raised, not moving but somehow seeming to beckon, arresting my headlong progress down the stony lane.

The scene is sharp and still in my mind, its details exact but its colours muted, a little unreal, magical, caught by a photographer with artistic pretensions. The afternoon sun is mellow upon the old stone house that stands alone in the landscape. Its façade, every dint and crevice accentuated by shadows, reminds me of an aging face. The tiny front garden is boxed in by a low ashlar wall topped with curlicues of wrought iron. Pillars stand at the corners like bullet-headed sentries. I wonder now as I wondered then what manner of incursion, in this remote and peaceful place, the wall was intended to repel. Or what confine. Not the dog, certainly. It is over the fence in one effortless bound, hackles up, teeth bared. All bluster, however. The tail is wagging in contradiction. By the time I get to the gate we are the best of friends.

The garden is full of flowers, crammed with flowers, as if by an over-zealous undertaker. Only afterwards, when I am leaving, am I struck by the oddity of this thought. And waist-deep in this turbulence of colour stands Martha, whose name, it seems to me now, I already know, having fallen in love with her likeness in a somewhat tawdry tableau in Sister María-José's Sunday School.

As I approach she sweeps away a strand of hair with the back of her hand, leaving a smear of flour across her face. It seals my fate, that clown-like smudge. Who can explain such things? Who can account for that lurch of the heart because . . .

The face itself is frightened. Appalled, rather, like a child's hurt by someone loved and trusted. The eyes are wide, brown, like Eliza's I become aware in this long, painful retrospect. I never consciously noticed their colour at the time. Not even when I looked into them later so ardently and at such very close quarters. But it is the dab of flour, remembered, that makes unbearable the childlike pathos of that softly beautiful face.

Without a word she goes in, the invitation to follow implicit in the way she turns. A large butterfly of polka-dot silk perches upon her nape. When I untie it, the long tawny hair falls in great profusion about her shoulders. But that is afterwards. Now, she crosses the room and stands by the immense kitchen range that casts a ruddy flicker over the table where she has been kneading a big ball of dough. The deep print of her fingers is still upon it. A man in late middle age sits in a rocking-chair beside the stove, staring at the fire, feet thrust out to the warmth. A cherry pipe clutched in one hand sends up a thin, expiring wisp of smoke. He is a big man, with the look of a farm labourer. His leather jerkin is shiny black and supple with age, his corduroy trousers are cinched with string below the knee. Shiny also his balding head, dome-like and a little comical. His discarded boots are under the stove.

When I turn from him I find Martha with her two fists, one white, one pink (both, I note, ringless), pressed hard against her mouth. Watching me watching the man. And it is what I see in her eyes, not anything I have observed about him, that tells me he is dead.

Then she is sobbing on my shoulder and my arm is about her, lightly, doubtfully, my hand crooked about the thick sheaf of hair at her back. Not a word has passed between us. I wait, smelling the salty vapours of her grief, feeling the fever of her cheek although it is inches away.

"I'm so sorry," I think I hear.

A subtle interplay between us, then. A slight, apologetic drawing away on her part that repudiates itself; the merest tightening of my hold, an almost-pressure that says, "You are welcome to the comfort but please do not fancy anything forward or disrespectful in it."

Over her shoulder, the dead man. On the floor beside him the book whose falling doubtless alerted her to his dying. *No One Writes to the Colonel*. No farm labourer, this.

"Your father?"

"Uncle."

Speaking breaks the spell. She pulls away.

"I came to him when I was five." Her sobs are gentler now. I see in her eyes the remembered pain of that childhood trauma, the sudden upsurge of memories she cannot share with a stranger, with a dark-skinned stranger who, she will never tire of teasing me later, "speaks so funny". Tears have etched a delta across the dab of flour on her face. She lifts her pinafore to wipe it away.

"I didn't know what to do. There's no one."

Never shall I forget the desolation of that "no one".

What to do, I decide, remembering an uncle of my own who did occasional odd (very odd, on occasion) jobs for an undertaker (*El Embalsamador*, a Dickensian character, one of the terrors of my childhood, who lurked, hunch-backed and shifty-eyed, in a smelly den full of coffins), is to lay the body out somewhere. It was Uncle Javier's only joke: "Sitting corpses don't bury well." So, having verified that Martha's uncle is indeed beyond recall, I steel myself to hoist him up and dispose him decently upon a sofa in the sitting-room. By which time I have found out there is no telephone. The doctor is three or four miles away, an old friend of her uncle who, she says, once summoned will take care of everything.

Maybe if I would be so good as to stay with *him* she could go on her bicycle. I have an unseemly thought about the futility of anyone staying with *him*, but somehow the request does not seem absurd. In any case she is plainly in no fit state to ride a bicycle, even on those quiet country roads.

So there I am a few minutes later wheeling the bike down the lane to the road. A very feminine affair with skirt-guard, embroidered basket, teddy-bear mascot on the handlebars. There is no one to witness how clumsily I mount. It has been a long time. I pedal away.

And, perhaps mercifully, here in the cell the light begins to fail before I can record the details of my humiliation before the townsfolk, wobbling down the small main street with my skirt-guard and my teddy bear.

"What's with you?" Paulo wants to know as my scribbling falters. As though, watching me Sphinx-like as he so often does, he has witnessed it all.

V

Considering the intimacy of those first moments—perhaps, indeed, because of it—things progress slowly and with great delicacy between us, my Martha and me.

Oh, yes, even as I pedal my shameful mount through wood-lands carpeted with bluebells and heady with the smell of English spring, even as two days later I steal shy glances at her across her uncle's open grave, she is my Martha. She knows it, too. But our very circumspection lends spice and intensity to our wooing. Wooing. How perfectly that good old-fashioned word characterizes the contrast between our scrupulously proper conduct and the smoulder of passion we were both aware of, augmenting beneath: I so eager to comfort, so solicitous of her grief yet so fearful of presuming upon it; she, desperately desiring the solace of my tenderness yet appalled at the thought of seeming too forward.

Paulo, the bastard, had no such scruples.

Look well upon him, my Martha, wherever you are. Witness what he has become, the godlike charmer who stole you from me. O Lord, if there is one iota of rationality underlying the chaos and corruption of the universe, one hint of reparation for all the wrongs of humanity, suffer her to look down upon her ravisher here in his ultimate degradation.

Not, I suppose, that I myself am any sight, now, to gladden the heart of such a one as she was then, during that enchanted time when she was still my secret. My jealous secret, although I dreamed, paradoxically, of showing her off to Paulo. But he was away most of that summer, cementing relationships of his own. What seems surprising to me now, though, is that although he wrote long letters (which, incidentally, I still have) about the two persons who had re-entered his life, I studiously refrained from any mention of Martha in my replies, even though I found it difficult to think of anything else. His garrulity and my reticence perhaps stemmed from a similar uneasy prescience: he at some subconscious level sensing a radical diversion in the path of his destiny; I foreseeing but refusing to countenance the inevitable.

When I say that I still have Paulo's letters of that period I am of course succumbing to the recurrent delusion that I still exist, in any practical sense. I *had* those letters, up until the last day that I had any possessions at all. They would have been seized in the inevitable ransacking of my house the day I disappeared. I know only too well how it works: a "burglary" by a gang of thugs with an uncanny nose for premises thus involuntarily vacated. Thugs who could not, if caught at their work, be linked to their political masters. Well, apart from those old letters, they wouldn't have found anything remotely incriminating.

I imagine Nina returning late, delighted with her day's shopping, to find . . .

But I digress, squandering precious daylight. Such dark thoughts repeatedly defeat my attempts to draw a little comfort from the memory of Martha. Or, for that matter, of anything pleasant from my past.

Another letter I kept all those years was the one from Dr. Loman, hand-delivered to the college by a neighbour's boy the day after my meeting with Martha. It was prompted by concern for the niece of his old friend, and by his feeling that she needed distraction from her brooding sorrow. The note "took the liberty", I recall, of informing me of the funeral arrangements for the late Simon Mallory. "Miss Mallory," it went on to say, "will be profoundly grateful for your attendance." If there was a certain presumption in that "will", I was in no mood to balk at it. A perceptive one, James Loman. He knew I would hesitate to show up at the funeral uninvited. He also divined, I suspect, the immediate bond that had been forged between Martha and me, and the barrier of diffidence resulting from those first moments of premature intimacy.

So there she stands in my memory, stark in her blackness against the sunlit dazzle of a white-blossomed hawthorn ("years a-growing", I declared in one of the puerile poems I wrote in those days, simply to produce that splendid cameo of her mourning figure against its sun-silvered whiteness).

The voice of the vicar seems intrinsic to the afternoon, like the hum of bees around the blossoming hawthorn. Martha calls it "may", and when we stand here again two Sundays hence its petals will drift down upon us like snow. Or confetti, she blurts out, and blushes furiously.

Others were at the funeral, of course, including the amiable doctor and his dusky-skinned wife, but in the half-dream, half-memory, that so often attends my drifting down to sleep, we are alone, Martha and I, in an immense contained emptiness, she with her spread wings of whiteness, leaning down a little to watch the brass embellishments of the casket flare valedictory in the sunlight. I see their radiance given back by the tears that pearl the lower border of the veil behind which her face lurks remote, unreal. As the casket winks one last time and vanishes she sways forward, seems about to fall with it through the bottom of the world. Sometimes I start awake with a cry, loud enough to pierce even Paulo's deafness. He quakes and curses. The lout bellows from somewhere above, "Cállate la trompa!" But when we have obediently shut up and all is still again I try to savour the memory to its end. Martha steadies herself. A hand steals up to lift aside the veil, and somewhere beneath the smother of her grief lies the earnest of a smile for me. I have a sense of immense privilege, seeing her weeping face, as if I had been allowed to look upon her nakedness.

But that is a blessing I dare not even dream of as we stand there beside the grave, a favour that is not to be conferred for a long time yet. And once, once only, before I lose her.

VI

"Of course," I hear in memory as the first faint promise of daylight comes, prompting me to take up my pencil.

There was cause for pride, I suppose, in merely *being* a Martínez, at least from Paulo's point of view, but the arrogance and presumption implicit in "I'm Paulo Martínez Alcina, of course" were sufficient, as we sped along in the train the day we met, to silence me for a long time.

Paulo. Even his baptismal name had a lofty ring. Why not Pablo, like my father? Ancient Portuguese blood, he would tell me later, from the time of the Braganzas. Awesome indeed to me, who could not name my great-grandparents.

As the slummy backyards gave way gradually to the gardens of semi-detached suburbia and then to dairy herds and hay-stacks, I sat staring sullenly out the window, swallowing the bile of my resentment. Paulo, riffling through *The Times*, tossing me tidbits of news and rhetorical questions about people and events I had never heard of, inflamed my anger by being unaware of it. Or was he? He had a disconcerting way, I soon discovered, of making off-hand remarks that had an uncanny relevance to my own silent thoughts.

"Ha!" he responded the other day when I recalled these disquieting insights of his, risking the lout's wrath to shout the question at him. "Ha, of course. That's why I'm so good at my business."

Something to consider there: the fact that he regards his multifarious activities as "business".

"Yes," he went on when the lout had gone back to his lair, "if you're going to be a good hunter you have to be able to second-guess your prey."

It was a name he was known by for a time, by the peasants of certain parts of his own country: *El Cazador*. The Hunter. Later he would become known as The Scourge. At every phase of his bloody career there was some fanciful *nom de guerre* to mask his true identity.

"You've got to put yourself in the place of the hunted. Think as he thinks. Feel as he feels. What would I do in his situation? you have to ask yourself. How far would I be capable of cold calculation and to what extent swayed by emotion, by panic? You have to feel his anger, his hatred, his fear. Slip into his skin. *Be* him." I saw only the changing shape of his shadow in the blackness, felt rather than saw the wry face of his mockery as he went on, "It's the one thing our two trades have in common, is it not? By the blood of the saints, Gaspar, I swear I'd have made a better novelist than you." Which I'd be willing to concede. Paulo has always been a superb story-teller, even from those first Cambridge days, when he evoked so vividly the scenes and events of his childhood that it some-times seems more real to me than my own. But there is one deficiency in that vaunted empathy of his, one nagging ques-tion to which there seems to be no satisfactory answer. How was he, the hunter, able to switch off the ultra-sensitivity he boasted of as soon as the object of it ceased to be merely a quarry, an abstraction, and became a victim? How could he share all the apprehended terrors of the hunted yet remain aloof from their realization?

He laughed at that. Answered it although I had not spoken.

"You, my friend, make victims of *your* puppets; create them, in fact, to *be* victims, so you can have your sadistic way with them. You and God both. Yet do I see you weep for them? Do you choose to stay your hand?

"Besides, your cruelty benefits no one, achieves nothing, advances no cause. The beneficiaries of your violence, like its victims, are no more than shadows on the flimsy curtain of your brain. Now *my* 'victims', as you unimaginatively call them, are instruments of a purpose. Unwitting instruments sometimes, reluctant sometimes, refractory even, kicking against the pricks of my higher intention. But I at least invest their mortality with meaning, allot them—against their will— a place in the pattern of history, in the working out of the grand design. In truth, amigo, they are no more victims than the woman who dies in childbirth is a victim, or the man who drowns while saving another from the same fate. They are privileged, did they but know it, to die in the furtherance of a great cause, instead of being overtaken by some futile, ignominious end, some pathetic accident. Walking under a bus, catching the clap from a whore."

"But they are innocent people, for Christ's sake!"

Some stray ghost of bygone daylight finds his eyes, cold and feral as a cat's in the darkness.

"Innocent of what? What the hell does innocence have to do with anything? There *are* no innocents, only insouciants. The rats and mice we murder are innocent also, are they not? But what is their innocence against their inconvenience in our sanitary scheme of things? And I wager you would not say no to a slice of innocent roast pig, did our hosts so far forget themselves."

He ranted on, but my attention wandered. It is not conducive to concentration, this life we lead. Especially when fantasies of roasted pig have been evoked. The mere words act so powerfully upon one's bean-abused stomach as to induce a mild delirium. The ghosts of appetizing odours conquer the prevailing stench and creep seductively into the nostrils. Against a background of Andean heaps of Brussels sprouts and roast potatoes one sees the succulent slices curl away from the carving knife and fall into the steaming ooze of gravy. Teeth anticipate the salty crunch of crackling. Vitals seized up since God-knows-when for lack of lubrication lust and gurgle for the fatty flow. Saliva moistens the lips, bedews the beard . . .

The carving-knife is wielded with surgical skill by Dr. Loman: a wry thought that does not dull my youthful appetite. Nor does the ache of love I feel for Martha sitting demure beside the doctor's wife. Smiling. Wanly, as yet, her eyes briefly offered and then away, enlarging only a little upon that graveside promise. The doctor beams at us both, pleased with the progress of his therapy. It is not flattering, perhaps, to be prescribed as poultice upon her grief, as prophylactic against her despondency. But there is flattery enough in that fugitive smile of hers to more than save my self-esteem. Anyway, I believe the doctor really likes me. His welcoming hand on my shoulder was fatherly. "My young friend Gaspar Sánchez Caramés," he said, introducing me. His wife clasped both my hands and seemed about to gather me to her stately bosom. Her eyes, however, were upon Martha. She, too, prizes me for my therapeutic value. But now, as she proffers her Yorkshire pudding, lighter than a cloud, I lift embarrassed eyes from the dark arrow of her cleavage to find warmth and genuine interest, as well as irony, behind her twinkling glasses.

It is something the Lomans have in common, that characterizes them, this coruscating bifocal benevolence. Indeed, as I lie here in this limbo, brought back by a seismic sneeze from Paulo, it is all I can conjure of their respective faces, handsome though they both were. It is only when I slip back into the dream that I see the exquisite, tawny softness of Sara Loman's skin, the sheen of her black hair with its one white lock arching up like a feather, the Latin darkness of her eyes behind the spectacles, the fine teeth that ought at her age to be dentures but, I will later in surprising circumstances discover, are not. Her age I take to be a well-preserved fifty. Another surprise in store. She is nearer sixty. Which her husband is also, and looks, despite the small-boy unruliness of his sparse white hair and the chubby pink shine of his face, so conspicuous in contrast with her coffee-and-cream skin. He fingers constantly his neat silvery moustache, as though it is a disguise he is afraid will fall off. He has a strange, onrushing manner of speech, his statements often ending on a high note so that they seem to be questions, or jokes with the punch-line still to come. I wonder how, in such whimsical tones, he contrives to pass sentence of death upon his patients.

I remember his voice, now, as a sort of *capriccioso* accompaniment that embellishes rather than contributes to the conversation, while Sara talks passionately, but with little trace of nostalgia, about her native Bolivia. She grew up, like so many of my own countrymen, in extreme poverty, from which Loman, to use his own phrase, "plucked her". I fancy she is a little nettled by this. She was at pains to tell me later, when we were briefly alone, that her family had not always been poor. Her grandparents had owned a fairly extensive farm, which was stolen from them piecemeal by grasping *hacendados* in league with the crooked politicians.

We tread lightly round the subject of Simon Mallory, now two weeks dead. Dr. Loman is inclined to reminisce, to extol his old friend's virtues and make affectionate game of his oddities, which apparently were many; but Sara, I assume out of consideration for Martha, skilfully turns the talk to other things.

This afternoon Martha and I have placed fresh flowers on Uncle Simon's grave. We have been snowed or confettied upon by the may tree, and walking along the fringes of the wood we have declared ourselves while talking about bluebells and primroses, my home and family, life in college. And my friend Paulo.

"He never married?" I ask as we take our leave of Simon Mallory. Innocent enough question, but too obviously prompted by her confetti *faux pas*. My turn to blush. She shakes her head. We are ten minutes down the woodland path before she says, "He was in love once, though."

To avoid the perils of that word she darts aside to peer into a thicket. A small bird shoots out. It soars and twitters overhead as she approaches its nest. Bending beside her to look, I feel the tickle of her hair upon my cheek. There is a small momentous touching of shoulders.

"Aren't they lovely?"

Two tiny white eggs, speckled brown. They lie there symbolic of something in their warm, vulnerable secrecy. They say the words we do not yet have for each other. We move some distance off and wait for the bird to return to its nest. The moment seems important, auspicious.

"He met her somewhere in South America."

"Him, too?"

"Yes. He was travelling. Squandering his inheritance, he said, and his youth. He was a bit of an adventurer. He dreamed of being a poet. I don't think there was ever any inheritance to speak of. Just a ne'er-do-well, was how he described himself. It wasn't true, though. He was a wonderful man. And she was a wonderful woman. He was always saying that. But he wouldn't talk much more about it, apart from that, that she was a wonderful woman."

33

"Ah, yes," I say, gently teasing. "There are many wonderful women there."

She acknowledges this with a slight puckering of her nose. Later when I torment her she will show the pink pointed tip of her tongue and pretend to flee from my reprisal.

What a small privation. What a frivolous thing to grieve over. When I lose her it will not be the ultimate intimacies that will haunt me to the edge of insanity. It will be the carefree trusting of that impudent *moue*, and the realization that no fond jest of mine can ever call it forth again.

But there is something I must not lose sight of in this resurgence of self-pity. After she wrinkled up her nose at me we stood watching one another. That almost-smile was there again, and while we stood there, for the first and only time in my life I heard the cry of a cuckoo.

So? I can imagine Paulo asking.

So I heard a cuckoo and Martha's eyes were—acquiescent. How can one explain these small epiphanies?

We walk on again, reluctant for a while to profane the cuckoo's sacring-bell silence. Then I ask, "And what became of her, that wonderful woman?"

"She found happiness with someone else."

"Ah," I say, teasing again, "they have a way of doing that, women."

She makes her rabbit nose again. "You know all about it, then?"

Not yet, my Martha. Not yet.

"He would speak of her sometimes as though she were still alive."

"You mean she wasn't? Isn't?"

"Well, maybe, somewhere, I suppose. I've no idea. But alive, I mean, in the sense of being still part of his life somehow."

As you, Martha, are still part of mine. You, too, are still alive.

"Which of course she was. An unforgettable part, as one's parents are, or as a wife would be who had died. You see what I mean? Conchita, he called her, but I knew that wasn't her real name, just a special thing he called her. 'That's one of Conchita's songs,' he would say, or 'Ah. Conchita's favour-

34

ite flower.' Even after all those years he would sometimes speak of her in the present tense."

Martha, what if I put my arm around you now? What if I make bold to kiss you here in this last leafy seclusion before we return to reality? Before we reach the Sunday-silent street where watchers behind lace curtains will presume we have been doing exactly that?

My hand steals out. Fingertips touch the white satin sash that relieves while affirming the severity of her mourning; a brush no heavier than the alighting of a moth but she senses it, stands alerted. Her face in profile has a waiting, listening look. Anticipation or apprehension? I lack the courage to find out. My hand falls away. She turns to me with that ghost of a smile again. There is gratitude in it, and promise.

We come out on the road not far from the Lomans' house. Sara is standing on the terrace in a long golden gown, holding a bunch of yellow tulips.

"It's a sad, sad story." Martha waits while my mind harks back to Uncle Simon and his fickle Conchita. "Very sad. I must tell you some time."

A moment to remember, to remember with irony, for it is not Martha who weeps and tells when the time of telling comes, but Conchita herself.

But this is Paulo's story. At least that is what I intended when I began. I saw myself merely as chronicler, sometime observer, only in the most incidental way a sharer; just as I was that day in the park as I watched Eliza's lovely inelegant walk and dreamed impossible futures. Imagining I *had* a future. But I am drawn into the story as I was drawn into the slipstream of that day's events.

Paulo is important in the cosmic scheme of things. I am nobody. Let others assess the dubious merit of what I have done. Let professors in pursuit of tenure and students driven by the thesis demon tease out the threads of my uneventful life and seek thereby to invest it with significance. Doubtless they will see the shadow of Paulo there, his dark star shaping and dramatizing the dull course of my days, and call my innocent fictions in witness to the self-evident fatality of my lot.

Paulo is a doer. I am a watcher. He influences, creates events. I in my elliptical way merely reflect and allegorize. Or dream up events of my own which I once with colossal presumption thought illuminated life by transcending it. Paulo *makes* history.

All of which should probably be in the past tense.

I see now that the only way to move this story forward is to take a leaf from Paulo's book. Slip into his skin. *Be* him. His youthful skin, at any rate, should fit me well enough. On many a sunny Cambridge afternoon I have lain beside him on a grassy bank while crazy Englishmen played cricket, half listening, half dozing while he evoked the scenes and people of his childhood. I have looked into his faraway eyes above countless tankards of bitter and seen there the re-enactment of his boyhood's escapades and tragedies. So eloquent and persuasive was he that sometimes, when the pints had been too plentiful and my bursting bladder woke me in the night, I would surface from some convoluted dream wondering for a moment who I was.

His adult skin would contain me no more comfortably than a hair shirt, although he has ranted on with spirit and eloquence enough, God knows. No, seeing into his mature mind will not be easy. But that I'll worry about when the time comes. If.

They have taken Paulo away for catechism. I miss him, strange though that may seem. Suffer with him, too, through the raw antennae of my own cowardice. I slip, now, all too readily into his skin, every nerve-end aflame with apprehension. For hours last night I lay listening for his screams with the craven ears of nightmare, thrown up now and then upon the shores of sleep to find the screams my own: mere croaks, however, in my parched and aching throat. I awoke choking on the stench of sizzling flesh from burning cigarettes applied to my body by a score of feasting mosquitoes. When the white-hot needle of daylight pierced my eyes I leapt up screaming. Now I crouch shuddering and sweating as the first tenuous thread of sunlight brightens and augments.

But Paulo by now has most likely been catechized into merciful unconsciousness. When life is a nightmare, any dream is sweet.

He dreams, I wager, of a high adobe wall at the edge of the world. Beyond the world are mountains and clouds and the waving tips of pampas-grass. In the early morning before the Snuffer descends there is also the white cone of the volcano called *El Gruñón* by Señorita Smith. She's a bit of a *gruñón* herself, but imagination redeems her. She may snap and snarl at Paulo's perversities and small stupidities but her malice has flair. She chastises with panache. The insults of Señorita Smith flatter even as they wound.

"Super-Pig crams in another cookie," she intones like a sports commentator as he sneaks his fifth macaroon. "He's going for the record. The fans are on their feet. Will he make it?" Paulo gags with rage and laughter, disgorges the whole masticated mess on the tablecloth.

He sits with bowed head, expectant of retribution, eyes averted. She never fails to drive a lesson home, the Señorita.

"Well? You're not going to waste it, are you, all that good food?" She passes him a spoon.

He risks a glance at her. Yellow goat's eyes, hair like ram's horns. *La Cabra*, he secretly calls her. She looks as though she means it. A sweetish odour rises from his vomit. Before she can come out with the inevitable line about the starving hordes that inhabit *el otro mundo* beyond the wall he flees to the bathroom and loses his dinner.

El otro mundo. It is a source of fascination and of a strange unease, that other world beyond the wall. From adult talk and his own rare glimpses, he has a confused impression of a place of great beauty and infinite extent, infested with creatures made in God's image like himself but devoid of heavenly grace and all other attributes of humanity. The beauty excites and disturbs him with its prodigality and voluptuousness, awakens in him feelings somewhat akin to those aroused by Ana, the peasant girl who comes to the kitchen door with honey and beeswax candles (a small chink in the vaunted security and self-sufficiency of the Hacienda Martínez: Paulo's father has a virulent allergy to bee-stings). Ana has cherub cheeks and plump, cherry-ripe lips. Ana has bold, bright eyes which out of modesty she casts down upon her immodest bosom. Ana, says Señorita Smith, has fleas. Or worse.

Within the wall, all things are ordained and under control. The parkland, although extensive, has precise and fanciful limits. Trees are drawn up in drill order along the avenues, arranged for effect in the orchards and arboreta, disposed about the *prado* like dancers poised for the baton. Crops and flower-beds conform alike to the prevailing Euclidean compulsion. Horses nuzzle the necks of mares beneath the carefully cultivated stand of eucalyptus at the edge of the corral. The dogs, sleek, aristocratic creatures capable of killing a man, deceptively supine before their strategically placed doghouses shaped like chalets, might have been worked into the fabric of the scene by some tapestry-maker with an abhorrence of empty space. Stretched asleep on window sills and balustrades, the many cats add a rococo touch to the all-pervading opulence.

Outside the wall it is otherwise. Animals, it appears, are neither pampered pets nor attributes of wealth and convenience. They are arbiters of existence. As witness the big black pig he often sees passing along the lane outside the disused south gate, padlocked and pointy-spiked, that is his only window upon the outer world. A rope, frayed, slick with the grime of ages, encircles the neck of the pig. On the other end of the rope, subservient to the gastronomic caprice of the pig, an old woman limps along talking unintelligibly to herself. The rope is cinched about her waist, leaving her free to manipulate, with great dexterity, a distaff in one hand and a spool in the other. She waits and works submissive while her charge roots among the stones for a few sere blades of grass, suffers herself to be dragged violently hither and yon as the pig espies a small clump of dandelions or some comparable delicacy, the rhythm of her spinning hardly faltering despite the clumsiness of her gait. One of the feet that show beneath her long black skirt has but one claw-like toe.

Paulo cannot imagine the woman apart from the pig. He cannot picture her walking pigless through the market-place, her hands empty and idle, ready to pick up and squeeze a papaya or slide covetous over bolts of imported cloth as he has seen the Señorita's do. His mind's eye cannot make her sit at a table, sleep in a bed, or pick flowers in a peaceful garden as the sun goes down in splendour behind El Gruñón. Once, in church, he finds himself wondering if she, too, is called to worship. He tries in his mind, lulled almost to sleep by the priestly drone, to pluck off her filthy felt hat, give her a bright floral bonnet and a Sunday dress like the Señorita's in place of her tattered homespun *mantón* and long, drab skirt; but still she comes swaying up the aisle in her workaday clothes (her only clothes, he supposes), her eyes not lifted up to the stained-glass Saviour but cast down upon her pig as it draws her up towards the altar, decked for Easter with succulent greenery. Too late he tries to disguise his laughter as a sneeze. La Smith is not so easily fooled, however. She hisses through her dentures. Her sharp elbow promises retribution.

Paulo thinks a lot about the Pig Woman. Not from choice. Especially at bedtime she is there at the fringe of his awareness. He resents and despises her, as though she were squalid and repulsive by choice, as though her vulgar presence is a personal affront, an accusation. She is a dark presence, a disquieting character in some story he lacks as yet the words to tell himself. The brooding anima of *el otro mundo*. He tries sometimes to see her face beneath the droopy hat-brim, to get a look into the eyes he senses rather than sees are dark, piercing, bird-quick, but they are intent always upon the pig, solicitous only of its insatiable appetite. She is aware, however, of his watching. The face is leathern brown, creased like an old shoe. He can read nothing from it; would not, likely, recognize her in a crowd, deprived of her pig and the crude paraphernalia of her ceaseless spinning. Except perhaps by the peeping forth of that curved, terrifying toe. What intrudes upon his half-awake reverie and sometimes pursues him into dreams is not so much a person as an animated bundle of clothing. But the bundle is symbolic, and somehow puzzlingly important. Perhaps it is merely the coarse texture of her rags that makes him think of the mendicant friar in the folio volume of etchings the Señorita sometimes allows him to look at but not to "get his grubby hooks on".

He thinks of the woman and her pig when Miss Smith (he is learning English now) tells him the legend of Sisyphus. He has (he will claim much later over a pint of Watney's in The Mitre) even at so tender an age a sardonic inkling that some day, as a reward for her diligence, and barring accidents of pestilence, predation, and drunken drivers, the old woman's pig will be fat enough to sell. With the proceeds she will buy another piglet and will sustain herself a little above the level of starvation while it, too, grows fat. But there are worse things, the Smith drily observes, than playing nursemaid to a pig.

On the rare occasions when he is privileged to venture beyond the wall with the Señorita and the chauffeur Ramón in the car, he has seen other animals tethered at the roadside, cropping the banks and ditches. It is their only pasture. They, too, have attendant humans, who periodically desist from whatever toil the Good Lord has meted out to them and trudge perhaps a mile to move their beasts along a little to where the growth is not yet nibbled to the roots. But these roadside horses, donkeys, pigs, seem unaware of their blessedness, of their superiority in the economic scheme of things to the women who shuffle along under immense loads of firewood or bamboo. It is no fun, Paulo supposes, being tethered by one leg, a tasty patch of thistle or fern a few inches out of reach, trucks and buses flinging up stones and thundering by only a hair's-breadth from your arsehole. Miss Smith tut-tuts as Ramón, echoing Paulo's thought, lets slip the word.

Paulo is vaguely but only fleetingly troubled by the dumb acceptance of misery by animals and women alike. Have they no hope or inkling that life might be otherwise? Only rarely, even when the car stops beside one of these creatures, is there any collision of eyes. A horse, a cow, looking up from its ceaseless search for food, shows awareness of his existence. Nothing more. No curiosity, no rapport. His is not the hand that, soon or late, will detach the tether and bring the coveted thistle within reach. The eyes of the women, likewise, concede nothing. If the ease and opulence enjoyed by the alien beings in the car hold for them an allure comparable to that of the thistle, they clearly expect no hand ever to come and unloose *their* tether. Nor does Paulo. They are born to their lot, as he to his, in the divine scheme of things.

They are blind also to the grandeur and to the many small miracles that surround them on every side, like the blue and purple gentians and the tall yellow-frilled puyas that find their sustenance among the rocks and screes of *el otro mundo*. The women beneath the bundles pass them by without a glance. Flowers are not edible. If the women's hearts are uplifted by the golden light that lies along the mountain tops, or by the soaring snow-covered peak of El Gruñón, they give no sign. If they are filled with awe and humility by the immense chasms along the brink of which they plod with their burdens, they do not exclaim as Paulo does, or comment like the Señorita how insignificant it makes one feel. Nothing, most likely, could deepen their sense of insignificance. The snowy summits and the plunging precipices may quicken the pulses of the well-fed, but they nurture no crops for the hungry. Even the young girls with their lesser loads, trailing along behind their elders, do not seem disposed to put aside their bundles and, out of sheer exuberance, hurl stones out into the void.

For Paulo the chasms exert a powerful fascination. Ramón, laughing, indulges his whim while the Señorita warns him with a hint of panic not to go too near the edge, and turns away her eyes. Her fear excites him further, engenders defiance. He casts the stones with all his strength, watches them bounce once, twice, three times on the naked scarp of the *barranca* and vanish long before they splash into the cataract that is no more than a wispy white thread in the gloom of the gorge bottom.

There is one place that fills Paulo with a tingly, exquisite dread. The road descends steeply, clinging to the curves of the cliff face, then swings sharply round a shoulder of limestone so that it seems to end abruptly in a blue emptiness of sky. Ramón roars with laughter as the Señorita clings to the back of his seat and averts her eyes from the abyss. Paulo wants to do likewise, but a chill fascination grips him. Some magnetic force impels him to that edge of emptiness. He almost shouts with terror lest Ramón succumb to the same deadly compulsion. Instead, he echoes Ramón's loud laughter and despises Miss Smith.

Then he sees the three crosses at the road's edge. P.A.M.A., it says on the one in the centre. Paulo Antón Martínez Alcina. And so begins his lifelong dream of being dead.

Just past the crosses a path drops over the edge of the cliff and can be seen winding down, vanishing, reappearing, to a narrow, swaying footbridge that hangs over the chasm on two ancient ropes. Another rope serves as handrail on one side. On the other, nothingness. As they approach, a woman on a donkey, plodding along the outer edge of the road, appears to sink slowly into the gorge. A few yards on, Ramón stops and they watch her slow descent. The footing is treacherous, the path in places no wider than the donkey's mangy rump. Where the path curves out around the outcrops and in among the vertiginous fissures even a courageous man would cower close to the rock face, but the woman sits unconcerned, apparently half asleep while the beast feels out secure places for its feet and lumbers leisurely down; unmindful, it seems, of the death-drop over which its single panier hangs. They watch her progress all the way down and on to the bridge. The flimsy structure sways and bounces until it seems that beast and rider must be catapulted clear into space. But the donkey carries on unconcerned and the woman hoists up her skirt to search her belly for one of their reciprocal fleas.

"Brave woman, that," says Ramón, eyeing her brave leg.

"Huh!" retorts Miss Smith, perhaps jealous of that shapely member. "It's hard to tell which one is the donkey. Neither has the brains to be afraid."

Which seemed not unreasonable to Paulo. Indeed, he was beginning to question whether the inhabitants of *el otro mundo* harboured any passions at all.

It would take the plump and pretty Ana to teach him otherwise.

VII

It was something of a mystery to Paulo how the lands of the Hacienda Martínez bloomed and fructified like the Garden of Eden while outside its bounds the land lay barren as the backyard of hell (Ramón again). Paulo didn't think that hell would have that sort of austere beauty, but he did imagine it peopled with the same kind of crushed, hopeless souls.

Miss Smith went about solving the mystery, in response to his questioning, in a characteristically discreet and round-about way. She had no intention of hazarding her position, distasteful and ill-paid though it was, by openly spreading sedition. The walls of the Hacienda Martínez had ears, and what they heard found its way to the ears of *El Amo*, Paulo's father. But the Smith was a mistress of innuendo. (Or, as Señor Martínez himself had been heard to phrase it, a cunning bitch.) She satisfied her pupil's curiosity in a manner so subtle that he was unaware she had done so. It seemed to him that he had arrived at the answers by the exercise of cunning and cleverness of his own.

She approached it by way of geography lessons. Together they pored over maps and charts as she explained the topography of the region: how the land varied in fertility from the rain forests of the lowlands to the bleak heights of the *tierra nevada*. Between these extremes were many gradations of terrain, great variations of fertility, and a wide variety of vegetation. At the altitude of the hacienda, lush valleys and tip-tilted pasturelands contrasted with the barren immensity amid which they lay. Something, she said, to do with glaciers and the winds that over the ages scoured the rocky expanses of their soil and dumped it in the sheltered folds of the uplands.

What she left him thinking he had figured out for himself was that successive generations of the Martínez dynasty had pushed the frontiers of their domain farther and farther out, a nibble here, a bite there, easing the small farmers and their *peóns* from their increasingly marginal holdings until the Hacienda Martínez encompassed just about every crumb of soil that would sustain a blade of grass. The more tractable of the dispossessed became tenants. The rest drifted to the city slums or took their chances in the desert. It did not occur to Paulo at the time that there was anything wrong with this. He saw it as the natural order of things: God's way of ordering the lives of His creatures each according to its allotted station and innate merit. The thorn that Miss Smith had slipped under the saddle of his complacency would chafe more or less unnoticed for a long time. It was not until much later that Paulo heard the saying, current among the local peasantry to indicate a desperate situation: *entre el desierto y un Martínez*: between the desert and a Martínez.

Señor Alberto Martínez Olmeda, Paulo's father, was a meticulous man. The order and efficiency prevailing everywhere on the estate were a reflection of his personality; and, it must be assumed, since such perfection is not attained overnight, the personality of his ancestors. Even during long absences made necessary by affairs of business and of state, his meticulousness continued to operate, as it were, by proxy. Its influence extended even down to Paulo, a Martínez and hence by nature proud and rebellious, although it seemed to the boy that he was lower in the domestic scheme of things than the asthmatic *peón* who cleaned the stables, and therefore beneath El Amo's notice. Miss Smith stood not much higher in the parental esteem, but one sure way to attract the great man's attention was to disobey her or to hint at disrespect. Which, when loneliness and boredom got the better of him, he was prone to do. There were times when being punished was better than being ignored.

"What that boy needs is a mother," he overheard the Smith say to Ramón one day, unaware that the boy was hiding from a band of assassins in a clump of datura near by.

It was true. He needed a mother more than he needed anything else in the world. Miss Smith was a poor substitute. Paulo did in fact have a mother, but he had not seen her since he was six. The mandatory euphemism was that she was sick, but even Paulo knew that she was crazy, that she was not being cared for in a sanatorium but was locked up in an asylum. Whether she was crazy or not, he yearned for her with a secret, enduring passion. She had been tender, indulgent, and, he had by now persuaded himself, gloriously beautiful. She must also have been desperately unhappy, for one of the never-talked-about things Paulo knew was that she had tried to kill herself, having first tried to kill her husband. Another, deduced from sharp looks and silences when Ramón was ordered to ready the car for the trip to the "sanatorium", was that Señor Martínez had driven her to it.

How had he done that? Paulo wondered, having no inkling of the tenderness of feminine sensibilities.

Once again it was Ana who, eventually, seemed to provide a clue.

"A man needs a woman."

Ramón had just driven one from town and delivered her to the summer-house (*la casa de verano*, so called although summer and winter were mere abstractions in that part of the world). The summer-house was off limits to everyone but El Amo. Except for the chambermaid when peremptorily summoned. Paulo's father slept there when he was working on his book.

Paulo, whose ears, according to Miss Smith, were bigger than an elephant's, took Ramón's words as an echo of the Smith's: that a man needs a woman in the same way that he himself needed a mother. This disposed him even more kindly towards the pretty, sweet-smelling visitor, who had smiled upon him. But Miss Smith had tut-tutted and made a show of righteous disgust, prompting Ramón to spring to the defence of his sex.

At Ramón's words she gave him a quick, perhaps hopeful, look, her yellowish complexion darkening a little. Ramón climbed into the car and drove off. No man, his brisk movements seemed to say, needs a woman that much.

Paulo's father only occasionally brought his women to the house. Indeed, he was not often there, and he presumably preferred to do his philandering elsewhere. But Paulo was to remember him as a man of peremptory appetites. His sudden gastronomic cravings, for example, were the curse of the cook's existence. After weeks of almost religious abstemiousness (in which the rest of the household were reluctant sharers), he would demand some exotic dish for dinner.

"How's a poor woman to plan?" Inés, the cook, would wail. "Do I have a magic hat, that I can pluck guinea fowl out of nowhere? Is there an ocean lapping at the steps of the *terraza*, that I can haul out sturgeon with a buttonhook, or scoop up lobsters with my chip basket?"

Paulo's affectionate imitations of the fat, multi-layered Inés enlivened many a Cambridge pub-crawl evening. Her body was a stack of tortillas waiting to be cooked. When Inés was angry or excited, all her layers would jounce and flap with an alarming cumulative motion, the illusion of which Paulo after a pint or two could conjure up with astonishing effect.

The Señor's hungers of the flesh were equally abrupt. Paulo envied him. When he "needed a woman" he had but to summon Ramón and within the hour his dream would be realized in the shape of a pretty perfumed angel. Hungers of the flesh were as yet a little beyond Paulo's comprehension, although he experienced a not-unpleasant commotion of the blood at the thought of the mysterious solace his father received from the motherly ministrations of these fair visitors.

Another thing not to be fully understood until much later was the readiness of Ramón to speed off on these errands of mercy at any hour of the day or night. He could be surly and sarcastic when ordered out on a mission not to his liking (although not in the presence of El Amo), but when Señor Martínez needed a woman he would snap out of a siesta or abandon his dinner with an equanimity very much at odds with his nature and go off grinning to do the master's "shopping". Many years later, when Ramón was grey-haired and reminiscent, and Paulo full of anarchistic fire, it all came out during an hour of tipsy good-fellowship beside a campfire in their mountain retreat.

"Well, now, amigo." He slapped the thigh of his erstwhile "young master" and gave a leering, gap-toothed grin. "It was one of the few benefits of working for your lousy prick of a father, God rest his soul." He savoured the recollection, crossing himself with exaggerated precision before tossing off his drink and smacking his lips. "I was the middleman, you might say, entitled to a small percentage. To show her appreciation for having been chosen in preference to the others to ride in the limousine to the hacienda and gratify my master, it was the custom of each girl to give me a little bit on the side. Most often on the way back to town, after El Amo had had his pleasure of her and the avails were safely tucked between her tits. But sometimes, when he'd been even more arrogant and bloody-minded than usual, I would get my trick in first.

I don't know why I found it so satisfying to score off him in that way, but I sure as hell did." Enjoyable in remembrance, too. They both laughed until the liquor spilled from their cups and their comrades in arms awoke cursing.

The Ana affair was different. No percentage in it for Ramón. Ramón, in fact, claimed he knew nothing of it until its consequences let loose a hubbub of rumour and speculation. Ana lacked most of the qualities of those gilded lilies that came to the summer-house; qualities that Paulo from his Oedipal fantasies had come to think of as mother-like. Ana had no smart clothes. Ana had homespun garments of some antiquity and dubious fit, over which her ripe flesh conspicuously triumphed. Ana did not leave in passing a waft of enticing fragrance. The Smith said she stank, but this was not true. She gave forth the warm, faintly musky odour of swaddled flesh. Miss Smith herself had a clean, antiseptic smell, sometimes with a hint of mothballs. Ana's small feet, pretty enough in a purely functional way though slightly splayed and often very dirty, had never known shoes, much less the impractical patent-leather sandals with high heels that made the city visitors, as Ramón remarked to nettle the Señorita, so fascinating in retreat.

Two more years had gone by and even Paulo was beginning to notice such things. The goings-on in the summer-house were a source of deepening mystery, of mounting curiosity not easily satisfied, even by lurking in the shrubbery, assuming one could escape the surveillance of Miss Smith. The nearby clump of azaleas offered only a glimpse of books and maps and the monumental oak desk where Señor Martínez, the whole world knew, was writing his monumental history of South America. There was a big north-facing window (put in long ago for the benefit of Paulo's paternal grandmother, who had painted pretty watercolours and was hooked on opium), but to take advantage of it you would have to stand on the broad exposed shoulder of the lawn, more seen than seeing. The nearest cover was a hundred metres or more away. Useless, unless by some miracle the Senõrita should happen to say at breakfast one morning, "It's time you got to know something about the world around you. The world is full of wonders—flowers and birds and small marvellous creatures.

Nature study is what you need, m'lad." And unless, after bringing from her satchel a series of field guides to this and pocket encyclopaedias of that, she should reach in again and bring forth *a pair of binoculars*.

She was not without ulterior motives, the Señorita. No doubt her desire to broaden her pupil's mind and her intention to awaken him to a due sense of his insignificant place in the cosmos were genuine, but sometimes she couldn't help thinking how nice it would be were he not so constantly underfoot. Fulfilling though it was to mould his character and feed his youthful intellect, he did tend to come between her and her crewel-work, her steamy epistolary romance with an undertaker in Detroit, and her penchant for crossword puzzles. He curtailed her living, in fact.

Ana did not, strictly speaking, fit into the course of nature study prescribed by Señorita Smith, although Ana was as fine a manifestation of the *anima mundi* as the most exotic bird or butterfly. Paulo could not have explained why he wanted to study her through binoculars when there were so many opportunities to see her close up. It had something no doubt to do with sharpness of focus, to the heightened perception whereby the bark of a tree, seen through lenses, becomes more rugged and real than it appears to the infirm unaided eye, even at a few inches' distance, or a face—Ana's, for example— leaps out at one with a sudden clarity and force, its details proclaiming themselves as though accented by an artist who sees through to the soul. Such details as the peachy fuzz between Ana's cheek, with its pinkish glow that triumphed over her native duskiness, and the intricate vortex of an ear half-seen under a recalcitrant loop of hair. This fuzz, to the naked eye, was fuzz only, a thing not perhaps quite feminine. But brought up close to him there in the bushes, furry, intimate, it suggested some silken moth strayed out from the rain forest. It bespoke mysteries. It cried out for the reverent touch of a fingertip. And the cheek itself, the ungovernable hank of hair, both hinted at something alien and mildly alarming, some Norse adventurer's blood bequeathed in the midst of smoke, looting, and carnage.

There was also the peculiar satisfaction of watching the antics of persons who imagine themselves unseen. Miss Smith, for example, taking out her teeth and lifting her skirt to wipe them on the hem of a surprisingly sexy petticoat. Ana's secret foibles over the weeks of his watching included blowing kisses to a donkey, or to a handsome prince ensnared therein. He also saw her on several occasions bend low over the polished surface of the fish-pond to study her reflection, not so much out of vanity, her rapt gaze suggested, as with bemused wonder that such a strange thing as a human face should exist. She seemed lost in the mystery of life itself.

But, Paulo confided to me in a tipsy haze all those years later (the hurt of Martha not yet having precluded such intimacies), above all he liked to study Ana from his leafy hideaway so that he could gaze and gaze upon her unabashed by the searching of her eyes; shy, bright eyes that were habitually cast down in the presence of her betters (Inés: "Don't talk back to your betters, girl!") but came up to encounter his own with an unsettling mixture of feral challenge and coy encouragement. It filled him with delicious terror, somewhat akin to his fear of that gaping roadside abyss. (You could *catch* things, hinted Miss Smith, from the likes of her.) Paulo's blush burned deep on these occasions, like a fever. He was weak and breathless. Her eyes avowed something special between them, a profound and dangerous rapport, inhibited on her side by inferiority of station and on his by the great mystery of her femininity. Her beauty (if indeed she was beautiful; Paulo four pints mellow would wax Socratic on the point), blooming from the squalor of ancient homespun and coarse linen handed down through several generations, seemed to cease abruptly at the tight, uncompromising collar. Only the fearful strain upon the thongs of her laced-up bodice, which rose and fell prodigiously as she and Paulo fronted one another like adversaries, hinted at some fleshly nexus between her face and her grubby hands and feet. But it was a hint that inflamed all his old mother-fantasies and left him seething with new and nameless emotions.

But it was her eyes above all that haunted him, then and for years after. They were a window upon that unimaginable outer world, toward which their ambiguous half-smile seemed to be enticing him, promising delights and dangers there, wonders. Her eyes had upon him the same disquieting effect as the wild land in which she lived, as if the sunlit mountains and the dark vertiginous clefts were all comprehended in the gold-flecked glow of her irises.

All of which, Paulo admitted somewhat sheepishly, having carried his skinful down to the bridge over the Cam, added up to the fact that he was in love with her. Agonizingly. Leaning on the parapet, watching a punt slewing unskilfully upstream, he even went so far as to suggest that, despite his pubic incapacity, he *lusted* after her. He said this with what seemed a disproportionate sense of self-disgust, which I would recall later when he described subsequent events. His yearning had at any rate a physical dimension, so that with a lot more courage and a little more encouragement he would have flung himself into her embrace and buried his face in the swell of her agitated bosom, fleas and mysterious maladies be damned.

As it was, the best he could do was to thrust into her hand when, astonished, she set down her honey bucket, the ebony crucifix inlaid with mother-of-pearl that had been his mother's. It was the thing he treasured above all else. The only thing worthy to express the painful emotion for which he could find no words. The crucifix had been his burning secret ever since the day they took his mother away, when Ramón had returned and handed him the package and said in a conspiratorial whisper, "She sent this for you to remember her by. She said not to tell anyone."

Ana looked flustered by his gift, and a little scared. People would think she had stolen it. How else would she come by such a valuable thing? She didn't know what to say, but she pressed the crucifix tight to her breast and looked at him for a long time with bright, moist eyes. Then she slid it into some mysterious place under her clothes and went on her way, almost running.

On the days she was expected, he would loiter near the gate, but out of sight of the lodge, at the place where the shaded drive forked to serve both the main residence and the summer-house, in the hope of seeing her; and of hearing her say "Hola!" with a funny flattening of the vowels that suggested intimacy, secrets. Her voice was low, slightly husky. Usually, between the "Hola!" and the "Adios!" they stood for a long time in wistful embarrassment, with that disquieting contention of eyes.

He wanted to talk to her, to ask her about beehives and honeycombs and the mysterious process of candle-making. He wanted her to tell him about the lavishly embroidered basket that contrasted so strikingly with her drab attire. Had she made it herself? The leaves and flowers worked into the weave were made of strips of brightly coloured cloth, relics perhaps of some garment that had gone too far even for her to wear. He wanted them to share secrets. Well, now they had the secret of the crucifix, but still they had no words. He would have liked to walk with her, carrying her basket up the winding drive and round to the back, where Inés would open the hinged lid of the wooden bucket and, after a sample fingerful, ladle the honey into an earthen crock, and lift out the golden candles—the colour of Ana's hair—from their cool nest of moist leaves. But after "Adios!" with a film-star flash of teeth and a darkening of those other-world eyes, she would leave him standing there. He watched her graceful barefoot walk until she vanished among the trees.

Just so, on the fateful afternoon, had he been waiting. This was the day when he would overcome his cowardice and break the barrier of silence. But Miss Smith flushed him out and sent him packing, with notebook and binoculars, up to the grove of cultivated willow and eucalyptus on the hill above the summer-house. He was to seek out and identify at least three kinds of birds. He had been deterred from going deep into the wood by the glimpse of a tawny flank vanishing into the undergrowth—an ocelot, he later swore to Miss Smith to excuse his lack of results, but more likely a squirrel—and so there he stood in the seclusion of the woodland's edge, looking idly downhill. He could see part of the drive and the main gate with the small inset wicket where, after jangling the big brass bell, Ana would be admitted by the grouchy guard, Miguel.

As he waited, he swept the scene with the powerful glasses. Two men were trimming the topiaries around the sunken garden. Ramón, clad in oilskins, was hosing down the limousine. Nearer, to the right, he caught sight of a white movement, fragmented by the foliage of the upper drive. The flecks of whiteness moved among the trees and drifted down towards the forking of the ways, where Paulo fancied himself standing, full of resolve to break the ice with Ana. The white shapes stopped, vaguely suggestive in their relation to one another, moved on; became, briefly, an arm and a shoulder, vanished. Señor Martínez at length emerged and stood bemused, striking the side of his boot with the plaited crop he carried like a sceptre about his domain. His boots were shiny and tall, shaped to his plump calves and burnished like the backs of beetles. Miss Smith called them "pistol cases".

Paulo brought the glasses up to his father's face. The features were handsome but hard, classical in the Spanish tradition. Paulo felt an irrational guilt, to be thus spying upon his father, bringing the power of the glasses to bear upon that familiar yet enigmatic face. Like Ana, he was accustomed to avert his eyes when El Amo looked his way. Moustache and shaggy eyebrows were all he normally saw before slinking off. When trapped, he looked away and waited to see whether his father's first words would portend anger or the grudging tolerance that passed for fatherly affection. And of course the scar. He saw the scar. It slanted an inch or so down his father's cheek. It made him, legend said, irresistible to women. The same legend had it that the scar had been acquired in single-handed combat with a gang of *bandidos*. His brother, however, long afterwards let slip in the presence of Paulo that it had been inflicted by their younger sister, who, incensed by his constant baiting, had thrown a vase at him. Paulo now studied this scar with interest. So much interest that Ana was already inside the gate before the sound of the distant bell claimed his attention.

Miguel stumped back to his lair. One could tell by the thrust and curl of his lips and the petulant shake of his head that he was cursing. Something must have upset him more than usual. Normally he would stand at his door and stare after Ana with undisguised lasciviousness. Thrusting out her tongue at his retreating back, she set down basket and bucket to pin back her intractable hair. It amazed Paulo how the details of this and her subsequent movements imprinted themselves upon his awareness. Almost as though events had already played themselves out, casting back upon these trivial happenings a lurid glow of significance. How she swung her head a little down and round so that the candle-coloured hair fanned and fell into the waiting snare of thumb and forefinger. How she swept it up with a twisting motion, almost savage, so that he saw for an instant, entire, the dark whorl of an ear with a golden fringe of wax around its delicate crater, and a small scratch, already scabbed over, across the tip of the auricle. She plucked the old-fashioned hairpin from her lips and plunged it into place with a quick, impatient stab. The hair immediately flopped halfway down again into its customary festoon, hiding all but the earlobe and the merest hint of golden fuzz. She bent to take up her twin burdens. A curious curtseying motion, graceful, as though rehearsed for the occasion.

Unhurried, pensive, perhaps with "Hola!" for him already at her lips, she comes on up. The glasses hint at something slightly coarse about her features but he dwells avidly upon them, making them mother-beautiful in his mind. When she looks up he interrogates her unresponsive eyes with a sense of shock, of intrusion, of daring. It is a glimpse of something that makes him feel suddenly grown up. He knows now that he can vie with her at this eye game and win. He watches, watches. Watches the parted lips and the moist peep of tongue-tip, the dusky curve where the softness of her throat merges into mystery. And the swell of her breasts, no longer afflicted with that disquieting agitation. A fugitive smile. A playful expectancy, head tilted birdlike as she comes to the corner, the "Hola!" already halfway out before—

El Amo steps from the shadows. Paulo is blinded by his whiteness. Ana's face is blank, with wide, innocent eyes. He will remember the word "innocent" being there in his mind. The eyes are innocent, are innocence itself. A page waiting to be written upon. He sees her start of surprise and a flash of something like scorn before she veils and lowers her eyes as is proper in the presence of her betters. Her face is again eclipsed by the white sleeve, swelling full to the wrist. "Gigolo sleeves", Miss Smith calls them, but Paulo finds them manly, elegant. They make him think of matadors. He admires as well as fears his father. He sees the sleeve fluted with shadows as it lifts and bends. The big hand emerging from it settles gently upon Ana's sleeve.

He sees them both small, comical in their remoteness, like marionettes. Their miming has some message for him, some meaning, but his mind is strangely passive and detached. Their gestures are intrinsic to the landscape, like the stir of branches above their heads. Or the shadowed tumble of water into the fish-pond where yesterday he went to look, as if he might find her likeness still there beneath the surface. His father's arm, starkly white against the tree-shade, is pointing. Ana's arms stretch darkly down to their burdens, candle basket and honey bucket. Her head inclines sideways, up towards the house. I must go, her impatient stance says, I am late. She takes a pace in that direction.

When Paulo brings the glasses up again, the hand on Ana's sleeve is clenched and knuckly, no longer gentle. Ana's eyes are cast down but she is shaking her head and holding back a little. Not fearful as yet, only demurring, puzzled but still respectful.

So they stand, it seems to Paulo, for a long, long time, their attitudes hardening, becoming statues of themselves, frozen in struggle. Silent, or making animal sounds. When El Amo moves again his gestures are abrupt, demanding. The girl, no longer the Ana he knows, seems appalled, twists this way and that, seeking deliverance. She looks, unknowing, into Paulo's eyes. Impossible to believe she is not imploring him, demanding his help as her due. But he stands rooted. Unthinkable to fight one's father. As well pit his puny will against El Gruñón's towering might.

Still he does not understand, cannot imagine, why his father is hurting Ana. What complaint has he that he should wish to punish her? Has she cheated on the bill, perhaps?

Ana looks away. El Amo turns her roughly to him, wrests the bucket from her hand and hides it in the shrubbery. The beautiful basket falls from Ana's hand, spilling its contents on the grass. Still holding her wrist, he bends to scoop the fallen candles up. Ana of a sudden shows fight. Up comes her knee into her attacker's face, once, twice. He staggers a little, straightens up, and strikes her hard across the cheek. Paulo glimpses his rage-disfigured face, flinches from the mask of wrath that leaps at him across the distance. His father seizes Ana's other arm and shakes her. Shakes till her hair falls down and clouds about her shoulders. Her head flings back and forward like a doll's.

Why? *Why?*

Señor Martínez picks her up and carries her kicking towards the summer-house. Her cry is like some small trapped animal's. Rage and terror made sound. A listening silence. Then the mountains send it back, rebounding upon itself like laughter.

Paulo's skin feels taut and frozen. The echoes tingle along the tunnels of his bones. All the world must hear it. He sweeps the glasses round. The hedge-trimmers stand alert, their heads turned up towards the source of sound. Their shears are still. He sees a flare of panic in the eyes of one. The other speaks, then shrugs. His free hand makes a gesture of repudiation. Blades glint as both men turn back to their work. It is not wise to hear such things.

Ramón has finished his chore and driven off. Miguel secures the gate behind the limousine, resolutely hearing nothing. Inés dumps out a pail of slops, stands for a moment all atremble, turns, and hurries in.

The heavy glasses shake in Paulo's hands. He cannot keep the scene in focus.

The pygmy shapes approach the summer-house, the captive's legs still beating up and down. They vanish, effaced and gone as if for ever, poor Ana carted off to Grendel's lair, devoured. Paulo blubbers in his shameful impotence. Hate wells up in him like old El Gruñón's lava. He curses the God who does not smite his father. He glimpses a great abyss of evil in himself, from which he turns away in fear.

He sleeves away the blindness from his eyes. The scene lies ordered, ordinary, everywhere at peace. The topiarists are out of sight. About the hacienda, doll's-house small, all is stillness save the rise of smoke where Inés prepares the dinner. Outside the southern gate, the woman with the pig stands black in silhouette against the sun. Beyond, the snuffer descends to veil El Gruñón's snow.

White movement at the window of the summer-house. Paulo steadies the glasses against a tree and brings the window into focus. White shirtsleeves cut off at the shoulder by the heavy curtains, the hands stretched out to Ana, Ana's throat. Her head, tipped back, turns in vehement denial from side to side. Her fists beat on the white extended arms.

All is flurry, confusion, struggle. Paulo, convinced she is being killed, shouts "No! No! No!" but even the mountains do not hear. His father's back is all he sees, hunched over, straining, strangling Ana.

But when their macabre waltzing swings them round again his father's arms are down. Ana, unstrangled, stands with puny fists upraised. Ana at bay, doomed animal, breast laid bare, shoulders pale and round against the shadows. Her ruined bodice dangles from one arm. Paulo is sick with the wonder of her nakedness. She becomes a blur of pallid round-nesses. Tears of rage and terror shut the whole scene out. He chokes them back and wipes his burning eyes: dares not look yet urgently has to see. Steamy ghosts, they grapple again. Ana floats, tilts, and slowly falls. His father crouches for the kill. She starts to struggle up. Roughly, he flings her back upon the bed and tears away her lower garments.

Something surges up, explodes in Paulo. A murderous fear. An abject fury. With coward sobs he starts from his paralysis, charges forward, armed to the teeth with hate, his father already murdered in his mind.

When he wakes, it is to blood, and stillness.

VIII

Paulo is back, tossed in the door limp and lifeless, carcass of some spurned and savaged dog.

Oh God! My turn!

But no, not yet. The tormentor had more urgent business elsewhere. The lout and the halfwit waited in the doorway, only too ready to pounce upon me cowering in my corner. But a third man, spectral in the shadows cast by the halfwit's lantern, gave a snappish command and strode away with ring-ing jackboot tread. Not, however, before fixing me with a contemptuous and somehow uncanny stare that pierced to the very core of my cowardice. I could see only his eyes, sardonic in the lantern's light. Eyes in a face without substance, nose and mouth more imagined than seen. A blackness below, perhaps a beard. A mere Cheshire Cat grin of disdain, afloat at the edge of darkness. Something, too, of sadistic promise. And a tantalizing hint of familiarity. Memory or imagination sketched in the lineaments of that scornful face but offered no clue to its identity. His boots rang on the stone steps down which I fell the day they brought me here, his tread receding, my ear in the midst of lingering terror recording (perhaps anticipating the dread hearing of it in reverse) the tonal ascent of his cleats upon the stone. One note short of the octave.

He shouted something back, his voice fighting its own echo, syllables of *Desvelarse!* or some such word swarming about like bats in this crypt-like place. Stay awake.

"Fine for him to say," grumbled the lout. "Big fancy dinner. All night in the sack. Sleep in till Christ knows when. What's to stay awake for in this shithole? These turkeys ain't goin' no place."

Slam went the door to emphasize the point.

"Not his own sack, neither." The halfwit laughed, sly and lascivious. "I know."

"Know what, cockroach? You don't know nothin'."

"This cockroach got ears. Eyes, too. Folks think I don't hear nothin', don't see nothin'. This cockroach see an' hear plenty."

While this gossip was going on outside the door, I took advantage of the light leaking in through the grille to drag Paulo to his bench and cover him. A trickle of blood overlay the bean-juice in his beard. Another tooth or two extracted in the name of sweet justice.

The voices were receding.

"Like what, you see an' hear, cockroach?"

The last of the light ebbed from the cell as the halfwit's reply trailed away.

"That bastard got some fancy piece o' tail in town. 'Bet you right lonesome in that big bed, *querida*,' I heard him say on the phone. 'Your man away an' all.' Seen her, too, I did once, his 'sweetheart'."

The words "plump" and "sexy" floated faintly back before the second door slammed, condemning me to silence and the suffocating dark. Silence except for Paulo.

I groped for the pages that had scattered when they burst in to startle me out of Paulo's boyhood skin. Then I lay down, trying to ignore the staccato sounds of Paulo's body teetering at the edge of life. Trying to repulse the swarm of dire thoughts and dread anticipations, trying against all odds to think of something pleasant. What a mulish thing the human mind is. How perverse and malevolent when it wants to be. How it mocks the heart's most desperate plea for equanimity, returning always to the source of pain like a dog to its vomit. (Dr. Loman, telling with mischievous twinkle about the folk-cure for some complaint or other: run three times round a church without thinking of a fox.)

In vain I paraded images evoked by those last, maybe imagined, words of the halfwit. Plump. Sexy. I called forth my Nina at her most voluptuous, wanton, tender. She slipped away, elusive as a wraith. Black imaginings slithered in to fill the void. So I dwelt by antithesis upon the skinny shape of Eliza. Projected her in exquisite detail upon the sooty ceiling of my hell. But she was walking away from me, always away, through the park, up the path towards the palace gates, the dark tunnel of trees . . .

I even, in my extremity, ogled the headless ghost of Clementina, willed my nerve-ends to know the torrid touch of her flesh. She fled me, grotesque and mocking, through a hall of mirrors in my mind. The grin of the Cheshire Cat filled the space where her head should be.

Martha it was who told me about the Cheshire Cat. And Martha who brought, thanks to that tenuous connection, some small relief into the hellfire of my torment. But that was hours later, in that part of the night when the dark settles thick upon one like silt at the bottom of a sunless sea. I suppose it was a dream, yet I was aware of my own volition in it. In my joyful greeting of Martha—the memory of Martha, of course, but she was so *real*—there was a poignant sense of the misery out of which I had escaped. A sense, too, of the precariousness of that escape. It was as though that heaven and this hell coexisted. I floated with Martha in that other time, sustained at an immense altitude above this living grave by the sheer intensity of my longing for her. One moment of inadvertence and I should plunge back into the present, into my bone-weary body; or perhaps, by the sport of some occult cross-wind, into Paulo's.

This seems an extravagant fancy now. It didn't then. I had lived so deep in his dreams for days as I wrote that my returning spirit may well have been confused.

Martha. Why do I dwell on her now, now that the daily dole of light is here and wasting? There is so much to tell and so little time. But I may be forgiven this one small self-indulgence. Given my present privation, is it so unreasonable that I should wish to—that I must—call up once more the only time in my life when I truly loved, and for all too short a time received love's fullest measure in return? Can you, lout, or you, Cheshire Cat, or whoever gets to read these pages before they are burned, can you imagine what it's like to languish here, a man in his prime with healthy loins and a novelist's penchant for romance, cut off from the natural affections as if no woman had ever walked the earth?

But how, the voice of conscience demands, can you indulge in these nostalgic ramblings with Paulo lying at the door of death? Well, Paulo is not so easily disposed of. I have used my ration of water to wash his wounds. Nothing practical remains for me to do. Now he is in the hands of the devil.

I should mention here apropos "the only time in my life," etc., that Nina and I have (had?) a "mature relationship". Ours was, in a sense, a marriage of convenience. Both past forty (she will not admit how much), we each needed the convenience of a compatible bedfellow, shared domestic arrangements, and respectability in the eyes of the world. But love? We were able to delude ourselves sufficiently to be, in every practical sense, happy. Love has little to do with happiness. There has never been between us, Nina and me, yearning so intense as to be capable of resurfacing, a lifetime later, as a crushing ache of the heart. Such as dictates my present addictive need for the memory of Martha. Such as might so easily have been kindled by a few more encounters with the vulnerable eyes of Eliza.

"Don't sit there grinning like a Cheshire Cat" was what Martha said.

She had dipped her nose into her ice cream.

Dabs of flour, blobs of ice cream, what is the secret of their power to inflict such tender retrospective pain?

I held up, beyond her reach, the needed handkerchief. When she pounced I seized her wrists and held her powerless. She bared clenched, beautiful teeth in mock ferocity.

"Bully! Beast! I bet you'd be a wife-beater."

Our struggle ceased. Locked in that improbable pose by the witch's wand of her indiscretion, I watched the blush ascend her neck and bloom beneath her splendid cheekbones. Her eyes—her eyes in last night's dark were like a benediction—were full of confusion that melted slowly into a great trusting warmth. We kissed softly, fleetingly, yet I felt the promise of forever in it. Then we went home and read *Alice's Adventures in Wonderland*.

That was all. But the fact of that first kiss—hardly a kiss at all—informed everything we did and said in the enchanted weeks to come. Of course there were other, ever more lingering, more passionate kisses, attended by more intimate caresses, but that shy brush of lips, endorsing as it seemed to do the involuntary image of her as wife (even though it cast me in the unflattering role of wife-beater), had about it something sacred, so that it endures in memory years after all those other kisses have merged into one long, blissful communion of lips and yearning flesh. It coloured everything, that kiss.

We went about in a state of wonder. Where before, on our walks, we took pleasure in watching and listening to the birds, admired the common flowers, enjoyed together the Cambridgeshire countryside and the distant, surprising prospects of the city, everything now seemed transformed, intensified, as though lit up from within; the more familiar, the more marvellous. The only analogy that comes to mind—inadequate though it is—is the experience of flying over a great city for the first time at night and seeing it all lit up. Where I had been accustomed to see the noble and not-so-noble works of man, there was now a veritable fairyland of riotous illumination: spiders' webs aglisten with dewdrops, necklaces of stars, nets cast by celestial fishermen in the black seas of night.

(What a load of romantic bullshit, I imagine Paulo thundering. The fanciful always provokes him to bellow.)

Nevertheless, it was so. We walked and walked in our Eden, and often we would arrive weary and replete with wonders at the Lomans', where the warmth of their welcome and their pleasure in our happiness set the crown on our contentment.

The cat sleeps beside me as I write, purring gently. She has become a regular visitor (it was Paulo, who is barely tolerant of her presence, who settled the question of her gender), and by saving her a little food I have succeeded in overcoming her mistrust. Indeed, she has become boldly affectionate. She has adopted me, I think, as her protector and friend, an unlooked-for *deus ex machina*.

I must find a name for her. "Peluche" Paulo tried calling her, but she disdained to answer to it. She wants no part of Paulo. No part of Peluche either. The fur stiffens along her back and her tail-tip stirs as though she senses a threat implicit in the word. As well she might. I have yet to tell you the story of Peluche. Like this cat, I want none of Peluche. Not now anyway. While yet a little light remains, I fight to win back the memory of Martha.

IX

There was, I now perceive, a certain desperate defensiveness in all that enchanted walking. We wanted, needed, to be alone with our blessedness, but we were disconcerted, perhaps a little afraid, at the prospect of being *too* alone. Of course, we could have made love in the woods. Such a small step, after all, from those tempestuous huggings and fondlings. But there was a prompting in us stronger even than desire. Not a moral thing, although Martha had scruples and I admired her for it. No, it was rather a fear of betraying something—

our love, each other, our future as presaged in that one unguarded word: wife.

If I make much of all this now, it is because it deepened immeasurably the anguish of what came after.

So for weeks we rise like gods above the promptings of our earthly passions. Then, one wet and blustery Sunday afternoon, when summer seems to have deserted us . . .

"My gosh," she exclaims. "You're drenched to the skin."

My shoes squelch as I step into the hallway. I stand there dripping audibly on the linoleum, cutting, no doubt, a droll figure in my blotting-paper raincoat and my wilting cap. I'm at a bit of a loss, deprived thus of the customary embrace. Martha's hand is still clapped to her mouth in dismay. We seem like strangers. Then she laughs, and leaps, literally leaps, into my arms. I hold her fiercely, in passionate denial of that fleeting sense of estrangement, until she shivers as the water from my clothing seeps through to her skin.

"Come by the fire. I'll find you something to put on while your things are drying."

I shed my raincoat. It falls with a moist plop to the floor. Martha takes my cold hand in both her warm ones and leads me to the stove. The fire leaps up with a joyful roar as she opens the damper and a white radiance flares at the heart of the embers. A grateful warmth steals through to my chilled flesh. I stand there steaming gently until she returns with a bathrobe and a towel.

We cling for a moment, and I have a strange extra-corporeal sense of floating several feet away, by the front door, seeing the two of us standing entwined, subliming slowly away in wisps of luminous vapour.

She breaks away, bringing me back with a queer little shock into my goose-pimpled skin, and goes out. At the door she pauses to give me a long, appraising look, as if it is important that she remember me this way. And as if she is making a momentous decision concerning me.

When she comes back I am sitting, coaxial with the ghost of Simon Mallory and wearing his robe, in the old armchair, bare feet extended to the stove, eyes closed, in an ecstasy of warmth. I feel rather than hear the descent of her steps on the ancient stairs. Then her presence is there in the room, felt, coming soundlessly nearer, stopping.

"I . . ."

Her voice is low, burdening that one syllable with an incredible weight of emotion. I remain with closed eyes, deferring the moment, but I know exactly where she stands, how she holds her hands, what an anguish of diffidence is in her eyes. When she takes another step closer, my sense of her nearness augments as if I had leaned a little towards the stove.

"I wanted you to see . . . me."

She comes closer yet. I open my eyes to the splash of firelight on her skin, ruddily golden on the long curve of her hip, dusky under the swell of her breasts, moulding to their shape like a silken garment and casting their soft shadow upward. Under lowered lids her eyes are bright as though with fever. I stand up to face her. Slowly, with effort, she raises her eyes.

I've no idea how long we stand there, outside time. I watch two large tears triumph over her rueful firelit smile, slide down to fall upon her breasts.

She bows her head so that I see the backward sweep of her hair and the wings of the polka-dot bow that binds it. As in a dance we each take one slow pace nearer. And another. She bends a little to me, divining my intention. When I untie the bow her hair falls in heavy firelit coils about her shoulders and encloses her breasts in long parentheses. I breathe the faint waft of its fragrance.

We draw together with tantalizing slowness. She lifts up her face, cheeks flaming, eyes dark behind the sparkle of tears. The first meeting of our flesh is as shy and tentative as that first Rubicon kiss. And we linger like that, flesh exalting flesh. I feel faint with reverence for her womanhood. Then we seem to melt together into one space.

I carry her with difficulty up the narrow, creaky stairs, uplifted by the press of her nakedness upon me . . .

Hell, it wasn't that way at all. Only in last night's desperate waking dream and in the remorseful dreams of all the years between. Many have been the nights when there was no hope of sleep, when my only hold on sanity was that imagined love-making rehearsed so often to myself that the recurrence has made it true. It has, indeed, a certain metaphysical truth, in that it could so easily have been; should have been, I think in my lowest, most cynical moments, had I not been such a diffident fool. For undoubtedly there was, as she stood unclothed before me in the firelight, having just said in that low, husky—yes, if you will, sexy—voice, "I wanted you to see . . . me," the possibility of all that. And much more. Years and years more. The possibility and perhaps even the promise. What sort of idiot was I? Why, that traitor voice inside me insists, would any woman—especially Martha, painfully modest Martha—invite a man to look upon her nakedness, if not with the implicit promise of all that?

Yet in my deepest soul I know it was not so. The possibility was there, yes. Even, in her readiness to take the risk, an acknowledgement of the probability. She would have submitted, perhaps with all the ardour I have imagined. As a natural consequence of that submission she would have become my wife, and doubtless our marriage would have been as happy and blessed as our half-formed dream of it. And the course of our lives, mine, Martha's, Paulo's, and so many others, would have been very different. I should not, most certainly, be here now in this stinking sarcophagus with a half-dead assassin. . . .

As for Paulo himself, who can tell what part his brief but calamitous encounter with Martha played in the shocking transformation of his character?

And yet. And yet beneath the placid surface of our years together, Martha's and mine, there would have lurked a deep, unacknowledged sense of betrayal, of my failure to measure up. For as I stood up, astonished to find her naked yet feeling the rightness and the immense tribute of it, I saw in the eyes she raised to me a great and childlike trusting. But no, that does her an injustice. She fully understood the situation. Was, in a sense, in command of it. But she had complete faith in my love and in my sensitivity to the courage and purity of her gesture.

So we joined hands and at arm's length I looked upon her. I think it is neither untrue nor impious to say I worshipped her. She blushed. How gloriously she blushed, her whole body aflame and rosy. There was no telling where firelight ended and blushes began. We bent to kiss, lips and fingers our only contact. Then she went away.

From the foot of the stairs she blew me a kiss. She said, "You dear, wonderful man." Then she put out her tongue, made her comical bunny nose, and the intimate secrets of her womanhood vanished for ever from my sight.

And although sometimes I rail at God for having cheated me, or having suffered me to cheat myself, I know that what I did that day was right, and that in some profound and inexplicable way I am the richer for it.

X

Paulo, as I have said, was away for most of that memorable, Martha-enchanted summer, having been summoned home by his Uncle Alvaro, who had taken over the Hacienda Martínez after the death of Paulo's father, and who now, in failing health, ordered his nephew home "to be schooled in the hard realities of being a Martínez". Paulo, who had planned a summer in Spain, cursed but obediently went.

I hardly missed him, I must confess, in my infatuated state, except perhaps in the mornings when we were accustomed to sit long at table and talk of home. We smoked and drank coffee so thick and black that even our Czech neighbour down the hall would grimace and go for hot water. The coffee beans came from one of the Martínez estates in the south. Paulo took it syrupy with coarse Cuban sugar (a poor substitute, he said, for Ana's honey), sent every month or so in big muslin bags by the doting but rapidly declining Inés. Paulo dwelt upon each sip with dreamy eyes and an addict's absorption. Seldom did that poisonous potion fail to prompt some boy-hood reminiscence.

Occasionally a letter from Paulo, left by Mrs. Clegg, who "did" for both of us, would relieve that early-morning emp-tiness. They tended to be flippant, those letters, even when their substance was grave. As when he announced, early in the summer, "Before I even arrived in answer to my uncle's peremptory summons, Alvarez had received a yet more peremptory summons of his own." Alvaro, I was to infer, was dead, and "buzzards were roosting already in the family tree."

The words were frivolous but the images they evoked were otherwise. I could see, as I read, the tousle-haired figure of Paulo leaning toward me over the table, his full lips reaching for the coffee with the covetous pout of a suckling's.

In time I began to sense something defensive in the flippancy. It is easy now to conclude that some profound change was taking place in him, a change with which he could not come to terms and which perhaps he did not even recognize; which, when he came back a little late for the commencement of studies that autumn, he certainly did not acknowledge. He seemed, if anything, even more set in his patrician ways. Perhaps this, too, was defensive, a refusal to countenance the forces of change.

It is only by an immense effort after all these years that I can call up words and impressions—lost on me at the time, so deaf and blind was I to all that did not appertain to Martha—to suggest that the dissolution of the Paulo I had known (and, yes, loved) might already have begun. This is a sort of paradox, for such small aberrations as I do recall, or maybe imagine, tend to show Paulo in a yet more favourable light. For example, once when he was short with Mrs. Clegg in his customary imperious manner, he called her back and apologized, to her evident dismay and disapproval. If he seemed a little more serious, less inclined to leap at every society invitation that came along, I would no doubt have put it down to the weight of his new responsibilities.

But, "Oh, the old place is in good hands," he said when I brought the subject up. He was headed for the door. I fancied I glimpsed a grin as he turned away. "My mother's."

And he went out quickly, leaving me with that.

We had talked of her, of course, his mad mother. Never for long. Paulo would conjure her wistfully up, wrestle for a while with words that would never quite fit the elusive, painful reality of her, and take refuge in his coffee cup, only his eyes lingering upon her disconcerting image. He had been taken to see her several times during his adolescent years, but always accompanied by (under the surveillance of, he would phrase it later) Uncle Alvaro. These meetings always took

66

place in the public room at the "sanatorium", surrounded by pathetic star-crossed creatures and their white-coated attendants. There would always be several inmates who circled them like coyotes, starved for the crumbs of their coveted intercourse.

There was nothing in his mother's appearance or behaviour to dispel Paulo's conviction that she was crazy. He was at first a little afraid of her. Had she not after all attempted to kill his father?

"And don't think," he said, "that I haven't wondered about that. The nature of the provocation, I mean."

There was a fanatical hunger in her embrace the first time they met, as though she wanted to reabsorb him into her soft, slightly sour-smelling flesh; a daunting experience for a youth of fifteen who had never been truly embraced before, by anyone. He was embarrassed by the bright, doting gaze of her eyes, imploring something of him that he did not know how to give.

Once in a dream he saw her leashed like a dog. She flung herself at him again and again, only to be brought up short at the end of her tether, again and again until she fell exhausted. He ran from her because he knew she was going to die of her insatiable yearning.

She was not beautiful as she had been in his childish fantasies; by the standards evolved, that is, from observation of his father's painted and perfumed visitors. But she had a chiselled refinement of feature that he could only characterize, setting down his coffee cup with a suggestion of defiance, as "bloody handsome". In, he would later amend, a ravaged, craggy sort of way. Their talk during those visits tended to be safe, banal, prompted by his uncle's questions about her health, the care she was receiving, the food, the weather; and by the information they volunteered about life at home. There was a hint of desperation about it all, as though only the tenuous web of words sustained them above the abyss of her madness. When, occasionally, she became unduly animated, her eyes burning with eager inquiry, her voice rising and taking on the vehemence of a frustrated child's, Alvaro would out-decibel her with some inanity calculated to divert her attention. He was very good at it. "It's very important, Chico," he would say afterwards, "not to let her excite herself." Paulo, for some reason, bitterly resented that "Chico".

So Paulo returning from Cambridge is picked up at the airport by a latter-day Ramón with a Castilian accent and bloodshot eyes. Not from weeping for his dead employer, however. Ramón, he confides with undisguised satisfaction, was "let go" by Alvaro for engaging in political activities. The wrong political activities, that is.

"He was a bit of a red," the new man says.

This is not news to Paulo. Ramón's political foibles had always been considered harmless, even amusing. Paulo's father was not above baiting the chauffeur as they drove along. Ramón, he once observed, did not have the brains to be dangerous (a perilous assumption, Paulo will later discover); besides, his political folly was more than atoned for by his competence. As procurer, for example. For Alvaro, this particular talent was not a consideration. An encounter with a belligerent dog in his childhood had severely diminished his sexual competence.

What the new man doesn't prepare Paulo for is the state of affairs at the hacienda. To be ambushed halfway up the drive by Jonatán, his father's black-sheep half-brother, is surprise enough. But to find himself, in a very short time, drawn to this skeleton in the Martínez closet astonishes him even more.

Known to Paulo only by oblique reference, Tán, as he was disdainfully known in the family, had cut himself adrift at the age of nineteen to follow his obsessive poetic and musical bent. He was a gadabout, a ne'er-do-well, as might be expected of one born (as he himself later confided) on the wrong side of the blanket. He went "gallivanting about the world" (this, years ago, from Señorita Smith) on an allowance from his father, which Paulo's father had grudgingly continued, with, of course, strings attached.

Tán had in fact, Paulo discovered, made a substantial reputation as a writer and singer of folksongs. His fame was downplayed in family circles, not only because he had committed the sin of escaping their exalted social orbit, but because his songs were politically distasteful. Downright sub-

68

versive, in fact. One could not laugh him off, as one laughed off Ramón. He sang haunting ballads in which farm workers, ditch-diggers, down-and-outs, and prostitutes laid bare their tortured souls in a low-key, unsentimental, but profoundly moving manner.

What he says, stepping forward from the very spot where Paulo used to wait for Ana and wrenching open the door of the limousine, is, "Le roi est mort. Vive la reine!"

This goes over Paulo's head for the moment. He is too overcome by the presence, the personality, of this stranger who yanks him out of the car, punches him playfully on the shoulder, and says, "My God, man, you've shot up. Last time I saw you, you pissed down the front of my favourite jacket. Another Martínez value judgement, I assumed."

Paulo is puzzled.

"Sorry. I'm your half-uncle, if there is such a thing. Jonatán." He takes Paulo in a big bear-hug. "Of course, you'd hardly remember your own christening. But I admired your style. You decided to do a little christening of your own. 'That kid'll turn out a rebel like me,' I told your mother." He propels Paulo up towards the house.

La reine stands white-gowned and indisputably majestic in what was always known as the music room. Her hand rests on the old piano that has stood there, unplayed and excruciatingly out of tune, for as long as Paulo can remember. Ever since, he now realizes for the first time, Tán left home. A sort of anti-memorial, silently admonishing any young Martínez who might be tempted to follow Tán's example.

"She blushed" I remember reading in my Cambridge digs while Mrs. Clegg fussed with the fire, an unseasonable chill having ousted the summer. What she blushed for, most likely, was the memory of those earlier encounters, seeing herself as he, through indoctrinated eyes, must have seen her at the asylum. One mad woman among many.

Mad, however, she was not.

"It's a wonder," one of the letters said, "she didn't catch it by contagion." We had a long discussion about this after he returned, punting down the Cam, wondering how one maintains some concept of normality in a world given over to the insane. Wouldn't one, we speculated, be afraid of free-

dom when the time came, the moment when one must relinquish the long-familiar for the unknown? Wouldn't one be
tempted to resist being cast forth into the insane world of
sanity? He did in fact quote her as saying it was like being
pushed out on the stage without having seen the script.

But if Elena Alcina de Martínez is unsure of herself, it
certainly doesn't show. Apart from the blush, that is. He, for
his part, stands there "gaping like a fool", incredulous. She
waits there in her long white dress, looking improbably
young, enduring his nonplussed stare.

Then something happens. An epiphany, according to
Paulo.

Her story comes out, of course, in the ensuing days. Or
as much of it as she wants him to hear. But in that moment,
even before they embrace, he seems to know it all. In essence,
at least. Simply by the way she stands, the way she looks.
And he is aware of the way that embrace—initiated by him—
atones to her for the indignity of all those others, and signals
a fresh start.

They study one another, hands joined, for a long time. It
is nothing like his boyhood dreams of this moment, yet it is
profoundly and satisfyingly right.

She says: "It's a long way back. Will you help me?"

The surprising thing to him, then, is that she is not bitter.
Or rather that her bitterness is buried too deep to manifest
itself immediately or to focus upon its ostensible object, Paulo's father. When they are easier together she tells her story,
not as a sustained narrative but in a series of piecemeal and
apparently random recollections of the "that reminds me"
variety, as any mother might. Her very composure should tell
him how far below the surface the fires of her resentment
burn.

God knows how Tán got her out of there. Nothing could
have seemed more improbable to Paulo at the time than that
Tán "had connections". Paulo's manner seemed offhand, the
day he spoke of it, the daylight already waning towards Tit
Rock. He spoke from the hindsight of his own later experience
of the web of "connections" that underlaid the social fabric.
Táns by the hundred tunnelled away at the foundations of
the world in a score of countries, not always their own. The

Tupamaros of Uruguay even I had heard of, but Paulo reeled off the names of a dozen or more underground "armies of liberation".

"At the time," he said, reverting to his mother, "I was so naïve that it never occurred to me that there might have been a problem. In springing her loose, I mean. The Martínez influence that got her in there, I thought, would surely be more than sufficient to get her out. In fact I discovered later that one of the things Uncle Alvaro was dying to impart to me, so to speak, was the absolute necessity of keeping her in. What appals me now is the thought that had he lived long enough to get at me I should probably have obeyed him. For the good of the family. At that point it was still something I believed in, the good of the family. I was still very much the Martínez. Which I suppose is why Tán didn't tell me how it was done. Getting her out, that is."

To Paulo at that point, it must be remembered, Tán was still, potentially at least, one of the "buzzards roosting in the family tree", while Tán had no grounds as yet to believe Paulo could be trusted.

"No doubt one of the 'connections' was a doctor who found her miraculously restored to sanity, or an administrator who contrived to lose track of Elena during her transfer to another institution. Or it may simply have become more profitable to the management to let her go than to keep her in. Tán was not without funds, after all.

"But one thing that didn't come out until much later, when my trustworthiness, I suppose, was taken for granted, was that the whole thing had been a bit of a charade. She suffered enough, God knows, but she did have friends—accomplices, I suppose you'd have to call them—in that place. She was given special treatment, kept apart from the more loony of the inmates, allowed the occasional illicit visitor. Oh, sure, they put on a show, during those visits of ours, and earlier, when my father used to go there to gloat."

His mother, Paulo had once told me, was not mentioned in the family except obliquely, when her embarrassing spectre could not be ignored, as "Alberto's little mistake". The family, like Alberto, had been captivated by her beauty and vivacity, although, one was encouraged to infer, they all suspected from the first that there was no depth of character beneath her charm. She had no lineage, no blood. Wealth, yes, but it was new money, and new money, ultimately, was never to be trusted.

Elena graced the social scene well enough for a while. Long enough, Paulo was able to testify, to make a scene when her son's curls were cut off without her consent. She had a strong will and a strong temper. Increasingly, over the years, she was critical of the Martínez "despotism". Which she soon discovered had a personal as well as a dynastic dimension. The more critical and recalcitrant she became, the more contemptuously and, in the end, brutally did her husband treat her. She was disgracing him in the eyes of the family. Jonatán witnessed one of their violent scenes when Alberto, inflamed by one of his sudden appetites, sought first to lure and then to drag her to the bedroom. She escaped by biting his nose and locking herself in another room.

"You're just a low-class slut," he shouted, hammering on the door. "You're fit to mix only with the likes of your Bolshie friends."

Her "Bolshie friends" must at that time have been a bit of a myth, since she had little chance to acquire any, but the discovery of a letter from Tán inciting her to "get away from that heartless bastard, that nest of vipers" and to join him in Europe was sufficient to precipitate the ultimate row, in which she seized a knife to defend herself against his savage attack with the ever-present riding-crop and thereby provided him with the excuse to declare her insane.

She is a shrewd woman, la Señora de Martínez. Although she makes no secret of her contempt for and hatred of the social milieu into which she married, she makes no direct attempt to "convert" Paulo. She and Tán discuss world news in a manner that is always coloured by their sense of universal injustice and their uncritical sympathy for the underdog, but their interest appears to be purely theoretical and, it seems at first to Paulo, naïve. If Tán tends on occasion to get carried away, to embrace an extreme position or to applaud some act of proletarian violence, she deflects his excitement in much the same way that Alvaro was wont to quell hers, and with equal success.

My impression is that she favoured the "softly, softly, catchee monkey" approach to her son's redemption. She didn't want to scare him off. Ultimately, any credit due to her for the subsequent astounding change in Paulo was probably more the result of her extravagant maternal affection than of any overt persuasion. And, of course, of her compassionate example. She was, if one could accept the image of her he brought back with him to Cambridge that autumn, little short of a saint.

And, like many a saint before her, she came to a bad end.

XI

Blood and stillness.

It was a long time before he took it up, that interrupted story of Ana. Since he had spoken those words, I had lived in a long, idyllic dream and Paulo had spent that surprising and perhaps germinal summer with his mother. Moving again amid the scenes of that youthful trauma, he had deduced, as much from her silences as from anything specific she said, that his mother was aware of that ultimate infamy of her late husband and had at least an inkling of the events that followed.

Paulo for his part must have been painfully conscious of the parallel between his father's abuse of his wife and his assault on the peasant girl Ana. Whatever other changes may have been wrought in Paulo during those weeks, he certainly lost any last shred of respect he still retained for his father's memory. That parental esteem had been innate, so deeply ingrained by generations of almost fanatical tradition that in the years following the Ana affair Paulo had been tortured by guilt for the resentment he bore towards his father, whose right to filial respect appeared in the Martínez dynastic scheme of things to be something quite apart from and unaffected by his conduct. But when he resumed the story, blurting out the same words he had used all those weeks before, as if that long interval had been but a thoughtful moment, I soon realized that the memory of his father fired in him a deep, implacable hatred. I seemed to detect an anguished frustration that his father was beyond reach of his malice. I have often wondered since whether Alberto Martínez was the devil by whom Paulo was possessed, the ubiquitous enemy against whom he waged his unholy war.

"Sangre! Quietud!"

We seldom spoke in Spanish, but the vehemence of his outburst seemed to demand the cogency of his native tongue.

The strange-looking couple at the next table, who had been unabashedly watching us, exchanged a veiled glance and turned back to their beer.

Paulo sat silent, remembering. I recalled the boozy haze of that earlier evening when he had recounted in disjointed fashion the details of El Amo's atrocity and Ana's dire predicament. That night on the bridge as he brought the story to that dramatic pass he shocked me out of my tipsiness by bursting into tears. He was certainly not one, as a rule, to get maudlin after a few pints. Maybe he had drunk more than I was aware of, for after blubbering in that uncharacteristic way for a minute or more, Paulo of the vaunted cast-iron gut bestowed a veritable Niagara of beer and Formal Hall dinner upon the occupants of a passing punt. To the accompaniment of a chorus of abuse such as the arch of that venerable bridge had surely never echoed before, we beat a hasty, stumbling retreat.

As we went, silent, sobered, and a little uneasy with each other along The Chimney, Paulo stopped, bisected by the moonshadow of the tower, fists raised as if to fight the world, and cried with Jeremiac fervour, "By Christ, a man has the right to be proud of his father!"

I glance across at him now, writhing under the extended torture of his dreams, and the retort springs twenty years too late to my lips: "Yes, and a father of his son!"

The unfinished story hung between us in the busy days that followed, together with the sour memory of that shameful episode on the bridge.

Our Freshers' photograph had for some reason not been taken during our first term, and it was during those fretful days that the omission was rectified, many, many months late. We were lined up five rows deep in First Court and our collective image was recorded for posterity; it being assumed, no doubt, that some of us would so distinguish ourselves that historians and biographers would have fun winnowing out the wheat of greatness from the chaff of mediocrity. Although I doubt whether anyone present could have foreseen the nature of the distinction Paulo would achieve, or the number of police archives around the world that this picture would find its way into.

I mention all this because in the many apartments and rooming-houses I occupied before I married Nina I would glance up to find Paulo looking down at me from the wall, all the petulant shame, all the repressed eagerness to have things out and amity restored, apparent in the sidelong way he looked at me instead of obeying the wag who said in a loud voice, somehow contriving to make it funny, "Watch the birdie."

And it was with something faintly reminiscent of that same look that, after the long separation of that summer, he sought me out after dinner one night and said, "Dammit, Gaspar, let's go down to the Mitre for a whet. I need to talk."

So there we were, the couple at the next table and I, agog with anticipation of blood and stillness. I, being at least partially "in the picture", waited for the whet to loosen Paulo's tongue. Our eavesdropping neighbours sipped and made small talk with an ear cocked in our direction.

It took some time. And the revelation, when it came, was something of a let-down. For me, at any rate, who had been left wondering for months whether the blood was his father's or Ana's, and by whose hand it had been shed.

As he told how he leapt from his hiding-place in sudden fury at what he had seen, he launched himself halfway out of his chair, causing our snoopy neighbour to spill his beer. He was in such a blind rage, he said, that he half killed himself on a low branch. When he came to, he had no idea how much later, all he could see was blood. Oceans of it, or so it seemed. And not a sound in the world. He was dead. The whole of creation was dead with him. Dead, unimaginably mute. He lay there, acquiescent in death, until the fire ants began to sting. Even then it took him upwards of a minute to realize this was not one of the minor torments of hell but evidence he might still be living. When he eased himself up he found that the sea of blood was in fact one of his own footprints in the mud into which his left ear was pressed. The other ear was full of blood, already congealing.

"I remember standing there swaying, groggy as hell." The grogginess was there again in his eyes as he gazed at me above his forgotten beer.

The sun was getting low, flaming along the ridge, lying red as his own blood in all the clefts and gorges. El Gruñón towered above the clouds, floated free of the world. It gave him a fearful sense of unreality. He, too, was afloat. One pace forward and he would soar up into the sky. So he sank to his knees, clutching the grass for anchorage, and watched the snow on the peak flame deeper and deeper red. El Gruñón was going to erupt.

"It didn't, of course. Hadn't for eighty years, in spite of its constant growling."

He stayed like that until the black and purple shadows crept up the volcano's flanks and there remained only the faintest glow at the summit. It flared for a moment, he said absently, like Ramón sucking on one of his cigars in the twilight.

"Then it went out and I felt suddenly cold. Deathly cold."

He went weaving down the meadow, remembering in agonizing detail all that had happened. Ana kicking and struggling in his father's arms. His father forcing her down on the bed. He saw it all there, like a movie, on the big window of the summer-house. Played over and over.

The man at the next table was unabashedly listening now, his great parrot-beak of a nose in the tankard poised at his lips. The woman lit a cigarette. I met her eyes, narrowed against the flame. But I sensed that their glint came from something more than that. Her glance made me uneasy. She shook the match and blew out the smoke, upward, her narrow lower lip thrusting out square, so that all I could see in the moment before I turned back to Paulo was the veiled predatory alertness of those eyes.

"In spite of my weakness," Paulo went on, "I was still fired up with my original impulse, whatever it was. To kill the bastard, I suppose. Crazy, of course. I couldn't have killed a fly, or those ants swarming around my legs. Anyway, it was obvious I'd missed my chance."

The summer-house was deserted and dark. He picked up a rock to heave through the window where the image of his father mocked him. It fell only a metre from his feet. He burst into tears of frustration as he felt himself falling into darkness.

That, one might reasonably assume, was the end of the story, apart from the desultory details he threw out as we played an inept game of darts under the sardonic gaze of the regulars: waking up in his bed with his scalp laced up like a soccer ball and feeling, he said with a rueful smile, as though it had been used as one. His father at one point, when he was half-conscious, looking down at him from an immense height, down into his soul, knowing what he knew.

But it wasn't the end, and Hooknose divined it. Or was it his woman?

Anyway, it was the man who sauntered up as I ended our game with a fluky double twelve.

"Care to make a foursome?"

"Sure," Paulo said without consulting me.

"I'm Hafiz Malik." As he crushed my fingers I had a good look at him. Hair slicked back from a centre parting like the folded-down wings of a great black moth. The parting ran improbably true as if laid out with a chalkline, continuing the line of his nose's bony ridge. The eyes that searched mine were dark, with jaundiced-looking whites. I had the sensation of looking at rather than into them. He had good teeth which were displayed a lot although I never saw him smile. Unlike the woman, who in response to his beckoning came up to us beaming. The teeth she flashed at us were slightly crooked, but pleasantly so. Fascinatingly so. I felt that she used them, consciously, to divert attention from the thinness of her lips. Her hands reminded me of talons, but her eyes were friendly, wide open, and ingenuous, perhaps inordinately so, as though she were passing through customs with nothing—for once— to declare. The somewhat oily complexion of her face I now saw was peppered with tiny scars of smallpox, which however did nothing to diminish its—well, yes, beauty.

Perhaps I am being swayed by hindsight in this account of my first impressions, but I am sure that even then something about the two of them left me with an intuitive sense of menace. When the hand with the long, curved nails clutched

77

mine I felt a quailing of the spirit, as though she had swooped upon some mousy secret of my soul.

It also seems to me now that our meeting was not altogether accidental, although they were already seated when we came into the pub and looked as though they had been there for some time. It would be a long time before I came to suspect how easily such accidents can be arranged. Paulo himself has admitted that after his stay with his mother he began to encounter, "by chance", a surprising number of people who would assume importance in his life, and who would contribute in their several ways to the growth of his "business".

There followed, between the pacing back and forth to the dartboard, a spasmodic exchange of information, the strangers baiting their hooks with snippets of their own history and circumstances to lure forth particulars of ours (definitely hindsight). Hafiz had been born in Haifa "before the troubles". Most of his life had been footloose, owing allegiance to no one, although he professed "a real fancy for the English ways", which in the light of history I found astonishing. When Paulo, who was surprisingly well versed in such esoteric matters, asked about his name, Hafiz roared with his peculiar mirthless laughter and slapped his thigh.

"Hell, no. I may be a Hafiz but I couldn't quote you half a page of the Koran. I'm a Hafiz in the same way Ellington is a duke."

The woman, whose name was Maar, came of Egyptian stock but had been born in a London slum.

"You have such places in your country, no doubt?"

Both she and Hafiz seemed more interested in me, during that first encounter, than in Paulo, sensing, perhaps, my lowly origin. Or perhaps they were merely laying the bait for Paulo.

"A few," I said.

She was quick to catch the irony. "And a few of the others. The filthy rich." Only the most fleeting of sidelong glances at Paulo, who was chalking up his score.

"Yes, a few of those. Not many in the middle. My father is an exception." I had an absurd impulse, which I resented even as I yielded to it, to explain my presence there among the university élite, to dissociate myself from the filthy rich.

"How so?" Genuine interest in her eyes. Warmth, even. I wonder now if I might have been a ready victim of her wiles if the spell of Martha had not been so powerfully upon me.

"Rural poverty is not the same as urban poverty. Slums beget despair." And much else, less innocuous.

"How right you are."

"In the country poverty encourages resourcefulness and cunning. Usually quite fruitless, of course."

"Eighteen from seventy-seven, fifty-nine. Nineteen double top." She was a score-keeping genius. "But not in your father's case."

"No. Excuse me." Suddenly I found myself resenting my own garrulity, antagonistic to whatever it was in her that coaxed the words out of me against my will, or at least against my sense of discretion. I resented *wanting* to confide in her. I made my play, split the double, leaving Paulo with three to get.

"He was lucky, then, your father?"

"You could say that. Resourceful, too, and cunning." Yes, you could definitely call him cunning.

We talked as we played, about my parents, about my early life, about her ancestry. She told me she was named for a goddess. I made the expected gallant reply. She spoke desultorily of politics, a subject on which I no doubt betrayed my naïveté and ignorance. She was cynical, I remember, about the United Nations and its failure to help the oppressed peoples of the world.

Paulo and Hafiz were talking earnestly, between their turns to throw. Hafiz was extorting, apparently, the earlier part of the Ana story. Maar, I could tell, had an ear for their conversation even while she was heaping abuse on the memory of Lord Balfour and prophesying doom for the state of Israel.

We finished our game and conceded the board to a couple of air force corporals. Hafiz called for another round as we moved our tables together and sat down. As we raised our recharged glasses Hafiz said, "She did come back, then, your little honey girl?"

Paulo seemed reluctant at first to pursue it. He gave a barely perceptible nod of assent and sat frowning.

"A very brave girl," Hafiz prompted.

"Or very foolish." This from Maar, who apparently hadn't missed much.

"Or perhaps she acquired the taste for it."

Stung by this, Paulo looked up at Hafiz and said fiercely, as though that ancient puppy love possessed him still, "She wasn't foolish. Far from it. *Very* far from it, as you'll see."

We waited.

"It was a month or more before she showed up."

He stopped again, seemed to be slipping away from us into a profound gloom. But abruptly he rallied and said, his hand on the table clenching until the knuckles cracked, "I'll never forget that month, never." His eyes were on me, but he wasn't seeing me.

"My father took a sudden interest in me."

I can hear those words now, across the years, and for the first time I perceive a link between that youthful, admirable Paulo and the human hulk with whom I share this cell. The savage irony beneath the casual, bantering words. The devastating understatement. The exact tone, the very same bland stare masking the pain when he said, soon after I came here, "A few days ago they took me away for catechism."

But after what he had told me of his mother's experience, it was not hard to deduce the nature of his father's "interest". The cat-and-mouse watchfulness. The subtle and not-so-subtle mental cruelty, designed to goad Paulo to the rebellious word or gesture that would be the signal for physical abuse.

"He drove me to the end of my tether. I woke up nights scheming to kill him. Next day of course I'd be sick with guilt and remorse. That 'honour thy father' stuff had been drilled into me pretty deep. But the next night I'd be back at it again. All sorts of crazy ideas for doing him in."

He sat silent, tracing the beer rings on the table with a well-manicured finger. (The nails remaining to him now are cracked and filthy at the end of blunt yellow fingers.)

His next words came so quietly they eluded me at first, and came back to me only by an effort of recall as he stood up like a sleep-walker and went to the washroom: "There was one crazy idea I didn't think of, though."

Maar's foot found mine under the table. I avoided her eyes. Hafiz was frowning, as if resenting the cryptic nature of Paulo's words.

As if he had drained off the rancour of his reminiscence, Paulo came back apparently composed and took a long pull at his pint.

"Anyway, as I said, it was a month or more. Then one afternoon Ana was there at the kitchen door with her honey bucket and her candles as though she'd never missed a visit, as though all that had never happened."

Inés, opening to her knock, took several paces back and exclaimed, "Gentle Jesus and Mary!"

Paulo's impulse was to run to Ana and . . . I don't know, embrace her, I suppose. What consternation that would have caused. But of course he didn't. Stood there instead "like a dolt", unseen in the shadows behind the stove, tears pouring down his face.

But the next time he was there at his old place, waiting. And wishing, as soon as he saw her, that he hadn't come. Nothing was going to be the same. The certainty of it struck him like a chill under the heart. He felt suddenly sick. Whatever had been between them was gone. Her "Hola!" was flat, impersonal, potentially hostile. He was a stranger. Worse, a mere child to her mature woman. And the estrangement was mutual. She had become a stranger, too, ages old in her mature womanhood. He fled into the bushes.

Only slowly was it borne in upon his grief and confusion that she had turned the wrong way. Not up towards the kitchen but in the direction of the summer-house.

As Paulo was telling us this, his tankard forgotten in the clutch of his hands, I intercepted a sardonic glance from Hafiz. She had, evidently, "acquired a taste for it".

Paulo was stunned, crushed. The savage hatred of his father boiled up in him again like bile. But now it encompassed Ana. A blind, unreasoning jealousy. His father had contaminated her with his filthy lust. It didn't present itself to him in those terms, of course. He had no conception of lust. In fact he had no thought at all. Just that murderous emotion. I suppose at the back of his mind was a sense of his father's having cast upon her some deadly adult spell, some curse. But it still didn't absolve her of blame. Didn't diminish his sense of betrayal. Which perhaps is why he began to follow her, with some wild, undefined vision of revenge in his mind. Against *her*, because he knew his father would not be back until nightfall. Whatever re-enactment of that former ravishing she anticipated, she was due for disappointment.

All manner of insane images swarmed in his head. Ana cowering under the blows of his miraculously powerful hand; Ana naked, violated by him as his father had violated her, although he had no very clear idea of what that involved. Her bloody corpse abandoned there on the bed for *him* to find.

When Paulo got there she was already coming out. The door was never locked—who among them would dare go in? Seeing him, she stopped. Then she came towards him, almost running. He cowered, his own belligerence forgotten, intimidated by that agitated, purposeful stranger, scared half to death by the look in her eye. She seized him by the shoulders. She had the strength of a man.

"You ain't seen me!" she hissed so violently that he felt the spatter of her saliva. "You ain't seen me, d'you hear?" She drew him close, her nose almost touching his. Her eyes were big and bright with menace. They seemed about to swallow him up. Then, seeing perhaps the imminence of tears, the hurt beneath his terror, she held him off. Her face seemed to soften, but that may have been only the blurring of his vision. "It's all right! It's all right!" Before his eyes she changed back into a child again. A frightened child.

He couldn't say which of them moved first, but suddenly his head was pressed hard against her breast and her arms were tight about him. He felt a great sob convulse her body. It seemed in memory as though they stood like that for a very long time, but it was probably not more than half a minute. He could smell the salty odour of her flesh and hear the soft sound of her weeping. Her hand stroked and fondled his head. Then she broke away, hurried to where she had left her basket and bucket, and strode off without looking back.

"I ain't seen you," he called after her, unconsciously imitating her peasant's speech. He couldn't tell whether she had heard or not.

What was he supposed to make of it? By that one resort to the mysterious power of her femininity she had deflected his fury, turned it back upon its original object with a new intensity. Yet his sense of betrayal remained. Mounting hatred of his father only made more bitter the thought of some satanic bond between them.

He walked blindly, bemused by thoughts like these. Perhaps for hours. He had no idea. Then, as though starting from a long sleep, he found himself pressed to the bars of the south gate, the one that was never opened. He'd cried himself out. His face burned with his spent tears. Only a few paces off, the pig woman stood twirling her staff. She wasn't looking at him now, but he knew she had been, perhaps for a long time. She was jabbering away to herself, as was her habit. Maybe it was some tuneless interminable song, for there was a suggestion of rhythm to it. And in the midst of that incomprehensible mumbling she said, or perhaps he only imagined he heard, a strange thing.

"Plunder the honey and suffer the sting."

At that point in Paulo's telling of it, I remember, the landlord dimmed the lights and called for last orders. I went to the bar. Maar was missing when I got back. Gone to render unto Caesar, Hafiz said as an aside to a discussion they had somehow got into about the doctrine of non-violence (Paulo was still, at that point, very much pro). Ana I could only assume had been satisfactorily disposed of. But as we rose from the table and were reaching for our coats, Paulo gave what sounded like a strangled laugh and said, "Plunder the fucking honey!"

We all stopped to look at him, coats halfway on, regarded with curiosity by several people waiting to pass. A strange enough tableau, to be sure. Paulo downed the dregs remaining in his glass.

"About noon the next day, Ramón found my father dead."

He leaned towards me and said it as though intending it for me alone, but in that strained silence it had the effect of a shout. The strangers around us forgot their haste, listening.

"Bloated up like a gourd. Naked. His body the colour of breadfruit."

We regrouped on the sidewalk outside. The eavesdroppers reluctantly dispersed. Hunched against the chilly night air, we waited. Paulo, standing a little apart, cast a fan of shadows on the pavement.

"Poison of some sort?" Maar prompted.

"Bees. Stings all over his body."

He didn't seem inclined to say more, although Maar was quick to say, "She put them there, of course."

He only nodded in an abstracted way, seeming impatient to be gone. We agreed we must meet again. A clinging handshake from Maar, an old-time tip of the hat from Hafiz. We said goodnight.

Maar phoned me the next morning. I was a little short with her, having been torn from my studies to take the call in the porter's lodge. And having, moreover, wrestled with a hell-spawned incarnation of her in a half-forgotten dream. She seemed not to notice, however, overriding my surliness with effusive good humour, calling me "Gaspar, my dear", as though we'd been friends, or more, for years.

"Well?" she prompted when the one-sided greetings were over.

"Well what?"

"Oh, come on, Gaspar. The bee girl. Did he tell you how she did it?"

He had, but I was prompted to thwart her curiosity. I put it down to an ungenerous impulse then. Later I realized that my reticence was instinctive, a response to the menace I sensed in her.

"Left a bunch of bees in the summer-house. He had an allergy."

"And did they catch her?"

"No. There were a lot of questions asked, of course."

"I bet there were. Clever girl, that. We could do with a few like her."

It was only after I had got rid of her by promising we'd all get together on Friday (weekends were for Martha), and was trying to come to grips again with Aeschylus and his intrepid Seven, that I found myself wondering about the constitution and implications of the "we" that needed a few like Ana.

Paulo, in truth, hadn't told me much. Surfacing from his early-morning megrims over a third cup of coffee, he was more preoccupied with the pig woman and her Delphic utterance, and with the network of communication and collusion this seemed to imply, reaching even into the ménage of the hacienda itself.

"How could she have known, that old witch? Surely Ana didn't blab her intention all over the *provincia*?"

He saw me smiling at that. I remembered how news travels like magic among the peasantry. But never travels too far. There is honour among the indigent, as well as among thieves.

"A veritable bloody *telégrafo subterráneo*," he said, as though reading my thoughts. He decapitated his boiled egg with a savage chop and watched with disgust as the yolk flowed down like lava.

"For a long time I was convinced she was one." He stemmed the offensive flow with a finger of bread. "Witch, I mean. I'm still not entirely sure she wasn't."

The conspiracy must have gone far beyond the pig-tending crone. He didn't suggest that it was in any sense an inside job. The servants, though, were tight-lipped as Trappists. Even grumpy Miguel at the gate. No, he hadn't noticed anything strange in her manner when he admitted her. He hadn't seen which way she went. He'd better things to do than watch her wiggle her ass (on that occasion, anyway). Couldn't say whether she stayed longer than usual. No clock in the lodge. Reckoned not, though. Must have gone out while he had the gate open for the deliveries from town. Didn't notice her.

María the maid was a little more forthcoming. And a lot more devious. She'd been in the summer-house that morning. It was her day. No, she hadn't seen any bees. Lord, yes, she'd have noticed if there had been. Scared to death of 'em. Wasps and the like. Couldn't account for bees in the summer-house. Except, well, maybe the door. She always left it open for a bit to air the place out. The Señor's cigarillos. He smoked a lot. (This was true. Paulo would watch for her emptying the waste-basket, from which he was sometimes able to salvage half-smoked cigarillos, envelopes with foreign stamps, once even a pair of frilly panties, torn.) No, bees had never come in before. A bird did once, though. Pooped all over the clean sheet. Why bees got in this time she'd no idea. Flummoxed her, she said. Although there were some potted plants just come into bloom. Smelled lovely when she watered them, they did. Real lovely. They'd 'tice her in, she supposed, if she were a bee. Which Mary be praised she wasn't.

Well, did she find anything unusual when she tidied up the place afterwards? *Si. ¡Pongo el grito en el cielo!* She hit the roof. Dead bees all over the place. Dead? Yes. She wouldn't go near until Ramón had sprayed the place. Made him stay while she swep' up the bees and set the place to rights. Real creepy, what with the bees and the ghost of *el señor* . . .

Which was all true, but not all of the truth. Paulo wouldn't have smoked a dead man's butts, even had there been any. Might even have thought twice about a dead man's discarded envelopes. But on this occasion there were only dead bees. What María had not deemed it necessary to mention was that two of the dead bees were in a paper bag. Paulo could see no logical explanation why María should pick out two of the bees and put them in a bag, especially as she had declared she wouldn't touch one o' them little *pícaros*, dead or alive, with a long-handled broom.

Paulo, pushing aside his breakfast and lighting a cigarillo ("one of the many peccadilloes I have to thank my father for"), left me to draw my own conclusions. Except for his comment, as we took our customary turn around the court before getting down to work, "I couldn't remember seeing Ana carrying a paper bag."

Of course I invented all sorts of explanations. But it took an unwary hornet, straying one afternoon through the hole I have dignified with the name of window, to elicit the rest of the story. Paulo downed the hornet with a deft clap of his hands.

"Ha!" He held it up by a wing and said with an uncanny echo of his words at breakfast all those years ago in Cambridge, "Well, my Gaspar, that's one failing my father didn't pass on to me. For which I thank him."

He studied the hornet minutely, as though he'd never seen one before. "It takes a bigger weapon than you have, *pícaro*, to kill *El Azote*." He tossed it aside and stretched out on his bench, closing his eyes. About his lips played the sadistic smile that once appeared on the front pages of the world. *El Azote*, the Scourge. And proud of it.

"Had a sting or two in my time. Like the day I put a wasp up María's skirt as she was washing her hair at the pump. I got stung but I didn't let on. It would have spoilt the surprise. You should have seen her go, round and round the yard, stopping every so often to do the cancan, hauling up her skirts and clawing at her bare arse. She never caught on, though. Probably thought it was God's punishment for not telling all she knew about Ana's revenge. She was a simple, devout soul, María. Inés came out, anticipating murder. Or another rape, maybe." He savoured the memory for some time before sitting up and saying, "I didn't find out the full truth about my father's death until a few years ago, when Ramón and I were holed up with some others in a ravine above the Cascada Humeante."

Ramón, too, had kept his mouth shut.

Paulo couldn't recall what had brought the subject up, but he remembered Ramón saying, "I saw you ferreting through that stuff after María emptied it. I thought, 'The little bugger's going to squeal.' " He gave Paulo a searching look. "Never understood why you didn't. 'Cept I figured you must hate the bastard as much as we did. And with reason, I suppose. I watched you pretty close for a while, lad, I can tell you. It was obvious you knew everything, and there didn't seem any reason why you wouldn't spill the beans."

Paulo let the silence speak for him. Shared danger and hardship had brought him close to Ramón, but not so close that he wanted to reveal his childhood passion for Ana.

"I mean, you were a smart kid. Too smart by half, that Smith bitch always said. I wonder what happened to her? Anyway, you must have put two and two together. You'd collected enough bugs, spiders, grasshoppers to draw your own conclusions about a paper bag full of pin-holes."

Paulo hadn't noticed the pin-holes.

"And from there it would be easy to figure out the rest. Someone had carried in a bag of bees, and under the circs it had to be Ana—although maybe you was too young to know about him screwin' her. But she was real clever, that little Ana. It was beautiful, the way she fixed it. I mean, putting the bag in the bed so the weight of the covers would hold it shut until he got in. By which time the little buggers'd be mad as hell. His tough luck that he always slept naked.

"He'd ordered the car for nine the next morning. When he didn't show by half past I went up there. No answer when I knocked. Didn't dare go in, though. But I peeked in. By God and all the saints, you should have seen him, right there by the window. 'Member the big man-shaped balloons they used to have at the *fiesta pascua*? 'Cept I never saw one o' them with a hard on. Purple as a beet he was, and blowed up fit to bust."

The aging Ramón relished these details. Señor Martínez had got what he deserved, but at the same time Ramón resented his death. Things had never been the same at the hacienda after that, and in the end he lost his job. His fortunes had declined steadily ever since. Couldn't go much lower, he said. Figured he might as well throw in his lot with this bunch. Least you got to eat now and again, and you had an occasional chance to take out your spite on *los puercos ricos*.

Well, there was one step lower Ramón could go, and did. With a little push from Paulo. But that's for another day's light, God willing.

Meanwhile, as the dusk descends, my feline friend comes to claim her tribute of beans. And suddenly, as she leaps through that last thread of light, I know what her name is. Conchita. Some fleeting, indefinable semblance, some long-forgotten glimpse, yet the name comes to me like a revelation. When I say it, softly, she looks up quickly. Ignoring the beans, she springs into my lap, gladly, as if she had been waiting just for that.

XII

Always my thoughts come back to the park, to the pregnant tranquillity, to the many small beauties of nature that surfeit the eye but ache in the memory like lost loves; to the fragrance of flowers and mown grass and the oozy resin of pine, to the cool oases of shade like manifestations of God's mercy in the midst of the inferno, to the ducks and the darting squirrels

88

and other small uncorrupt creatures; and to the almost mythical figure of Eliza that moves continually across my mind's eye but never reaches the raw, unguarded edge of my remembrance: Eden before the Fall.

I try to remember how she became a part of my life. If indeed she did. We moved in two worlds, treading separate but occasionally meshing figures in some complicated interminable dance, seeing one another now remote, now tantalizingly close. Only rarely and fleetingly face to face—Nina of course always on the *qui vive*. Our encounters were tantalizing only to me, I must grudgingly admit. Yet assuredly there was something between us, something that defies definition. On my part a great incomprehensible tenderness. On hers? She must have seen me as an aging man. Personable, I like to think, perhaps even distinguished. Not that it matters now. A man greying about the temples (my hair, grown now long enough for me to see, has the sickly whiteness of a plant bereft of light) and perhaps slightly stooped after years of desk work, but still the one to beat at the faculty squash tournament. Well back in the marathon pack but always sticking it out.

She came into my life, of course, that day in the Café del Rey, but I never expected to see or hear of her again. Had that been our only encounter, I idly wonder, should I be haunted still by the pallid nudity of her hands and the depths of her vulnerable eyes? Likely not. In the bustle and the somewhat forced euphoria of the wedding preparations, the sense of something momentous in that meeting of eyes would doubtless have passed into oblivion along with a score of other "unforgettable" experiences. But as the weeks went by I became aware of Eliza orbiting my existence as one becomes aware of a dripping tap. Not a happy analogy, but the repeated reminders of her presence somewhere out there made just that sort of insistent and cumulative claim on my attention.

Images of her from those days invade my mind and vanish like the slides my colleague Juan Moreno used to flash before his students to demonstrate his theory of subliminal imprinting. Eliza getting off a bus (my first inkling of her lovely legs). A curtain swinging aside and falling in the window of a house on the Avenida Albeniz, unveiling her, enfolded in soft light, for an instant so brief and so miraculously synchronized with my glance in passing that I could not but take it as an augury. Eliza at the theatre, rapt and pleased as a child by some stale Castilian romance. And something perhaps of the same absorption in my own expression as I watch *her*, for Nina's elbow strikes me in the ribs and she says with an edge of petulance, "Let's go, Gaspar. This is insufferable." On the way home she adds pointedly, "I don't know how *anyone* could be taken in by such rubbish."

Other glimpses of Eliza, fortuitous, not yet contrived, vanishing round corners, swept along in crowds, wandering bemused among the pigeons before the Monumento de Liberación.

Then she is proffering canapés and I am standing confused, with no hand free to take one. I say, nothing else coming to mind, "Thank you." And then, finding myself surprisingly possessed of her name, "Thank you, Eliza."

She looks startled at that. I have a foolish urge to apologize. Not because I have taken a liberty but, I sense, because I have acted out of what she perceives to be my character. She perhaps expected my mind to be on more weighty things. There is, however, something in her eyes. A sort of appeal. I remember our eyes' first encounter—does she?—and have the same vertiginous sense of destiny.

I recover my composure and look down at her tray, then at my hands, Nina's gin fizz in one and my Cerveza Jaguar in the other. I open my mouth to speak, but there are no words ready. But then she does a preposterous thing. Or so it ought to be. She takes one of the tidbits from her tray and thrusts it into my mouth. For an instant we face one another, eye to unguarded eye.

Only afterwards do I analyse and seek to understand her look. Maybe there is mockery. Certainly defiance. Curiosity? Yes, but of a strange, seemingly agonizing kind. Diffidence, of course, but something more. Anxiety. Fear, of a sort. Not of me as a person but of some possible outcome, perhaps, of this encounter. I stand there effectively gagged with anchovy on rye, on the brink of outrageous behaviour of my own. The urge to put my arm about her is almost irresistible. I want to *comfort* her. (Who in this stiff-necked gathering would swallow such an explanation? Yet somewhere in my past there is a similar experience that sanctions, prompts, such a gesture of compassion.) I have no idea why, or indeed if, she is in need of comfort. And in any case there is the tray, and the drinks, and the barbed barrier of propriety, between us.

It was all over so quickly that no one seemed to have noticed. There was no titter at what she had done, no clucking of tongues (no subsequent sarcasm from Nina, either). I reawakened to the surrounding hubbub, and as Eliza passed on with her tray I caught the word *protégée*.

Our hostess, Señora de Bedoya, who likes to be called Doña Sofía, is one of those middle-aged women who in widowhood cling desperately to the fringes of the social milieu to which they have been introduced by their husband's station in life. She maintains her entrée to the houses of the middling rich and the blue-blooded poor by giving lavish parties she can ill afford. The sense I receive from the make-up of the crowd on this occasion is that she is losing ground.

One economy Doña Sofía practises in her struggle against inflation on one hand and the insouciance of society on the other is the exploitation of her protégées, of whom there has been a long and interesting succession. God knows where she finds them, or how; all well-educated but in varying degrees indigent, foreigners mostly, seeking to establish themselves in this strange land. They are only slightly her social inferiors, worthy sharers of her roof and table, but willing on occasion to assume the duties, if not the status, of servants. Hence Eliza.

The gossip Nina picked up and presumably edited for my benefit was that Eliza, having been orphaned at a fairly early age, had been raised by foster parents who took her to live in Spain for several years. While there she acquired both a fluency in the language and, from contact with a series of interesting exiles, a passion for things *latinoamericano*. Having worked variously in England and Spain as tutor, translator, children's nurse, and secretary to amass a little money, she had foolishly (in Nina's opinion) cast herself adrift on this continent in the hope of finding employment, a long-vanished relative, and (Nina again) a rich husband. She had now lived for six months upon the charity of the widow Bedoya and appeared to have little prospect of achieving any of these ambitions.

When it came to husbands, rich or otherwise, I had neither the means nor the inclination to help. But in the matter of employment I could at least exert a little influence. Not directly, of course, since she had no qualifications that would admit her to my narrow world. And there was always Nina. But it was here that the quadrille-like structure of our society came into play. I never knew precisely the chain of events that resulted from my initiative. It sufficed for me to hint to the wife of a certain coffee broker (whose son I had been able to help find a junior place on the faculty) that it was a matter of some importance to me that Eliza be rescued from her dependence upon the Señora de Bedoya. The broker no doubt had his own share of unrequited favours, and so over a period of several weeks the virtues and accomplishments of Eliza were touted from one sphere of influence to another until she found employment.

And so it was with a satisfaction bordering on the smug that I watched her wheeling her carriage that day in the park. My pleasure was perhaps clouded a little by an ungenerous regret that she was unaware of my part in her good fortune. Unaware also of my presence there on the bridge, or so it must have seemed to anyone watching. The jackal, for example, or the parasol-toting frump on the bench. It appeared so even to me at first. Or worse, that she deliberately ignored me. Even now I cannot explain the manner of my divining that she knew I was there. Not only knew but cared. And this conviction of her caring gave rise to all sorts of extravagant, half-formed hopes. Hopes, I now all too plainly realize, that must have shocked her had she known of them. What a fool I might have made of myself, had things worked out otherwise.

What, I wonder, did she make of my interest in her? Did it occur to her that we saw each other more often than might be explained by coincidence? Did she assume my presence there on that particular day was contrived? It wasn't really, in truth, although I might so easily have gone by way of the

Calle San Fernando instead of through the park. I merely played the odds, shall we say, on my way back from the bicycle repair shop where I had left Nina's English Raleigh some days before. It still wasn't ready. Overwhelmed with work, he said, the queer fish called Alejandro. Enough jobs piled up to keep three men busy. Hadn't had a day at the races in more than a month. Couldn't even, he said without cracking a smile although he was the most notorious backslider in the city, take his wife to church.

He was by repute the best cycle mechanic and fixer of small contraptions in the city. I say "by repute" because I always harboured a certain doubt, suspecting that the legend of his superior skill sprang from his singular hold upon the imagination of the people. Including Nina. When it came to replacing a worn sprocket, no one else would do. It must be Alejandro.

He worked, this putative genius, surrounded by an extraordinary clutter. In the midst of which had stood, when I wheeled in Nina's toy several days before, conspicuous as a pearl in its slimy abode, a burgundy-coloured, chromium-bedecked baby carriage; or, as the maker's discreet decal insisted, perambulator. Half blinded as I was by the glare of the noonday plaza, it struck me with all the force of an apparition. It stood there among the rusty frames, the hunting-trophy handlebars, the greasy chains festooned like the webs of monstrous metal-eating spiders, giving back the stray beams of the bench light by which Alejandro, spider-like himself, worked on, unmindful of my entry, or pretending to be. It stood there, that carriage, as if demanding obeisance. Minus a wheel.

I waited. It was some power he had, something in his priestlike preoccupation with—and mystification of—the task at hand that moved the watcher to reverence and humility. Persons who set far greater price upon their time than I—lawyers, dentists, prostitutes—have been known to feign interest in last year's calendar or the instructions on the side of a long-defunct fire extinguisher rather than distract Alejandro's attention from the assembling of a three-speed hub or the arranging of ball-bearings in their annuli of grease. I at least had, courtesy of Prescott Perambulators, Manchester and Kilmarnock (By Appointment), the splendid carriage to contemplate.

It was in fact my interest in it, my move forward to peer into its sumptuous interior, that seemed to penetrate the shell of Alejandro's abstraction. Something in the abrupt way he swung about left me disconcerted, with a caught-in-the-act sense of furtiveness. His eyes, unblinking, seemed no bigger than sequins above the half-lenses teetering at the end of his nose.

"Qué desea?" Curt, guarded. He held up the wheel to the light and spun it critically while I explained about the sprocket.

He said nothing.

"When, then, do you think . . . ?"

He went through the rigmarole about the races, the sabbath deprivation of his long-suffering wife, regarding me dispassionately through a blur of spokes.

"A couple of days, maybe? Three?"

He drew down the corners of his mouth, which always struck me as reptilian, just perceptibly lifted his shoulders, and turned back to the bench. I leaned the bike against a battered locker and strode angrily out. Perhaps it stands there yet.

Alejandro, according to Paulo, now somewhat recovered from his catechism, is dead.

His reply, when I asked how he knew, was cryptic. "One cannot ask questions without giving answers."

He relented a little later, pitying my obtuseness. "They spoke of him in the past tense."

I waited for more, but Paulo turned to the wall, gave up the ghost of the day's beans, and muttered, "A great loss to the profession, Alejandro." He composed himself for sleep.

And I? My mind wanders these days, I fear. Instead of pursuing the interesting paths of speculation opened up by Paulo's remarks—the nature of "the profession" for example, to which the demise of Alejandro would mean so much— I drifted off into idle thoughts and random memories of Nina. Beginning with her annoyance about the bicycle, and my failure to get an answer out of Alejandro. She is prone to a childlike petulance on such occasions, which she visits upon

94

the nearest person. Almost invariably me. Was I, she demanded, man or mouse? Was I afraid of that . . . that . . . ?
But she couldn't bring herself to revile Alejandro. A fact that
I drew to her attention. Even I had to laugh at the image my
insinuation suggested.

"You're disgusting."

"I know, but other men are wild about you, why not him?"

Nina did not, to my knowledge, encourage her admirers,
but their homage, however unflattering it might be, seemed
in her eyes to entitle them to her respect.

She turned her back on me, determined to sustain her anger,
or at least to exact a penance. Ah, how well I have come to
know you, Nina. How appropriate the pet name you carried
with you from childhood: Niña, one spoilt little girl in a batch
of brothers, the "little mistress" to a succession of doting
servants; shedding the tilde with great difficulty only in your
late teens when it became too great an embarrassment. How
easily your scolding is checked by a little flattery, your anger
appeased by a caress. I have but to come to you as you stand
there in your attitude of scornful hostility and whisper your
real name, used only by strangers and by me in the most
intimate of moments, so that it has assumed for us a sort of
arcane significance. Angélica: the ultimate endearment. The
face I see in the mirror will soften; reluctantly, and only a
little. You will resist my first gentle touch, your flesh tense,
unyielding as wood (how do you *do* that?), but your rigidly
folded arms will lift imperceptibly to admit my hands, and
as soon as they shape themselves to the prodigal fullness of
your breasts I shall feel the first augury of your surrender. If
surrender is the appropriate word for the violent, demanding
passion the merest caress will unleash.

It made us late for dinner. We lay long together in the
twilight, in that blissful dreamy afterwards, serenaded by cica-
das, the fans stroking our bodies with cool beams of air. If
images of Eliza intruded, they were as shadowy and remote
as the angels that, according to the tapestry text made by
Nina when she was a *niña* and which hangs above our bed,
watched over us while we slept. Or didn't. At the time, the
half-formed idea of a ghostly Eliza watching over us while
we didn't sleep was not without a certain piquancy.

I believe I was in fact asleep, angel-watched or not, when I became aware of Nina's hands caressing, inciting, coveting. At the first inkling of response she rolled atop me and gave a long, moaning sigh of pleased anticipation.

Always ready for a romp is Nina. I remember the very first time I found the courage to kiss her. She seemed so regal, so secure in her ripe femininity, that I was as gauche as a teen-ager, full of foolish trepidation. Anticipating, perhaps, a slap in the face. Which could not have shocked me more than the aggressive hunger of her response. Nothing coy about Nina.

So, as the darkness fell that afternoon, she engulfed me with the savagery of her desire and filled the room with the loud, wailing sounds of her rapture. We soared and soared, making the moment endure as though we knew it was for the last time. And she cried out at the height of her abandon, "Gaspar! Gaspar! Gaspar! What would I ever do without you?"

What, indeed?

XIII

Since we have been here Paulo has talked little about our time at Cambridge. He has shown a strange reluctance on those occasions when the ache of nostalgia has prompted me to try, by some scribbled reference, to bring the subject up. I concluded that his character had undergone so great an inversion in the years between that his mind shied away from the remembrance of happiness as others shy away from the remembrance of pain. Or that, sensing my pleasure in dwelling upon those days, he chose to deny me the satisfaction. He is capable of that.

But suddenly all is changed. It is as if, having summoned all the refractory (I almost said heroic) forces of his being to frustrate his interrogators, to deny them information there is no longer any point in withholding, he has exhausted all his powers of reticence, as if he no longer has the fortitude to hold back the flood of "despicable sentiment". Not, of course, that there is anything sentimental in the way he relates it, but the reminiscent urge is unmistakably there. For hours he rambles on. At times it seems a sort of delirium. Despite the occasional "my Gaspar" I am convinced that from time to time he loses all awareness of my presence. The Gaspar he addresses is some Socratic extension of himself. I have awakened in the night to hear him still at it. Impossible to remember, let alone transcribe, it all. Next to impossible sometimes to adjust to his leaps in time and the twists and turns of his thought. But phrases, anecdotes, whole long tirades have invaded my consciousness, and will out with as much force and conviction as if they sprang from my own experience. I am as involved, mentally and emotionally, as when I was drawn into those harrowing recollections of his childhood. Except that then it was an innocent Paulo with whom I could readily identify; now I find myself parroting the words and repeating unchallenged the opinions of a man whose mind was already beginning to open to, if it was not already tainted with, ideas that I find repugnant.

"Good people," I heard him mumble in the midst of the night (night being defined for us not so much by darkness as by stillness), "the world has nothing to hope from good people." He said it with a faint echo of the strange Arabic lilt that redeemed Maar's elided London speech. That the world had nothing to hope from good people was Maar's credo.

He had said more than once of Maar: "What a formidable bloody woman she was." Formidable indeed. She might have been a consummate actress. Or a high-class courtesan. Or a cabinet minister. As it is, she combined the talents of all these in the service of Hafiz, or of the cause for which he stood. I could never fully understand the hold he had over her. I had sensed very early on that he possessed her as a hunter possesses and exploits a falcon: chained to his will but capable of predatory flights of her own. I sensed also that without her he would be nothing. I remember remarking to Paulo that she was the one who should have had that nose. Beak.

They were lovers, of course, although they were never demonstrative in the presence of others, and I eventually came to realize that even their love was subservient to the Cause. Subject, that is to say, to betrayal. And I don't mean mere infidelity. Maar's body was as much a weapon or a bait in the furtherance of their aims as a bomb or a proffered bribe. But I became convinced that if the Cause required it, each would have renounced or sacrificed the other without hesitation.

I call it a cause, but even now I cannot define what they stood for, or to whom they owed allegiance. They were anarchists of a sort, but their rhetoric offered vague glimpses of tomorrows which, if not exactly golden, were free from struggle and distress. This millennium of theirs seemed exceedingly remote, somewhat akin to the Christians' heaven except that the toilers in the Cause for generations to come had no hope of sharing in the felicity. It was a purely secular paradise, although they were fond of the word *jihad*. They seemed to have no religious convictions, but they exploited and when expedient even encouraged the convictions of others. Anyone anxious to die for the Cause in expectation of a reward hereafter was subtly incited to do so.

Yes, the fruit of their endeavours would be long on the vine and would be harvested by the unborn. In the interval there was no villainy so dark, no cruelty so inhuman, that it could not be glorified in the name of the Cause. It seemed that at that time the organization had not progressed far beyond the recruiting stage. They schemed and theorized. It is probable that many of their early disciples became enmeshed in the web simply because they found the inflammatory talk agreeable and stimulating, and realized too late that they were committed to action.

We didn't, of course, walk into all this cold. Everything I have said is hindsight. I did, as I have intimated, have qualms, serious forebodings, but it could not possibly have occurred to me that we were walking into quicksands of that sort. Most certainly it could not have occurred to Paulo. Whatever seeds of repudiation may have lain dormant in the deep subsoil of his psyche he was still, to all outward appearances at least, very much the patrician. My own worst fear was that Hafiz and Maar might be a couple of con artists. Which in a way they were, but even that scruple of mine seemed far-fetched. What pickings, after all, could they anticipate from us? From me, especially.

No, despite the menace I had sensed (and thought I might have imagined) when I met Maar, we went to their place that

Friday evening "to meet a few people" in the belief that they merely found us agreeable and interesting. Youth I suppose is prone to that sort of conceit. So we walked wide-eyed as lambs into that roomful of polyglot humanity. A web full of foolish flies I see them as now.

"That tower of bloody Babel" Paulo characterized it as at the time. It had more than a metaphorical truth. Their flat was under the eaves of a tall, silo-like structure clinging precariously to the corner of a run-down building not far from the river. A garage, I judged, for the sound of engines being revved up added to the already considerable difficulty of attending to one outlandish accent among many.

"What a motley crew," Paulo said during one of those nocturnal ramblings. "If it hadn't been for you, my Gaspar, I'd have got the hell out."

"Me?" I said, astonished, but of course he didn't hear.

"Thought I'd walked into a refugee camp. But I saw the way Maar looked at you. Had you halfway to bed in her mind. Didn't want to do you out of a lay, even though you were moonstruck over that piece you were always slinking off to see. Just leading you a dance she was anyway, Marjory, or whatever she was called."

"You *bastard*!" I shouted, rising to the bait. Later I decided that perhaps he really had, in spite of everything, forgotten her name. To think that after all that happened she was no more to him than "that piece" whose name he could not be bothered to recall!

"But it wasn't your body Maar was after, was it? It was your soul."

He was only half right there. She was after my "soul" all right, but if her aggressive attempts to seduce me were merely bait to trap me into total commitment, she put on a pretty impressive act. But I've already said she was a superb actress. Like all great performers, she made no distinction in her mind between the pretence and the real thing.

"The soul," Paulo rambled on. "We had a few down-and-outers over that, Maar and I."

For her it wasn't something that existed apart from the body or that lived on after death. It was something you had, a sort of moral bank account which you could be persuaded to invest in the work of the Cause. They argued about it, according to Paulo, even in bed. The faith that Smith woman had pounded into him was wearing thin by that time, but he defended it all the more fiercely for that.

"Remember that prick of a priest we had at Cambridge? Sean McClarty his name was, or something equally outlandish. What a mindless turd he was. But he got one thing right."

I heard Paulo struggling to sit up in the dark. The old Cambridge skill at mimicry briefly resurfaced and he gave a comical rendition of the priest's fruity voice. "You can always pick out the backsliders. They'll be the loudest in defence of the faith."

Well, Paulo wasn't that loud, normally, but there was something about Maar's smug certitude that drove him into the pulpit. He trotted out all the stale clichés and specious claptrap of a thousand years. In all seriousness. Or so he imagined. He was a hopeless case, as far as she was concerned. How she must have chuckled, later. Hopeless cases were her specialty, anyway. She saw the cracks in his façade right from the start, or so she claimed.

"Remember how interested she was when she heard me telling you about Ana? She and Hafiz both, but her especially. Saw a sore she could pick at until it bled."

Only first she had to contrive to have him available long enough to do the picking. Which was where I came in. The easy target. Oppressed peasant written all over me. *Upstart* oppressed peasant. The most desirable kind. Your *chusma*, your rabble made up of cowherds and stable-shovellers, are fine when you want to set a mindless rabble in motion. Just goad the backsides of one or two and they'll stampede like the beasts they tend. Just be sure they're pointed in the right direction, that's all: a mob on the move's got no ears, no reins, no brakes. You can't call it back any more than you can call back a bullet.

"Can't you just hear her holding forth? For her sort of work, she said, she needed people of intelligence and education. Not too much of either, mind you. Just enough to make them governable. She saw you as the ideal recruit. A dormant volcano of proletarian spleen with a guidance system and a shut-off valve. She certainly had you figured wrong, didn't she? Not your suitability, I mean, but your vulnerability."

He fell silent, seemed to sleep. I thought I heard a snore. But almost at once he took it up again.

"Your soul slipped through her fingers. Why? A thousand times we could have used you. You weren't exactly heroic, but that's not always a bad thing. A few of my best jobs were blown by reckless bastards. Your kamikaze is a bomb with a short fuse. But you didn't succumb to her spell, did you? Too much intelligence or not enough? Or was it just that she never got you into bed? If she had, man, she'd have sucked the soul right out of you once and for all. God, what a woman! She'd have taught you to beg, roll over, play dead, fetch and carry, jump through a hoop. And when you were thoroughly besotted she would cut you off. But you'd perform anyway. No longer just for her but for the Cause. Wanting to do it because your soul was oriented that way, stroked by the magnet of her sensuality. And because it was the only way to fill the abysmal emptiness she'd left inside you."

Is that what happened to you, Paulo?

"With me it was a little different. It was a power struggle from the start, although perhaps neither of us recognized it at first."

For some time she paid little attention to him, overtly at least. Afterwards he had reason to believe she had been watching and assessing him all the time, even that first evening at their place, as one studies the habits and temperament of a potential quarry. Looking for the constants that can be counted on no matter what, and the idiosyncrasies that can wreck the preparation of months. After a few years of doing that sort of thing himself he realized how intense her observation of him must have been and how far back it must have gone. He remembered trivial things that she would have noticed and filed away in that incredible brain of hers for future reference. Like the way he reacted when we walked into that poky apartment full of the riff-raff of five continents.

As we groped our way up the dark stairs Paulo sniffed the rancid air, the stale odours of squalor, staying well clear of the walls in his Savile Row suit. I could sense the aversion mounting in him, the mutiny. Several steps down from their door he balked. It was a fence he was not about to take. He half turned. I wouldn't have been slow to follow. We lie here now on the threshold of God-knows-what horrors because at the instant of our flight the stairway was flooded with light, the hubbub of voices poured forth, and Hafiz, divining our intention, ran down and seized me by the shoulder. The easy target. Paulo followed as our host literally dragged me into the room.

It was full of social misfits of both sexes. Skins of all colours. Every garb you could imagine: headgear from turbans and burnouses to gor'blimey caps; dress from dhotis to oily dungarees. There was a woman in what today would be called a jump-suit, purple and green, of unutterable vulgarity. They all swung round to look at us with the precision of a shoal of fish. At Paulo, to be precise. Paulo in his elegant suit. Their stares were so frankly astonished that I turned to look at him too. His own surprised expression was hardening into that mask of lofty contempt that only the true aristocrat can command, and that oppressed multitudes the world over recognize and resent more than all the wrongs of tyranny. But before that look could freeze upon his face his eyes widened and he stepped forward as though entering a room full of friends. And it was at that moment that Maar came in from the kitchen. I glanced, as she came forward to greet us, in the direction Paulo had been looking. A young woman stood there. She might have been a *granjera* from our own mountains, the wife or daughter of some impoverished rock-scratcher of the eastern Andes.

"Ana. I could have sworn it was Ana," he said later, confessing to feeling a little foolish. "It wasn't, of course. Very little like her, in fact, when I got close." But there was a nebulous something, perhaps not merely physical, that brought it all back.

It's all pretty confused in my own head now, but from what I recall of the time when Paulo was still, to use his words, "soft in the heart", as one might say "soft in the head"—and when, it seems safe to assume, his testimony on such matters was more reliable—he must have experienced something like a revelation. When he saw his pseudo-Ana there in the midst of all those (to him) socially unacceptable people, the hard shell of his gentility began to crack and fall away, leaving him naked, exposed, a sort of spiritual *tabula rasa*.

It didn't show much on the surface, that I recall, beyond a certain taciturnity. At least I wasn't astute enough to notice. It is only now, sifting through the detritus of that dead past— fossil fragments of our old intimate relationship—that I see this, above all, as the point at which his social and political convictions began perceptibly to veer. There are half-remembered snatches of conversation, fleeting images, gut feelings which, held up to the light of my present knowledge, suggest that as we beat it homeward that night in the blustery autumn darkness, Paulo, unbeknown to both of us, was changed for ever.

"Those poor deluded bastards," I remember he came out with. I could barely hear him against the background of the chucking-out-time revelry of the pub we were passing. Maar's guests, he meant, of course, not the tipsy revellers. And it bears analysis. They were still deluded, still bastards, but now they were "poor". They had elicited sympathy. You see my difficulty? Paulo has spoken of it since, here, but he no longer knows what sympathy is. "Poor", in his current vocabulary, is a term of contempt.

"Who can blame them for being so bloody anti?" was something else he said that night. He startled me out of a long daydream, so I knew he'd been thinking about them as we walked. "Anti" still implied error. They were "anti" what he stood for, but he was now conceding some measure of justification.

There arises an image of Paulo, sharp and true upon my mind's eye as though it had lain all those years in a mislaid family album: Paulo sprawled in his big leather armchair— sitting, as we used to say, on his shoulder-blades—smoking a nauseating Turkish cigarette foisted upon him by one of Maar's disciples. We must have stayed up well into the small hours, because what comes back with the image is the gist of the story he was telling and the sound of the clock in the nearby tower measuring out the hours of the night with sonorous strokes that echoed in the Andean valleys to which Paulo's words had transported me.

The anguish of those Ana days still lay with him, heavy, undigested. He was willing in those days to admit as much. Reminded of it recently, however, he came back with some sneering dismissal of "what you romantics call 'heartache'. The gas pain you get from larding life with too much sentiment."

But seeing that girl at Maar's place that night brought back not only a twinge of the old heartache but something else, something he had forgotten. At first as he began to speak of it he had so much trouble putting it into context that it was as though he strove to recall a nightmare. There were enough of those, God knows, in the months after his father died and Uncle Alvaro took control of his life. Later, he has since told me, he confirmed the events with Ramón, who had a prodigious memory.

Once, on the way back from town, they took the road that ran north of the hacienda, a track barely wide enough for the car, and rocky, hard going even for a mule. Ramón remembered the specific occasion because he had trouble explaining the leak in the gas tank.

"A little business to look after," Ramón had said as he swung the car off the main road.

Paulo had no idea of the nature of the "business", but Ramón's one remaining eye had a lascivious twinkle all those years later when he was reminded of it.

When the road got too rough to go any farther, Ramón told Paulo to wait in the car and went ahead on foot. He must have been a long time. Paulo wriggled and squirmed and fretted until he could sit still no longer. Right in front of the car was a big rocky bluff, swelling out and sagging over the road "like Padre Ortíz Franco's paunch", he said. His curiosity about what lay beyond the bluff got the better of him. He didn't have the will to resist, in spite of all his father's warnings about what would happen if he ever disobeyed Señorita Smith, or Ramón when he was in the latter's charge. Smith was gone by then—Uncle Alvaro would have none of her. But the fear instilled by Paulo's father was still there. And anyway, Alvaro had sucked at the same tit.

I must have half dozed, passed into a sort of semi-hypnotic state, for although I could recall no more words, the substance of what Paulo went on to relate was so vividly with me when I awoke to the new day that I lay for a long time disoriented, as though I had mislaid my soul somewhere during the night. There was nothing especially harrowing about what happened to Paulo. (Or, as it seemed in that strange, dazed state of mine, to me.) In fact, little or nothing did happen, in the existential sense.

Paulo climbed out of the car and stole along the track, furtively, staying close in under that sagging belly of rock because he was terrified of the chasm that yawned on the other side. And because he expected at any moment to hear the thunderous voice of Señor Martínez, who had ousted God from his throne and was just waiting for a chance to send down one of his sudden hot fingers of lightning. It was a long way round the bluff. Beyond, the track widened a little and dipped downward. The rock face leaned away to the right, far enough from the vertical to permit a tethered goat to graze, and a man, held to his task by a tether less tangible but no less restrictive, and only moderately afflicted with arthritis, to struggle up, hoe on shoulder, to a small irregular field that hung from the sky. The rocky slopes over which he passed with crab-like gait were veined and splotched with yellow where flowering weeds grew in the fissures. These were poisonous, as any child knew, but their blooms touched that barren place with beauty. The air was vibrant with the hum of bees coaxing sweetness from that noxious growth and carrying it back to a row of hives below. Glancing up to the right, seeing only that colourful patchwork soaring up to a skyline humped against a fleeced blue heaven, one might have found the scene idyllic.

Leftward, it was otherwise; a prospect of appalling squalor. A large lip of rock, some three hundred metres long, leaned out over the abyss like an immense bracket fungus. Around its perimeter, at the very edge of emptiness, a row of shacks so crude and chaotic that they might have been mistaken for the debris of some natural disaster, or the refuse of a nearby metropolis. They were cobbled together from everything imaginable that could be scavenged from the creations of God and the trash-heaps of man, neither of which were prolific thereabouts. Branches of dead trees, dragged in with enormous labour from God-knows-where, lashed together with ends of rope, wire, and lianas that did not grow within a week's walk of there, were interlaced with decaying fronds, pampas-grass, and stunted bamboo such as one saw heaped high upon the backs of women along the highway. These flimsy structures were given an illusion of substance here and there by sheets of rusty metal, salvaged scraps of half-rotten lumber, and tattered canvas. On one, the uncured hide of a donkey, tail still attached, was aswarm with flies. On the side of another the panel of a long-ago truck proclaimed—with excruciating irony, for the stench overlying the place was foul beyond belief—the merits of a certain PERFUMERIA FOR-TEZA, FUENTE DE LAS FRAGANCIAS.

Beside the first house an old woman squatted with her buttocks overhanging the cliff. In the semicircular space before her two dogs contended for a huge bone, possibly another remnant of the donkey. Naked children stood about the yard listlessly waving away the flies. Several girls had a boy backed up against a rock and were flicking and prodding at his genitals with the woody stems of weeds. From the fetid interior of one of the shacks came the sound of someone softly moaning. A woman's voice was repeating words of ostensible comfort but her tone was petulant, resentful.

To Paulo these sounds, combined with the smells that seemed to shimmer visibly in the noonday heat, were like the living, suffering spirit of the place reaching out to ensnare him. Half-remembered words of priestly menace rose and echoed in his mind: Gehenna, Golgotha, Purgatory. Yet there was a deadly fascination, a compulsion to peer into the watchful dark of those hovels, as one pokes and pries at the lairs of night creatures, half in curiosity, half in terror. The solemn eyes of the children followed him, inviting yet defying encounter. The girls ceased their sport and turned to stare, perhaps in hope of a new victim. Clothes were no defence against the scorch of their speculative gaze.

This place, this nightmare scene induced in me by Paulo's half-heeded narrative, shocked and terrified me, whose early childhood surroundings had been but marginally better. What, then, must have been its effect on him, so long accustomed to the order and opulence of the Hacienda Martínez, so long insulated from the encompassing squalor? He must have stood there bereft of will by all those dispassionate eyes, overwhelmed by the noxious emanations of the place.

The old woman at the cliff edge rose and dropped her skirt. She approached Paulo with a bizarre, dancing gait, her bare feet kicking out at each step, imparting a birdlike motion to her body. It ought to have been ludicrous but it was terrifying. He wanted to run, but he was bound there by all those eyes, by that ensnaring ambience. The yellow stare of the woman fixed him with the glazed intensity of a belligerent rooster. Impossible to say what evil he anticipated from her. His fear was physical but it was his soul that quailed, shrank in upon itself so that as he stood there watching her approach it seemed a matter of small moment that he wet his pants.

What freed him from that dread paralysis was a scream, so sudden in the midst of that tense waiting that he almost fainted with fright. And then words. Agonized words rising into a second scream, as though dragged from the sufferer with instruments of torture.

"It's coming! It's coming!"

The words and the scream seemed to persist in the still air, becoming one with the pressing heat, presaging whatever dread thing it was that was coming.

The old woman swung about. All the children ran to crowd about the hovel from which the scream had come. The moaning resumed, more compulsive now, prophetic of screams to come. Voices inside were shouting. The old woman drove the children away with cuffs and kicks but they pressed close behind her as she went in.

Paulo ran.

Screams pursued him round the bluff. He ran regardless of the gaping void, fearing only the phantom *it* whose coming could implant such terror in a human soul. He sat cowering wet-assed in the car, waiting for Ramón, reliving that horror.

But it was not until that night, when he lay sweating and afraid to sleep, that a detail of that chaotic scene came back to him, came back first to tease and then to torment him with doubts of its reality. Was it memory or imagination? On a nail beside the opening about which the naked children swarmed, craning to see into the shack, something was hanging. Memory made it a basket. But was it really brightly embroidered with leaves and flowers, or was this merely a foolish fancy, an illusion engendered by the odd conviction that he'd heard such screams before?

XIV

Another thing Maar might have excelled at was psychiatry. Not only did she get that story out of Paulo but she let him stew in the emotions that welled up from that deep-drifted past. He was profoundly shaken by it at the time, to the point of being sick for several weeks, but still he saw it as an isolated event, an interlude of terror such as might be occasioned by getting lost in the swarming crowds of the market-place (thus giving Uncle Alvaro an excuse to fire Señorita Smith), or by spending several hours on a barn roof in a rising wind, unable to get back on the ladder by which he had ascended. That glimpse of the dark underside of human society shocked him, but it did not strike him as a judgement upon the Martínez way of life, nor did it demand from him any direct involvement or concern. It did not present itself to him as a situation about which something might be done, least of all by him, any more than it occurred to him to offer to feed that old woman's pig. Or, for that matter, the old woman herself, who obviously needed it more.

No, the life of the hacienda went on. If its tenor was not smooth, it at least resumed after a time some semblance of normality. Uncle Alvaro was harsh, but fortunately was absent a lot, as Paulo's father had been. Two attempts to fill the large shoes of Señorita Smith having proved disastrous, it was decreed that Paulo should be sent away to school, and in the ensuing trauma the tragedy of Ana and the plight of the local peasantry were alike forgotten.

Only to be revived and subtly exploited by the resourceful Maar. Those ancient sources of anguish, along with others more immediate in our lives, Paulo's and mine, were all grist to the relentless mill of the Cause.

Whether or not Maar came into the room on that occasion in time to see Paulo's incipient contempt for her other guests, it was only a matter of weeks before he had come, under her guidance, to recognize those unfortunate people with their various obsessions as part of the universal misery of which Ana, the pig woman, and the residents of that mountain shanty town were exemplars. On that first evening he unbent only so far as to exchange a polite, bored word or two with a few of them and to behave with a certain stiff gallantry towards the woman Laura of the Ana soul. Later, from motives more compassionate than romantic, he even cultivated her acquaintance, but one of the characteristics she had in common with the original Ana was a certain insouciance in matters of personal hygiene. At that time he was still very far from being ready to repudiate, along with all the other attributes of aristocracy, the extreme fastidiousness that sometimes irked even me.

That symbolic renunciation of the habits and conditioning of a lifetime would come much later, long after I had lost touch with him. He adopted his new, uncouth persona along with the name El Azote. It was probably a pose at first, a histrionic gesture of rebellion against the society that had produced him, but long before fate threw us together again his nature had hardened in the mould of vulgarity and slovenliness as a body long constrained takes on a permanent deformity. He was quoted somewhere as saying, "You can't fight the people's war in a Savile Row suit. You can't kill with conviction got up like a tailor's dummy."

I was too taken up with Martha to have much interest in what I thought of as Paulo's passing association with Hafiz and Maar. I would occasionally go with him to one of those evening gatherings, but the talk bored and sometimes irritated me. I am not (Cheshire Cat, please note) a political person. Their motives seemed more vindictive than remedial. I had no inkling of the extent of the web of machination and intrigue of which that smelly apartment was the centre. Even the events that involved or in various ways affected me are still confused in my mind. I cannot arrange them in any logical sequence of cause and effect.

Was it mere accident, for example, that Maar appeared at that precise moment on that particular street corner in Cambridge where I stood waiting for Martha? Is there some satanic stage manager of such accidents, who contrived that Maar should rush up and clutch me in an embrace so passionate as to seem almost indecent in that public place, just as Martha came round the corner? What had got into the woman? My astonishment was genuine, but it did nothing to placate Martha. How could I convince her that there was nothing in our relationship, mine and Maar's, to warrant such an extravagant display of affection? Apart from that touching of feet under the table at the Mitre, I was not even aware that we had a relationship.

Before I could recover my breath or my wits, Maar had kissed me and rushed off, leaving me to face the music.

"Well!" Martha said with that edge of sarcasm only a jealous woman can command. "And who might *that* be?" *That*, as if in reference to something unsavoury underfoot on the pavement.

"Her name's Maar. She's . . . she's a friend."

"I can see that." I had not believed her capable of such bitterness, my sweet, mild Martha.

"A friend of Paulo's, actually."

"Well, she acted pretty friendly toward you, I thought." But already her tone had softened. There were tears in her eyes when she said, "If she really means a lot to you, I—well, I mean, we're not engaged or anything. If you'd rather—"

In my anger at Maar and at what I saw as the injustice of fate, I was quicker to protest my innocence than to reaffirm my love for Martha. Blundering and inept, I succeeded only in making matters worse. In the end we let it drop and went to our movie. I spent most of the time watching the play of shadows over Martha's set, sullen face. When at last I captured her hand, it lay in mine stiff and unresponsive, as though dead. On the way home I again endeavoured to plead my innocence, and this time I tried to convince her of the singleness of my love for her, but in my bewildered resentment I could not find the words to reach into the depths of her hurt. How well, now, I know the extent of her suffering, but then she merely seemed impervious to reason. Her silences seemed to turn my protestations against me. At the door she offered me her cheek to kiss. The cheek of a marble statue.

It was while this hurt was festering between us that the devilish manipulator of human affairs decreed that their paths should cross, Martha's and Paulo's. I have said that she was my secret, and in a sense she was. Paulo knew I was seeing her, of course. That I was, to use his own expression, "moony as a *muchacha*". I had long dreamed of showing her off to him, of letting him see the extent of her devotion, of basking, perhaps, in the pleased awareness of his envy. But I made no effort to bring them together. I suppose I even sought to preclude, or at least to defer, such a meeting, although at the time it seemed simply that our respective busy lives afforded no opportunity. Now, it seems that some jealous intuition, some fearful insecurity, prompted me to keep those two compartments of my life insulated one from the other. My blessedness was so precious, so fragile a thing. I had to shield it from the chill winds of reality.

Yet the meeting was inevitable, was it not?

On a lunch-time stroll one day, Paulo and I met the Lomans. A casual enough encounter. Small talk. A little banter about the black eye Paulo had given himself with a tennis racquet. Gloomy speculation about the weather, straightway justified as a few large drops starred the pavement around us, hastening our parting.

Sara gripped my arm and sparkled at me through her glasses. "Dinner on Sunday, then, eh?"

It was while I was glumly anticipating the inevitable awkwardness and pain of that occasion that Sara shouted back, "And bring your friend along, why don't you?"

He didn't seem especially eager. I believe he was already enjoying his battle of wills with Maar and would have preferred her dingy sitting-room to the Lomans' pleasant, well-appointed bungalow. If I pressed him, it was less out of a sense of fellowship than out of a hope that his liveliness might atone for my lack of it, and thus salvage what promised to be a disastrous evening, and of course it did. The Lomans were charmed. So was Martha. Warmed by the wine she

laughed with the rest of us at Paulo's stories of schoolboy
pranks and at his impersonations of the college dons. In her
mirth at one point she leaned to me in the old familiar way,
her hand on my arm. Our eyes met, suddenly sobered, remembering. Then I felt her fingers tighten and she patted my arm
before turning to speak to Sara.

So all was going to be well. In that warm conviction perhaps
I took a little more wine than was prudent. I suppose we
all did. In the general good humour, the only part of the
conversation that comes back to me seemed to be no more
than harmless banter. There seemed nothing calculating in
Martha's casual remark to Paulo.

"I saw your friend Maar in town the other day."

Apparently not surprised, he said, with a wink at me,
"She's more Gaspar's friend than mine. He's a real Lothario,
that Gaspar."

The conversation and the mirth rolled on. The words, it
seemed, had been accepted in their intended, teasing sense
and at once forgotten.

Near midnight we walked Martha home, Paulo and I. He
waited at the gate while I took her to the door. When I took
her in my arms for the goodnight kiss that was going to
assuage the anguish of our misunderstanding, she beat my
chest with her fists.

"You're drunk. You're drunk. Please go away."

She tore herself free. The door closed. But not before she
burst into tears.

I see now only too clearly what I should have done. The
very next day I should have taken Paulo to her. I should have
made him explain that he had spoken his foolish words in
jest, not dreaming she would take them seriously; that there
was nothing between Maar and me, that I had in fact been
less than friendly to her up to that point. He would have been
ready to do that—then. But I let the situation drag on, my
stubborn pride augmenting as my misery deepened. I went
in search of Martha several times. She was always out. Or
she pretended to be. The letter I wrote went unanswered.
Little wonder. It had hardly slipped from my fingers into the
pillar-box (which I thereupon kicked from sheer vexation)
when I knew that its tone of recrimination and self-pity could

only make her more angry. I burned with shame at the thought of her contempt.

Weeks went by. Obviously it was all over. I stayed away from the Lomans' and avoided the places where they might be encountered. Out of bravado, I suppose, I went about my daily life as though some vital part of me had not shrivelled and died. I went pubbing with Paulo, played tennis, even tried out for rugby. At which, inevitably, I was woefully inept. The second time out I suffered several broken ribs and a back injury.

Martha, I naïvely thought, lying there in my hospital bed, will surely come to see me. Day after day as the visitors filed along the corridor I waited and watched for her, daydreaming our passionate and tearful reconciliation. She never came.

Maar did, though. Every day. After the first week, that is, when she got to hear of my injury. My welcome that first time was not warm. I spent her whole visit in a state of suppressed panic. What if Martha came in answer to my constant prayers and found her there? Maar, however, had a thick skin. She also possessed infinite patience. And an endless fund of simulated sympathy. She brought sweets and fruit and books, and stayed until the nurse chased her out.

By the end of that second week the Devil herself would have been welcome, come visiting-time. I found myself listening for Maar's quick, determined tread.

She would read to me until I foundered in drugged, dream-filled sleep. She would still be there, smiling, when I awoke. Her softly accented voice would coil around and caress my bleary mind, implanting images that I carried down again with me into that troubled sleep; images of oppressed and famished multitudes roving the earth in search of something they could not imagine and would never see. I remember with terrifying clarity the images of a herd of starved, gazelle-like creatures roving a vast plain in which there were oases so lush and beautiful that I felt the ache of those beasts' insatiable longing. Whenever they reached one of the pools and bent down their human faces to drink, the water would become solid as glass. When they reached for the fruits that hung so prodigally within their grasp, the fruits would burst and vanish like bubbles.

When I could speak without pain, Maar encouraged me to talk. She was so earnest and flattering in her interest, so perceptive in her questioning, that I rambled shamelessly, reliving my childhood, evoking for her the splendours and squalors of my native province. I described, with perhaps a foreshadowing of my novelist's passion for narrative, the people, the customs and traditions, the unstable institutions, the turbulent politics. It all seemed to pour spontaneously forth, but it is plain to me now that my recollections were being prompted, my sentiments orchestrated, by that judicious questioning.

"You were going to tell me about your lucky father."

I couldn't recall having made such an undertaking, but it was a good story, not likely to start her off on one of her political tirades.

"Ah, yes, my resourceful father."

"And cunning," she reminded me.

"And cunning, as you'll see." She drew her chair close so that I caught the slightly oppressive fragrance of her perfume and the faint aftermath of her Egyptian cuisine.

"Well," I said ignoring the hand resting on mine, "I was about five at the time. As ragged, snotty-nosed an urchin as you would find anywhere in your part of London. It all began the day Father stole a ride to town on the roof of the bus, with two goats and a sheep for company."

Father was fond of the story. You could see the bus from a long way off, snaking along the road that was no more than a ledge following the winding contour of the cliff face before it vanished into a tunnel. When the bus entered the tunnel, my mother was to lead the donkey out into the road on the far side so that the driver would have to stop. It called for nice judgement and not a little courage on her part, since the bus had to be brought to rest halfway out of the tunnel, and there was no guarantee that the driver would be alert or even sober. Father meanwhile was perched on a projection above the tunnel mouth ready to drop onto the roof of the bus.

His arrival caused some panic among the livestock (when Mother told it, it was "the other animals"), but since the beasts were already terrified by the thunder reverberating from the rock only inches above their heads, the driver was not likely to notice. In fact it was only the danger of bashing out their brains that reduced the speed of the bus and made the whole enterprise feasible. Father landed on his arse. Not until he got home did he discover that he had been walking around town all day with that part of his anatomy plastered with sheep manure, looking, Mother would testify through a rising shriek of laughter, like a *pudín inglés con pasas*. A plum pudding, I translated for Maar, and explained that it was an analogy that could not have struck Mother until much later, such delicacies being far beyond our means at the time.

Such acumen always encourages imitation. A neighbour somewhat less shrewd than my father some weeks later tried the same ruse at the far end of the tunnel. It cost him a leg, a wife and a donkey. The bus returning from the market town, unburdened of its roof passengers, was going at a fair clip when its driver was blinded by the westering sun at the tunnel mouth. He braked, but not before he had sent wife and donkey to perdition over the edge of the *barranca*. The man rolled off the bus and lay writhing only inches from the brink. The driver had no idea where he had come from, or a long prison term might have been added to his list of misfortunes.

Father, plum-duff posterior and all, wandered about town, hoping to scrounge a cigarette or earn a few centavos by beating some tardy bellhop to a tourist's luggage. He was walking along the Avenida de Jordan when he saw a woman, a North American, stepping out of a big black car. The man holding the door for her was handing her a flower. An orchid. At first it was only the beauty and elegance of the woman that arrested him. (Mother at this point always snorted "Men!".) Because he was watching her face so intently ("lust-fully"), he noticed how she shone with a sudden radiance when she saw the flower. Clearly in her eyes it was something rare and precious. And, he supposed, costly. It earned the man a big all-the-way-down hug and a smile in which there was the promise of much more to come.

Now Father, who had drifted about a lot in his youth, working cane-fields, loading bananas, harvesting coffee, knew that flowers such as that grew wild and in great pro-fusion along the lower eastern slopes of the mountains and on the lowlands at the fringes of the rain forest. For a couple of weeks after that chance encounter these two visions coexisted in his mind: the glad, beautiful smile of the woman and those masses of orchids blooming in prodigal, unseen splendour. He went about, said Mother, like a young girl in love, in a sort of blissful daze. Mother, I suspect, was only partly teasing when she maintained that Father's euphoria during those first days was occasioned solely by the naïve belief that any woman in the world was ripe for seduction through the mere offering of an orchid. He had, she was fond of saying, very big ideas in that department. The thought of all those women and all those orchids just waiting to be brought together was like a preview of Paradise. And, in view of the distances involved, about as difficult of attainment.

Father, on the other hand, swore that from the very first moment it was the market possibilities alone that absorbed him. As for women, he was wont to retort, placing a finger under Mother's chin and looking playfully into her dark, feral eyes, who would need orchids if one had money?

Whatever the truth of it, it was clear that Fortune had smiled upon him through the eyes of that unknown woman, and however fickle he may or may not have been otherwise, he wooed her until she was won, and remained true to her despite all the obstacles fate placed in his way. The greatest of which was penury. Or as Father called it much later with unconscious irony, lack of working capital.

"So," he would say, pushing back his plate and reaching for the brandy he now affected in the place of Mother's home-brewed *pulque*, "I decided to liquidate my assets." One donkey.

"Your best friend, eh?" Maar broke into my reverie, squeezing my hand. "The donkey, I mean."

I ignored it. Resented the insight. How the hell did she divine that, anyway? How could my casual, even flippant, reference have betrayed any hint of the anguish I suffered over the sale of Suegra, who had always been there, on whose back I spent as much time as on the ground? I'd as soon they had sold one of my sisters.

Anyway, off went Papa, leaving a little of the donkey money with Mother to keep four bodies and four souls together until he returned.

"I'll be back soon," he shouted back, riding now *in* the bus as befitted an up-and-coming business man, "to take you to a big new house in the city."

"Well," said Mother, unaware that I was listening, "That's the last we'll ever see of him."

It wasn't, though. Not only did he come back, he made good his promise. But it wasn't soon. And it wasn't easy. He hitch-hiked, walked, and connived his way down to the low-lands and haunted the hangouts of truckers until he found one who, for an exorbitant "modest consideration", would transport him and his first cargo of orchids to the city, con-cealed behind a shipment of bananas. Since it was a long drive to the city and he had no other way of keeping the blooms fresh, he dugs the plants up and took them soil and all.

The "consideration", it turned out, did not include the *propina* for the soldiers who inspected the cargo at the frequent barricades. These handouts, to Father's dismay and disgust, "ate up the hind legs and tail of the *maldito polino*". He did not even recover his costs on that first trip, but, as Mother never tired of declaring, he was as stubborn as any donkey himself. He would have died rather than admit defeat.

So he stuck at it, and at the end of six months he had acquired a ramshackle truck of his own and had hired a woman to sell his orchids at a booth in the market. The next year he rented a shop in the better part of town, where there were fashionable ladies and lovesick suitors to buy them orchids at exorbitant prices. We moved in over the shop and lived there for seven years until the "big new house" mate-rialized, by which time Father had four greenhouses and was growing not only his own orchids but every exotic plant the whims of the rich could encompass.

"So," said Maar with a faint derisive smile, "you became part of the capitalist élite."

"Well, not exactly. Father became middling rich and he liked to put on the dog, as they say over here, but you didn't need to scratch very deep to find the peasant in him. Or the *malcontento*. There was always a point in the evening when, no matter who the dinner guests were, he pushed aside the brandy and called for the *pulque*. After a glass or two he would boast about the time he was arrested for inciting a riot among the cane-workers, or the time he started an avalanche that buried a troop of soldiers who had set fire to the village where his parents lived because it was thought to be a rebel hideout."

Maar said nothing, but I was aware of an alerting in her, an enlarging of her presence in the room, like feathers bristling. I avoided her eyes, afraid of their fascination, but I could feel their dark, compelling gaze. Her hand with its long, curving nails tightened on mine.

"And then there was Mother. My mother came of Guajiro stock. Her family had been driven out of Venezuela in some past upheaval and had made the long trek south. She remained a Guajira to the last black hair of her head. She loved to dress like a lady, but the social graces were beyond her comprehension, beneath her very considerable dignity. She would pass up an invitation from the mayor's wife any time to visit the God-forsaken *pueblo* in the mountains where her friends lived in crushing, louse-infested poverty. Where wealth was a couple of scrawny goats and where, next to a bellyful of *pulque,* a bellyful of maize *potaje* was life's greatest happiness. Roaches and other vermin swarmed in those hovels, but rats, my father used to say, knew better. They made a welcome addition to the *potaje.*"

All this no doubt merely confirmed what she had already heard from Paulo about the poverty prevailing in our native Provincia Montaña, but it also shed upon it the harsh light of personal experience. It was one thing for pampered Paulo to be horrified by the squalor of that row of shacks on the very edge of the Martínez estate, but what of the inhabitants themselves? What could he possibly know of them? How could he even begin to imagine what life looked like to them as they chafed like roasting chickens on that rocky spit by day and shivered under threadbare sarapes by night as the chill air slid down from the mountain snows?

Were they, Maar skilfully dissembled her eagerness to know, docile under the yoke, crushed and spiritless? Or were there among them potential demagogues, Anas with a political dimension to their vengefulness and cunning?

At this point a nurse politely shooed her out. She left a kiss on my brow that lingered like a brand.

It was Hafiz, who had been "abroad on business", who came to visit me next, on the day before my release. I can't recall much of what passed between us. His manner seemed to suggest some purpose beyond the merely altruistic, but I had no inkling what it was. I remember lying there, vulnerable, in the regard of his yellow bedouin eyes, glancing *at* them from time to time and experiencing the odd sensation I would encounter later when looking into a television camera, of communicating with a remote, only half-believed-in presence. He sniffed a lot, with that beak of his, and such was my sense of being under investigation that I could have sworn that Maar's heady perfume lingered in defiance of the day's Lysol, that the print of her lips was as clear as the mark of Cain upon my forehead.

He was friendly enough, even effusive, but it was a politician's effusiveness, or a priest's in pursuit of a convert. Eventually, having stayed long enough to satisfy the demands of courtesy, he stood up and said heartily, "Promise you'll come to see us just as soon as you're up to it. Next Monday? Is that too soon? Good. Nothing special. Just you and Paulo. Mustn't overtax you. It's a promise, then?"

If there was a promise in my guarded "Thanks for coming in," it was one I had no intention of keeping. I told Paulo as much next day when he came with a taxi to collect me.

"Maar will be hurt," he said, but he didn't pursue it. He knew only too well the snake-and-bird fascination she held for me; knew me better, evidently, than I knew myself.

He was going to London that week-end. A pressing invitation from friends of Tán. He was to be back by the evening train and would go straight to the "dark tower". Hafiz, he said, was most anxious that I should go.

"See you there," was his parting shot.

"You bloody won't," I muttered.

He didn't. But only because *he* wasn't there.

The week-end was wretched and interminable. I fretted away Saturday in my room, slept late on Sunday. By the afternoon I could stand the boredom no longer and went out for a walk. Which led me, inevitably and against my strongest resolve, in the direction of Martha's house. She was not home.

So there I was on Monday evening, wending my way like a sleep-walker through the damp, deserted streets and up the smelly staircase to Maar's apartment, steeling myself for an evening of radical claptrap.

Maar, however, was alone. It was evident as soon as she opened the door that she had more than talk in mind. She wore a silk, kimono-like gown of considerable splendour. Somewhat faded and frayed, I would notice later. An embroidered band encircled her forehead. There were large bangles on both her wrists. It was like coming upon a bird of gorgeous plumage in a squalid backyard.

"Hafiz said to give you his apologies. He had to go to Harwich. Some trouble over a shipment. I don't know."

"And Paulo?" He should have been there an hour ago. She look up quickly at my tone of suspicion, sarcasm.

"Just this moment phoned."

"He's late?"

"Can't come. His friends had tickets for the opera. They insisted he stay."

Her lips brushed my cheek, light as the touch of a trout-fly on the water (so as not to scare the fish) and she drew me in.

"So you'll have to make do with dull old me." She spread her arms and stood mannequin-like, inviting me to study dull old her. She had a good figure, slightly full, that prompted the word "voluptuous". Offered thus for my appraisal, it could not but kindle a small flame of desire. But I remembered Martha, standing so shy, so painfully abashed, saying, "I wanted you to see . . . *me*." Suddenly I wanted to fly from this woman flaunting her body. She was beautiful, in a mystical, Arabian Nights way, but the desire she awakened despised itself, was afraid of itself.

"Well, then, sit down and tell me more about your father while I pour us a drink."

There wasn't much more to tell. Despite his tipsy boasting about youthful exploits, Father was pretty much the armchair revolutionary. In his cups, he liked to stir the embers, but the fire was long dead in him.

"But it burns in you a little, no?"

I lied. Why did I lie? I confessed to that non-existent revolutionary fire in my breast because, in spite of my revulsion and my vague sense that she was the bait in some inescapable trap, I hesitated to repudiate with too much finality the fire in my loins.

So, "Yes," I said. "Yes, I suppose it does."

Even the smallest of our sins will find us out. As a consequence of that harmless little lie, intended only as a stop to keep the door of her bedroom open, my name found its way on to her list of "converts", and thence into the files and "little black books" of seditious factions around the world.

"How could it not," Maar went on, "given your background?"

How indeed, given my background. But it didn't. Doesn't. Believe me, Cheshire Cat, that fire never got going in me. The tinder was too damp with selfish preoccupations, fantasies. I never saw it as any business of mine to redress the wrongs of humanity. We all have our vocations. Yours is to persuade birds of such ill-assorted feather as Paulo and me to sing in unison the songs you wish to hear, the songs that will absolve you. Mine is—was—to celebrate life, not to tinker with its faulty mechanisms.

Maar handed me my drink and sat beside me. While I spoke—perhaps a little breathlessly in my anxiety to defer the moment when my power of resistance to her charms might be put to the test—she watched me and listened with the wide-eyed fascination of a child being told about Santa Claus. In which, however, there was nothing ingenuous. She was weighing the words I used, not for their truth but for what they revealed of my emotional response to the things I spoke of. I rambled on about my youthful experiences in a country peopled by power-crazed politicians, excessively wealthy *hacendados,* and peasants living on the edge of starvation in an economy bled dry by greedy foreigners. Everything I told her was true, but I was acutely aware that I was telling her what she wanted to hear and I was afflicted with an irrational sense of improbity. I resented her interest in my country's misfortunes. Our shames, I felt, were no business of hers.

But she sat so confidingly close, the predatory glint of her eyes veiled behind that flattering concern, her lips a little open upon the pleasant imperfection of her teeth, her scarlet talons hidden in my hair. I felt my breathing quicken to the perfume that rose to my head with the fumes of the sweetish, potent drink she had poured me. I was oddly at war with myself. I talked to incite—or at least not to discourage—the seduction she seemed bent on, yet also to defer and perhaps to prevent myself succumbing to it. Dire would be the consequences, I had been painfully conditioned to believe, of coveting another man's woman. Although "covet" in this case seemed hardly the appropriate word. Hafiz was not a man one would want to be caught double-crossing, either. But it went far beyond all that, my unease. It went beyond even my dream of being miraculously reconciled (unsullied, of course, by any sordid liaison) with innocent, undefiled Martha. It had to do with something in Maar that produced in me a sort of intellectual, or perhaps spiritual, goose-flesh; an apprehension of some impending hell at whose gate she was the siren. The song of her flesh was sweet. Another drink would do it.

As if divining this thought she took my glass.

"Another wee one first, eh?"

This "first" confounded me. But not so much as her next words.

"Hafiz is really sweet, you know."

Hafiz and sweetness were not easily reconciled in my mind, at this or any other moment. I suppose I raised my eyebrows.

"Such a dear. Look." She set down the glasses. "Look what he brought me back from Germany." She crossed to an expensive-looking camera set on a tripod in the corner.

"Looks complicated."

"Not really. I've been nuts about photography for years. Portraits, mostly. And animals. Scenery I'm not good at. But I've never had a really good camera before." She made as if to fetch the drinks, then stopped and said, "Say, why don't I try it on you? D'you mind? You have a very photogenic face."

I stared at the floor, still having a little trouble with sweet Hafiz, reminded of the delicacy and indignity of my situation.

"Oh, come on, Gaspar. Let's do it now, before . . . While you're undishevelled, shall we say."

She fussed over the camera, then over me. My belligerent ardour was beginning to ebb away. I did not smile for the birdie.

"And now one of us both. I'll show you what a clever machine this is. Wouldn't that be a lark?"

Wouldn't it, though? I imagined sweet Hafiz beating me up. Or worse.

"Now, you keep perfectly, perfectly still until I tell you." She set the timer and walked leisurely round the old sofa to stand behind me, slightly to my right. After a moment her hand settled on my shoulder. "Quite still," she whispered, as though the camera was not in on this conspiracy. The shutter whirred and clicked.

"Good," she said after what seemed a long interval. "You can move now." She restored the camera to its corner. "Now, let's . . . relax."

I stood up. She came to me quickly, her eyes smouldering with desire. Clearly relaxation was not what she had in mind. Her arms came about me and she pressed close with subtle motions of her body.

"Look, Maar, I'm sorry. I'm just out of hospital. I shouldn't have come." I thrust her away. "I like you. I like you a lot. You're a wonderful woman. Some other time, maybe, when . . . "

God knows how I got out of her clinging arms, out of the house, out of her life, without giving vent to some insane, violent manifestation of my self-disgust. My shame could not have been more bitter had Martha herself been there as witness. And what, you may well ask, has all this ancient sinful-soul searching of mine, who make such protestations of innocence, to do with this alleged history of Paulo Martínez, El Azote?

Who knows?

Who knows, for example, how that photograph, taken as a "lark" with Maar's new camera, which I did not get to see because I could not bring myself to enter the place again, came to be here in this country, in this very place (wherever it may be), all these years later?

"So," sneered the thug (evidently a minor thug) into whose presence I had been thrust by the two men who had arrested me. "So, you're innocent of all this. No idea why you're here, fine upstanding citizen that you are. Never been associated with any murdering sons of bitches who call themselves *sol-*

dados de justicia. Nor with other murdering sons of bitches around the world who just happened to have your name in their files. Then how, *Señor Profesor*, do you explain this?"

And he thrust it under my nose. It took me a while, in my distraught condition, to recognize it, but now I see it as though it were projected permanently upon the dank wall before me. There I sit, minus jacket and tie (it was always so damned hot in there), drink in hand, a little wooden with the effort of protracted stillness but with an expression very much out of keeping with what I remember of my sensations at the time. Out of keeping, certainly, with my subsequent conduct. An expression decidedly lascivious and moony. The expression of one who knows and relishes the nature of the "lark". Behind me and a little to one side stands Maar, hand on my shoulder, looking fondly down at me but presenting enough of her face to the camera to show that her thin lips have a pout of urgent anticipation. She leans a little down, so that her big breasts, naked, appear to rest upon my head. A matter of camera angle. Looking very closely at the picture it is possible to see part of her gown, shrugged back off her shoulders, hanging from her arm beside my head, but to any but the most painstaking observer she appears completely naked. As if it makes any difference.

Even in the extremity of my terror as I looked up into the eyes of that gloating bully I felt a twinge of that ancient shame, that sick feeling of having betrayed myself. But only now, when the terror has been with me long enough to numb the faculty that feels it, do the questions come. What was Maar's motive? Why did she want to take the picture in the first place? What possible reason could she have had to expose herself like a Hyde Park flasher and then cover up while I was still frozen in that "perfect, perfect" stillness? And did Hafiz get to see the picture? I know the answer to that is yes. And why, I wondered at the time, didn't he come and break my stupid neck? But the question which so illogically causes me pain and humiliation now, when there is no one left to care, and to which I intuitively know the answer, is this: did Martha ever get to see that picture? Memory answers with the look in Martha's eyes the last time I saw her. Where before, since our quarrel, I had been accustomed to see anger, hurt, resentment, I was appalled at that final encounter to see hatred, a depth of anguish that could only have sprung from a comparable depth of love. I knew in that moment that all along she had hoped, that she had had it in her heart to relent, that reconciliation had been as necessary to her as it was to me. All the time there had been hope and I had killed it.

Conchita comes stealthily and curls up on my knees. She purrs loudly as I stroke behind her ears. Something in me purrs responsive. Something like peace descends upon my soul. We purr in acknowledgement of our need for each other. She is my only friend, my only link with external reality. I live in terror lest the lout should discover and evict her.

XV

"Insurance," Paulo said, having picked up and read these last pages while I was at the bucket. My mystification must have been obvious but it was some time before he went on, in the middle of a sentence as though he had been carrying on the monologue in his head, ". . . almost as if she could see into the future. She always just happened to have an ace up her sleeve. All that stuff she stashed away somewhere. Something on just about everyone she'd ever had dealings with. All catalogued in her head with an efficiency that made Dewey look like a pack-rat. Whenever she wanted something done, something perilous or nasty that no one wanted to do, or when she or Hafiz got into a tight corner and wanted a way out, she could always produce evidence that so-and-so had poisoned his wife or that a certain judge had been in the habit of frequenting a cathouse. Photographs were her specialty, but she had great wads of press clippings, thrown together at random, you might think, but she could always sniff out what she wanted in a matter of minutes. She had tape recordings, letters, documents, cancelled cheques. Uncanny it was, her nose for what might prove useful. Or maybe it's not so surprising. She made her own opportunities. Having got the goods on someone, she'd lure him in deeper. Or her. She loved to manipulate women. It was more of a challenge.

"Remember that case of Antoinette Picard?" (How well you remember the names of strangers, you who profess to have forgotten Martha's!) "She ran the French minister of justice through with his own antique sword. They put her away as insane. Which she may well have been after all Maar had put her through. It seemed an incredible coincidence that after the press had received and published threats that the minister would be killed if he extradited that Libyan—what was his name, now? no matter—that he should happen to die by the hand of his best friend's wife only hours after he signed the papers. There was a lot of rumour and speculation, but no one ever established the connection. Just too damned far-fetched. But all that goes back to the time Maar happened to see the Picard woman pawning some jewellery.

"Most people wouldn't have given it a thought, but Maar was the shrewdest judge of character I ever met. She knew from the woman's manner that she was nervous as hell about what she was doing, and that the knowledge that she *had* done it might some day prove to be a valuable commodity. So she got hold of the jewellery. I'm not sure how, but it's not hard to figure out. The pawnbroker was a crook anyway, a fence. Maar probably had something on him, too. At any rate, it was safe to assume that Madame Picard was not in a position to raise a stink about him disposing of the stuff before the due date. And Maar had ways of raising money for schemes like that, even though she was usually broke herself.

"When Picard was just about frantic, Maar contacted her and offered to return the jewels. With a little condition attached, of course. Picard was to pilfer some papers from her husband's files. Maar didn't give a damn for the papers, but for Antoinette it was the second step into the quicksand."

The light was dwindling fast, the sun's last shrunken beam spanning the cell, a taut candescent wire anchored to the wall an inch to the left of the granite nipple. In that expiring glow we must have looked to the lout like grotesque oriental sculptures. A pair of starveling Buddhas. I was too preoccupied to turn and encounter the cat's glow of his eyes at the grille but I was aware of his scrutiny, as my thoughts followed two divergent lines of speculation, becoming lost at last in a dreamy limbo between the two.

One part of my mind was obsessed with sunlight. It followed that attenuated beam through the window and out into the half-forgotten, almost mythical world where people trail shadows like bridal trains on the shimmering sidewalks; where lovers sit long under café umbrellas sipping their *con leche* and squinting against the fiery eclát of the streetcar windows as the cars swung west around the monument; where newsmen stand watching the rain of diamonds on the children braving the cold fringes of the fountain, cameras ready, hoping for a spectacular shot to fill the censored voids of tomorrow's *Democracía*. The first faint breath of evening carries the promise of coolness. My skin prickled with vicarious pleasure.

At the same time I was seeing a vast Balzacian horde of characters twitched and tugged by invisible puppet-strings leading back to Maar, all strutting about in their pathetic delusion of freedom but constrained by growing burdens of guilty secrets. Poor Antoinette was but one of many who took the second step that led to calamity rather than face the unpleasant consequences of the first. In my somnolent state I heard the hysterical shriek of headlines crying the dire events of a decade or more, but behind them I saw the shadowy figure of Maar, recognizable only by the look in her eyes, the same look I found trained upon me that night of our first meeting at the Mitre. The look from which I failed to take warning.

"You were lucky," said Paulo, as though taking his cue from the confused spate of my thought.

The last thread of light snapped. In the crepuscular gloom that followed I could see him sitting there, defined only by the faint sheen of sweat on his skin and the glow of his eyes deep in their craters of shadow.

"Oh, sure. Lucky as hell." I frequently answer Paulo, futile as it is. It prevents the atrophying of my vocal cords and reassures me of my own existence.

"One of Maar's few failures."

Which I suppose was an accomplishment of a sort, even though it resulted from my weakness rather than my strength. It wasn't so much that I got away as that I was thrown back, not even useful for bait. I was let go as being unworthy of pursuit.

"Thank God for that." But I felt, even in my present predicament, a tiny paradoxical twinge of wounded pride. What a rank, persistent weed is the human ego!

"You screwed up her strategy, of course."

"What?" He heard my incredulous shout all right. So did the lout. The door at the top of the steps clanged open. He stood silhouetted there for maybe half a minute, his jaw working in a slow rotary motion like a cow's. Satisfied that he had daunted us by his mere presence, he slammed the door and went back to his meal.

"What d'you mean, strategy? How did I . . ."

"Well," he resumed halfway through my question, not hearing me, "I guess you could say we screwed it up between us, eh? You were supposed to stay arse-over-head in love with that Marcia. Marry her. Sire a brood of kids on her. Settle down to domestic bliss. Then one day when Maar wanted a dirty job done she would trot out the photo. Sweet and friendly as hell, of course. What a genius she was at that sort of thing. 'Gaspar, how nice to see you. I've always remembered that wonderful time we had together. Are these your children? How sweet. Look, here we are, the love-birds. Remember? I've carried it about with me all these years. And how is your dear wife? D'you think I might call? I'd love to meet her.' "

Even this fantasy contained the seeds of pain.

"But she was the one who . . ."

"There was an element of risk. She had to throw a temporary wrench into your little love affair. Get you upset enough to let her work on you and take the picture. She wasn't averse to a little pleasure in the process. There would no doubt have been other, more interesting pictures. And then of course she had to set the scene, so that your 'wife' would have a memory to reinforce her potential jealousy."

I could hear him chuckling and scratching. Somewhere outside the window a small animal screamed and there was a loud beat of wings.

"Not that you gave her much, from her telling of it. Pleasure, I mean. Big disappointment all round, eh, my Gaspar. And then instead of patching things up with your popsy you went into a fit of the sulks and spoilt the whole plan."

I could no longer see him except when he moved, a restless stirring of the oppressive darkness on the far side of the cell, on which I focused my impotent rage.

"Anyway," he went on, "you were wrong about her."

Outside, the sudden swish and gurgle of rain. Earthy odours of renascence wafted through the window hole.

"María, I mean. You had no chance of getting her back. You were too late. All that stuff you just wrote about what you saw in her eyes, crap like that. That's all it is, crap."

The wet stones around the window shone livid with the flicker of remote lightning.

"That show that prevented me from being at Maar's that night. She was it."

I leapt up, ready for murder. But the sudden unaccustomed exertion sent me toppling against the wall, my head spinning with vertigo. I collapsed back on my bench. What was the use, anyway? A black, crushing hopelessness descended upon me. All I wanted was death. But I had no way of killing myself.

"She cried for you, sure. Cried in my arms, afterwards. The first time, I mean, while you were in the hospital. 'Poor innocent' I think was what she called you. But poor fool is what you were. All she needed was a little persuasion. The dominant male stuff. They like that."

I tried in vain to shut out the nightmare image.

"All your fine scruples were for nothing. You were too late. You might just as well have had your little romp with Maar. It would have made a man of you."

"Shut up, you bastard!" I screamed, and waited for the lout.

XVI

Sara Loman.

She stands at the base of the Boatie Tower, looking lost and lonely. A great yearning for her old friendliness and compassion rises up in me. I start towards her but a cowardly impulse prompts me to turn away and seek escape. My hurt has been slow to heal. Even after a lapse of months I am not sure I can stand the sympathy. I'm not even sure that I deserve any, or that she has it to give. I prefer to be alone with my guilt, my wretchedness. What could talking bring but further pain?

She sees me, however. Has in fact, I intuitively know, been waiting for me. She comes half-running, arms outstretched as if afraid I'll make a bolt for it.

"It's been so long."

We cling for a moment, all that has happened during that "so long" harrowingly between us. Then we walk a couple of miles along the Cam, exchanging hardly a word, wanting only the comfort of one another's silence. At one point she reaches for my hand. A childlike gesture, immensely touching, as though it is she that craves sympathy.

When she speaks there is such intensity in it that we stop, her words there before us like a hurdle.

"You were so perfect for one another."

I look at her. Tears well up along her eyelids. I look away before they spill over.

"I wanted so much for her to be happy. I don't know why it seemed so important. A sort of atonement to him, I suppose."

She makes no attempt to explain this further as we move on. Any curiosity I may have concerning this unexplained "him" is immediately submerged in mourning for that lost future.

I find myself sitting beside Sara on a bus, not by invitation, not because of any conscious decision by either of us, but simply because it seems impossible for us to separate.

She says again, as we stand in the familiar hallway and she takes my coat, "It's been so long." Her words seem to imply a past that goes back far beyond our last meeting, seem to hint at other, more ancient sorrows. It shocks me, some-how. She has always seemed so jovial. She and her husband both. So secure and content. One of the reasons I have been avoiding them is that I could not bear to face their twinkling good humour. And as if aware of this, as we move into the living-room she takes off her glasses.

I am not prepared for the vulnerability of the eyes thus exposed. They are strange to me, yet I seem to have known the person they reveal from earliest childhood. There is something cat-like in the way her features and the dark sweep of her hair converge upon those intense blue eyes, which have depth and clarity where one might have expected the blankness of myopia. My turn, now, to take her hand. She smiles. It is a rueful smile, but it has a warmth that soothes my troubled spirit.

"There's so much to be said, isn't there?"

And no way of saying it. Not yet. The words are locked away somewhere, full of potential for pain.

"It will come."

I sense suddenly an immense compassionate wisdom in her, a wisdom not of words but of emotion. Of sensuality, I am surprised to find myself thinking. The wisdom, I suppose, of eternal womanhood. Then without shame or self-consciousness I am weeping on her shoulder.

She, too, has tears. They outlast my own, and we cling, sharing our unspoken pain, until she is quiet. Impossible, now, to find words for the slow mellowing of that shared grief, first into a spent calm and then, very slowly, into a warm, wondering awareness of each other. Man and woman.

I dare not dwell upon it here, that bittersweet loving. Loving, or whatever name it might be remembered by. It is a memory too fragile to profane with words. Gentleness. Such tender conferring of comfort, one upon the other. For yes, she too craved comfort, perhaps more desperately than I.

Let it suffice to record that in the midst of her passionate abandon she cried out, with a strange unworldly urgency, "Call me Conchita!"

"Conchita?" I said as we lay together in that tranquil afterwards. It was part endearment, part praise for the consummate Woman she had just been. I was bemused, listening to the word itself, trying it on her like an exotic garment. But I was also plumbing the past in search of the name's echo.

Martha at the grave of Simon Mallory.

"Conchita, sí, let us start with that."

We lay close. While she looked inward for the words, I studied what I could see of her, astonished, of a sudden, to find myself clinging skin to skin with this aging matron and feeling so *blessed*.

With drowsy interludes of silence, her story came out.

Her family had scratched an inadequate living from a mountain farm not far from Potosi. As long as she could remember she had toiled in the fields with her brothers, who took pleasure in bullying her. She was slow. She was a dreamer. She was a girl. It was a shameful thing to be, a girl. Her father, a hard man, resented her. Her mother, too, was harsh and demanding. And religious. Childish follies were magnified into sins. Sara heard no laughter but the cruel mirth of her brothers.

When she was fifteen her mother grew lame and could no longer carry the loads of produce to the city for the weekly market. This chore now fell to Sara, since it was not man's work. She was not good at it. Instead of crying her wares like the other women, she would sit among her produce on the sidewalk and fantasize about how one day she would have a stall, where she would sell not onions and corn but gorgeous silks and tapestries and embroidered *rebozos*.

She had other fantasies. She was going to be a great artist. She made charcoal sketches on sheets of cardboard salvaged from the cartons behind the stalls. She made drawings of the people and scenes around her and set them up for sale beside her produce. She never sold any, though, and had to throw them away, since she dared not take them home.

There was another, recurring, fantasy.

"But he was something of a surprise, when he came, my handsome *caballero*."

He began as a pair of badly worn boots that shuffled into her line of vision as she sat there sketching. They did not move away, and at last she was forced to look up; over a pair of twisted knee-socks topped by knobbly knees, over khaki shorts, too long and probably none too clean, although she was not conditioned to notice such things.

Not a promising start to the delineation of one's beau ideal. But at the summit of it, seeming as she squatted there an incredibly long way up, was a tousle of blond hair fired by the sun, and under that a sunburnt, blue-eyed face.

"Well," Sara said, "you must have seen the sketch I made of him."

It had looked down at me from Martha's piano the day I laid out the body of Uncle Simon. Simon as he must have appeared to Sara on that first day. The bony knees were there, and the ill-fitting shorts and the sweaty armpits. But reflected also, somehow, was her own wondering perception of him. She found him, she ventured after a long, frowning quest for precision, "comically godlike". The skin was peeling from his nose.

She sold him one of her sketches. She was elated. The excitement of the discovered artist. How could she possibly imagine that it would prove to be her life's most tragic mistake?

He was there again the next week, as she knew he would be. She saw him several times during the day, and when she was packing up to leave he came up to her and said in his atrocious Spanish, "*Puedo servirle?*" It was a store clerk's question, but clearly he was requesting the privilege of being allowed to help.

After that he always walked her home, but she insisted on saying goodbye (ah, the growing sweet torture of those goodbyes!) at the bridge a kilometre away, not wanting him to see the hovel where she lived. Not wanting her family to see her with him. She knew she would be found out sooner or later, but in dreams there is always room for miracles. Those walks home with Simon had become the *raison d'être* for her whole existence.

Then one evening she was greeted by a stream of self-righteous abuse from her mother. She endured it with bowed head and waited in terror for her father's arrival. But to her astonishment he shouted, "Hold your holy claptrap, woman! Let's hear more about this young man before you damn your own daughter." He wanted very much to marry her off. Perhaps this illicit suitor would turn out to be a rich *norteamericano*. All *norteamericanos* in his experience were rich. But Sara already knew he was a penniless *inglés* with poetic pretensions. She dreaded the day when her father would discover this.

Other events saved her, at least from that calamity.

Simon had shown her sketch to a friend, the nephew of a medical missionary in Potosi. This young man came with

Simon to see her. He and his uncle both agreed that she had talent, he said. She ought to be properly trained in drawing and painting. He was nice enough, but his enthusiasm made her uneasy. The English word she would later learn for the quality that disturbed her was "pushy". In any case, dreamer though she was, she dismissed his suggestion as impossible. It was therefore a great shock when her father announced that she was to be enrolled in the missionary school.

But how could that be? There was no money for such things. Had there been money, it was on her brothers, not on her, a mere girl, that it would have been spent. Arrangements, she was told, had been made.

These "arrangements", she later discovered, included payment to her father for the "loss of her services".

Simon had to return to England. One day he would come back and marry her. He would write every week. But she never received any letters.

It soon became evident that James Loman was interested in more than her drawing. She was cool to his advances, dreaming always of Simon, but James was not easily discouraged. And he was the next best thing to a rich *norteamericano*. A little of his pushiness and a lot of his money were enough to win the consent of Sara's father to their marriage when she finished school.

"So," she said, turning to stare at the ceiling, "here I am."

After a long silence she sat up, severing the bond of intimacy that had seemed impossible to break. I could see only the long curve of her back and the greying hair curling about her shoulders. Her next words seemed to come with immense effort.

"The day before the wedding, Simon came back." She ran to the bathroom to escape the painful implications of that ill-timed return.

Her calm restored, she brought tea to the fireside. She sat close, taking my hand.

"James is a good, a wonderful man. We have come to love each other in a different way. A way that is not betrayed by what I have given you. I shall treasure our moments always."

Implicit in this was the agreement that "our moments" were unique, incapable of repetition. I smiled to show that I understood, with mingled sadness and relief. I merely said,

"Conchita." The word seemed to epitomize and explain whatever it was that had sanctified those moments. It also prompted a question.

"But how was it that you never told her? Martha, I mean?"

She thought about it for a long time.

"A conspiracy of silence, I suppose. It seemed the best thing. The only thing, in the circumstances. Not that we ever discussed it, Simon and I. It was something we both took for granted, tacitly agreed on from the start. One doesn't pick at wounds of that sort. Or flaunt them."

"She knew about *his* wounds, though."

"Yes. I'm thankful she never knew it was I that inflicted them."

I made as if to protest, but she gave a small gesture of deprecation, of dismissal. The time had come to talk about Martha. I realized with a pang that we had been speaking of her in the past tense.

"She has wounds of her own, now."

Once again that small gesture of denial.

"And she knows who inflicted them."

"No, in her heart she never believed that." Sara studied my face. I wondered what she read there. "Especially after . . ."

We stared into the dying fire, balking at the portent of that "after". After she was seduced, or worse, by Paulo. After he had exacted a tortured sort of love from her and then abandoned her. After he took up with Maar. That would be the cruellest cut. After he vanished so suddenly and mysteriously. After . . .

"After you went into hospital she came to see you."

"What? She never did. I prayed she would, but she didn't."

"Well, no. She saw that woman coming out."

Sitting here now, I smite my head. My whole life, it seems to me, has been directed—misdirected—by such coincidences. I have been, again and again, the victim of cruel chance, the sport of unpredictable syzygies in my personal cosmos. Would I be here now, in this rat hole, with this—this monster, had I but taken the direct way home from Alejandro's? Might I not even now be happily married to Martha, had not Maar appeared on that Cambridge street corner? And I burn with shame all these years later, to think of Maar emerging from the hospital door just as Martha was about to go in.

"Even then," Sara said, "she didn't really believe that you— that you and that woman . . . So she phoned him. You didn't know that? Well, all she wanted was to be reassured that there was nothing between you and that . . . Jezebel. There wasn't, was there?

"Anyway, he agreed to meet her. At her place. Her first mistake."

Sara sighed and closed her eyes, as though visualizing the train of Martha's tragic mistakes.

"Her second was to break down and weep on his shoulder."

Just the way she did on mine. But on this occasion *I* was the dead man.

"The rest she couldn't tell me. Wouldn't, anyway. By the time I got to talk to her, when we got back from Yorkshire, she had already developed a twisted sort of loyalty to him. Queer, irrational creatures, we women. The ancient pragmatic urge to submission. Not just submission but acceptance, self-delusion, active complicity. It's a delusion that surprisingly often imposes its own truth. Some instinct for self-preservation, and I suppose a desire for stability and security, trap a woman into a sort of retrospective collusion in the crime. And it is a crime, however larded with endearments and uninvited caresses. 'Well, yes,' she said, when I tried to get to the bottom of it, 'he *was* rather insistent.' Insistent. My God! 'Forceful, you mean?' I said. And at that she burst into tears and ran out of the room."

She fought like a tigress, was the way Paulo put it.

"Oh, and yes," he said, after the lout had roared his idle threat and retreated to his lair. "She did see the picture. Maar's, I mean. What else could I do? She kept coming out with that 'poor innocent' crap. Cried all the time. Which inhibited her performance. Not that she was all that good anyway. Lukewarm. Very English, you know. None of the old Latin fire. You should be thankful I saved you from a lifetime of that." I turned my back on him, tried to shut him out. But he had to have a last word. "No, a boudoir bombshell she wasn't. Unlike Maar. Even after she got you out of her system."

Which according to Sara she never did. At least until the time she faded out of the picture. She faded out because after living for a month or so with Simon's relatives (a sour-faced Methodist minister and his mousy little wife whom I remembered meeting at the funeral) she removed herself from their household without explanation and did not communicate with them again. Or with anyone from whom I might have received word of her.

I saw the Lomans several more times, always together, always full of the old twinkling good humour, always the devoted couple. No conspiratorial glances between Sara and me, no secret pressures in her welcoming embrace. If I read something sardonic in the glint of the good doctor's glasses, it was probably only a figment of my unease. I had, strangely, no sense of guilt. There was a bond between Sara and myself, stemming from the memory of "our moments", but it was something spiritual and remote that would have been profaned by the least word or sign of acknowledgement.

And in truth we no longer seemed to have much in common, the Lomans and I. I had continued to go there because they sometimes fed me a crumb of news about Martha along with the Sunday roast. Martha, I now realized, had been the catalyst in our relationship. When they lost touch with her, they also in a sense lost touch with me. My visits became infrequent and desultory, and at last ceased altogether. Sometimes I would see them in town. I remember very clearly the last time I met them, walking arm in arm along Hobson Street. We stopped and spoke of some new crisis impending in the Middle East. Paulo's name came up, although I cannot recall in what context. We had of course no idea that there might be even the remotest connection between these two topics. Sara was planning—or maybe merely dreaming of—a sentimental journey to Bolivia. She spoke with great wistfulness. Suddenly all that had been between us, the doctor, his charming dusky wife, and me, seemed very long ago. As I watched them walking away, with a solemn sense of the finality of the occasion, they both looked old and frail. The thought that Sara, that elderly woman leaning on the arm of that elderly man, had once lain warm and passionate in my arms was like an ancient dream. She had spent, for my solace, the last, long-husbanded fire of her youth.

PART TWO

XVII

All is changed, yet all is harrowingly the same. How long a time has passed? So much has happened. Yet surfacing from a sort of delirium, finding myself when the day's sun smote my eyes still in this place, I felt as though time had ceased, run down, broken its spring, and expended itself in one instantaneous convulsion. So it must seem when the brain of one dying discharges its burden of remembrance into the black pit of oblivion.

Alone? Or was Paulo still there and all that lay so agonizingly upon my mind merely another of the nightmares this place spawns as soon as one half-closes an eye? I was afraid to look. Afraid lest he sat there still, watching me with his basilisk stare as he has done so often and for so long. Even more afraid lest he did not.

Where begin again? Where pick up the thread of the narrative interrupted aeons ago (or so it seems)? All I previously wrote has been taken away, perhaps destroyed. Who knows? In which case further writing is futile, toil in vain. I labour to bring forth a cripple. Yet write I must. If not this feeble attempt at truth, then some work of fiction (for which, in a long-ago life, I was renowned), a necessary flight into fantasy to maintain my hold on reality.

Well, at least I have an ample supply of paper. And a dozen pencil stubs which the lout has orders to sharpen daily. Courtesy of the Cheshire Cat.

"Qué es Cheshire Cat?" he wanted to know. "Quién?" He looked down at me, even more Cheshire Cat-like, backlit as he was by the painful glare of a naked electric bulb.

You see how my mind wanders? Forgive me. I am distraught. Who are you, anyway, my perhaps not-so-gentle reader, poring over these grimy pages, most likely after I am dead?

As far as I can recall, I was about to record what I remembered, and what I have since learned, of Paulo's departure from Cambridge and what became of him thereafter. Which is the core of what I originally set out to do: to trace the course of his transformation from the admirable friend I knew in Cambridge to the abominable El Azote who terrorized half the civilized world. But when I began, it was with the intention merely to portray him, and in so doing I suppose to condemn him. Now that he is dead . . .

Forgive me. The manner of Paulo's death and my over-active mind's eye between them have conspired to relieve me of the morning's ration of beans. No great loss. The Cheshire Cat's promised improvements in the cuisine have yet to materialize.

Now that he, Paulo, is dead, it comes to me like an afflatus that I—we—might aspire to understand him.

But first I must unburden myself of all that has befallen since I was snatched so violently out of my world of maudlin reminiscence. The world peopled by the ghosts of Martha, Sara, the poisonous Maar. The chaotic series of recent events demands regurgitation as irresistibly as did the beans; reluctant, fearful though I am to thrust my finger down the throat of remembrance.

I have been catechized through it all, of course, by the Cheshire Cat. This is not conducive to another telling of the story. Each word makes its own involuntary connections, so that I experience again in the recapitulation all the gratuitous agony that accompanied the first recital. I say gratuitous because, coward that I am, I was only too anxious to spill the beans. (Unfortunate metaphor!) What, after all, was there to hide? Who, now, could it harm?

But I must strive for some sort of chronological order, blurred though my impression of sequence is. First, find a beginning.

We had been talking once more of Martha, Paulo and I. Well, you know what I mean. Martha was on my mind, as she had been increasingly, almost to the point of obsession. Divining this, Paulo did the talking. Not, you will by now appreciate, with any benevolent intent. It was still light, but I could not compose myself to write. I stood under the window, seeing in that sliver of daylight a symbol of the whole beautiful sunlit earth. I saw the sun shining on the peaks of my native province, on the park before the gates of the *palacio* (with, unavoidably, strobic flashes from the wheel of Eliza's carriage), but above all I saw its soft radiance overlying the Cambridgeshire countryside through which we loitered so often, Martha and I. The more ardently I dreamed, the more maliciously offensive Paulo's remarks became. Oh, I can remember the words. How in the name of God could I forget? The Cheshire Cat extorted them, every one, with relish. But they are too painful to repeat.

Paulo described in sadistic detail how he first had his way of her. In the coarsest language he boasted how, after a while, he could make her beg for what he had originally imposed upon her by brute force; for the gratification I could have given her with such loving tenderness but which I had withheld out of reverence for her chastity. He described the indignities he made her suffer before he would satisfy what he called her "rampant desire". He quoted word for word her cries of supplication and the loud paeans of her impending release. Yet he pretended that he could not remember her name.

He could not hear my curses but he could not fail to notice my near-apoplectic fury. Stung beyond endurance by his taunts I rushed upon him, raining feeble blows. If he had struck me back, knocked me senseless to the floor, I would have felt my attack had some foolhardy merit, but he held me off with contemptuous ease despite his enfeebled condition. He shoved me away as though I were a child. As I staggered back, Conchita leapt from the window and alighted on my shoulder. Her momentum was too great, however. She was forced to jump again, and fell sprawling at the feet of Paulo.

"Ha!" He stooped to pick her up. "Gaspar's furry friend, who adds fleas and cat piss to our long list of blessings."

Conchita bit and clawed his hands. He dropped her with a howl and a volley of profanity.

"Vengeance you're after, eh? Vengeance for Peluche?"

The words meant nothing to me, but I truly believe that in that moment he was possessed by some sort of superstitious dread. Before she could escape, he kicked her with all his strength. I had the absurd and inappropriate image, as the cat's body rose into the air, of Paulo converting a try for the college team at Cambridge. Conchita struck the wall and fell in a limp, twitching heap on the floor.

It was while I stood frozen, hearing the piteous sounds of the cat's dying, that my glance fell upon Tit Rock. I remembered how it had moved to my touch. It came away from the wall with surprising ease. Perhaps for an instant I gained strength from my fury.

Paulo crouched over the cat, sucking his bleeding hand.

I repudiated the act even as the heavy rock descended. The sound it made was obscene, indescribable. A soft mashing sound, at the heart of which was a dry click of bone. Almost at once small petals of blood sprang out from the rock, set comically nipple-uppermost on Paulo's head.

XVIII

"You saved us the price of a bullet," a voice was saying from the sky as I floated up from a dream of flowers: my father chin-deep in a sea of scarlet azaleas. "But then, you also cost us a canary."

The significance of all this passed me by. The word *canario* evoked a fleeting blur. My mother had one once. She wept to see it caged but would not let it go.

"You sure he's awake?"

An excruciating pain exploded in my loins and sent waves of agony through every nerve of my body.

"He is now."

The face above me was the spectral hub of a blinding radiance, Christlike.

"You are forgiven."

I began to succumb gratefully to the delusion of death.

"He was not worth a bullet, that one. But you, *garañón*, you are different. Wake him up."

Again that consuming agony.

"What happened, *garañón*? Why did you do it?"

I opened my eyes. The face was closer now, darkly visible, still with a fiery fringe. Definitely not the face that should go with that word. *Garañón*. It echoed tantalizingly in some far, far past, but it slipped away.

"Why did you kill him? Tell me. I want to get on to more important things. Tell me. Just for the record, you understand? No one blames you. I marvel that you waited so long. Now, please. From the beginning."

I cast about for it, that beginning, in a confused welter of warring impressions. What beginning did he want? Beginning of what?

"The cat. What about the cat? Start with that."

My eyelids were drifting shut again. The many cats of my life prowled at the perimeter of my consciousness. Then with amazement I heard the voice of Paulo coming from my own mouth.

"Peluche."

Pain brought me once more shuddering awake.

I focused on the face, fading away at the hairy edges into darkness, like water into weedy shallows. The whole slightly indistinct against the light, framed in long hair; a Norman arch held up by a brow of the sort commonly called noble, as seen in certain medieval portraits. A glitter of eyes, which pored over me as over some hieroglyphic puzzle. Scholarly, but with a strange, sad-whimsical cast. A poet *manqué*, perhaps.

"Peluche," I said again, but from far away. I was foolishly wondering whether he ever collected his sandals. Part of me was there in the park, luxuriating in the sunshine, seeing the sandal-maker busy at his work. But the part of me that lay on the table in anticipation of the ordeal knew with a fearful quailing that the events of that day were among the "more important things" the Cheshire Cat was anxious to get around to. Sooner or later he would come to that.

"Peluche," he prompted, with an edge of impatience. But he held up a hand to stay that other, unseen prompter.

Peluche was a martyr of the revolution, Paulo had said. The unsung hero of the Dominguín affair.

"Dominguín," I heard myself say.

The eyes above me widened with surprise. A hand gripped my shoulder, as though it would shake the words out of me. The tall forehead creased as he strove to make the improbable connection. No doubt he was trying to decide whether I was delirious, whether my mind was unhinged by those searing bursts of pain, whether I was more cunning than he had given me credit for, or whether I was simply trifling with him.

"What of Dominguín?"

"The cat. Peluche was Dominguín's cat."

Anger flared in his eyes.

"Don't play games with me!" His hand came up to signal his fiendish helper, but before the agony engulfed me I saw his eyes' fury subside, and what I encountered in them as I was coming out of that ordeal was cunning. And something like jubilation. The grip on my shoulder became almost caressing.

"Evidently," he said, "we are considering another cat."

An unexpected bonus, he must have been thinking. The "Dominguín Mystery", as it was popularly known, was now almost a decade old, and a mystery still. It was one of Paulo's greatest triumphs of inspired assassination. His own term, of course. He took an overweening pride in the uniqueness and variety of his means of dealing death and inspiring terror.

Hazy-minded as I was, I had my own flash of cunning. If I made him the gift of that coveted knowledge, conferred upon him the distinction of being the one to solve that ancient puzzle—and took my time about it—I might win myself a respite.

Alfonso Dominguín Gómez was the leader of the shaky "democratic" civilian regime that preceded the present military dictatorship. The chaos following his death was the perfect pretext for General Carrero to step in and take control. A step on the road to the political and social destabilization that was the goal of Paulo and his kind the world over.

Although he styled himself a socialist, several inept attempts had already been made on Dominguín's life by various insurgent factions. He lived, as befitted one of his democratic pretensions, in a modest villa at the edge of town, using the *palacio* only for bureaucratic purposes and social functions. The villa, however, was surrounded by a very high wall and guarded like a fortress. The only thing unguarded was Dominguín's tongue. He was obsessively fond of his cat, Peluche. At cocktail parties he would bore the company with endless accounts of the cat's cleverness and devotion. Dominguín was not a likable man, and while he extolled Peluche in one corner of the room, sycophants in another would be whispering, "Well, at least he has one friend," or "That's not the only cat he's slept with." It was rumoured that Dominguín had syphilis.

One thing Dominguín liked to boast about was Peluche's sexual prowess. Every night without fail he went marauding round the neighbourhood, siring a progeny that now must number in the thousands, as witness the tortoise-shell faces that looked out from every window and every *terraza*. Only one thing, it seemed, exceeded Peluche's randiness: his affection for his master. Worn out by his night's gallantry, he would head for home in the small hours, enter the ingeniously constructed cat door giving on to the balcony from Dominguín's bedroom, and curl up on the pillow beside his master's head.

These fascinating details had been recounted *ad nauseam* to anyone who wished to listen and to many who did not, but it took the creative mind of Paulo to perceive Peluche as a loophole in the president's iron-clad security system. He perfected his plan after several weeks of close observation of Dominguín's comings and goings, and after arranging for a couple of attractive female accomplices to cosy up to the domestic staff. He installed one of these co-operative ladies in an apartment in the vicinity, together with a desirable and amorous female cat.

When Dominguín was found in his blood-bespattered bedroom, minus head and hardly recognizable as human, it was assumed after an exhaustive investigation that it was an inside job. Which of course it was, but the fact that there were tufts of cat fur adhering to the far-flung gobbets of the presidential brain was not considered to have any bearing on the case. Peluche was seen as having paid dearly for his devotion. One magazine even ran the headline: Heroic Cat Dies With Master.

Peluche had to undergo intensive training for his mission. He was ensnared with fishy delicacies and promises of sexual dalliance. Over a period of two weeks he was conditioned to accept without demur the small body-belt made from an old bedsheet, which would eventually contain the plastic explosive. They would keep him in the apartment for an hour or so every night, then remove the belt and set him free. On that last night he seemed surprised that the belt was left on, but after a little coaxing he streaked for home. The plan almost ended in disaster when, as they watched from a darkened window, Peluche went aside into a neighbouring garden as if bent on some incidental romance. The bomb, kept cool in the refrigerator, was designed to be detonated by the cat's body heat when it curled up on the bed. Habit triumphed over temptation, however. Paulo estimated that Peluche could not have been in position more than two minutes when the detonator reached its critical temperature.

I've no memory of the words I used to convey all this to the Cheshire Cat. No doubt my account was fragmentary and punctuated by bellows of pain each time the invisible prompter jolted me back from the edge of oblivion. It required immense effort to surface from the black slough of my fatigue.

"Very ingenious. He had more than shit for brains, your friend Paulo." He looked smug. I could imagine him announcing to a group of reporters that *he* had finally fathomed the mystery of the death of Dominguín. But if he was eager to be gone, to savour his moment of glory, he was not about to let me off the hook so easily. He seized me by my long hair and yanked up my head to fix me with his inquisitor's stare.

"The *other* cat, *garañón*."

Little by little he grubbed it all out of me. All the way back to the original Conchita. All the way forward to the squashy sound of Tit Rock sinking into Paulo's skull. He pieced it together I suppose from my incoherent blurtings, in more than sufficient detail for "the record". He harped long, with sadistic glee, on Paulo's cruel recounting of his conquest of Martha. It amused him that I wept. Wept for a dead woman.

"Dead!" It sounded in my own ears like another of my shrieks of pain.

"Ah, yes. Dead. We all die, no? Some sooner than others, eh, *profesor*? Dying is no great thing."

As if to lend force to this intimation of mortality, the unseen persuader gave me another small jolt.

"Dead? How do you know? How could you?"

As if it mattered. As if Martha alive could have any meaning for me now.

"We know. You'd be surprised what we know, *garañón*."

He was watching me narrowly, perhaps to observe the effect of this repeated "*garañón*". But before I could train my slippery attention upon it he said, "She had a baby, by the way, your Martha."

"Baby? Ah." Why had the possibility never occurred to me? Now, sitting here, wasting long minutes of light in bittersweet reverie, I see Martha big with child, walking hand in hand with me through a might-have-been future. But as I lay there under the sardonic eye of the Cheshire Cat, hearing the snuffling and shuffling of the unseen tormentor impatient for action, my mind could encompass only the tragedy of her situation and impotent rage at the perpetrator of it. I wished him alive to be killed again.

"You were not the father, then?" the Cheshire Cat readily deduced from my reaction.

I grimaced in repudiation.

"The child thought so. Assumed so. Hoped so. It was understandable, no, given the alternative? Not that the mother would talk much about the alternative. She talked about you, though. You, her lost love. Romanticized you, no doubt."

How, I ask myself now, over and over again, could he possibly know all this? Such intimate things from so long ago, so far away? But at the time his omniscience seemed a natural, an inevitable, thing. Godlike, as Paulo once said.

"The child is still alive?"

It seemed, for an irrational instant, vital. As if in the child's being alive lay my way to redemption.

His face came very close, bringing a faint waft of garlic.

"Unhappily, no." His words, as he gazed into my eyes, seemed burdened with a connotation far beyond the mere statement of fact. But my mind, fatigued beyond endurance, could not cope with it. I felt myself plummeting down to sleep. "Very unhappily, no."

I came abruptly awake, partly because I sensed a movement of the man (woman, as it turned out: *Women, they are the worst, my Gaspar*) with the apparatus of persuasion. But partly also because my fuddled mind, spinning in a blur of memories, impressions, fantasies, stopped abruptly at *garañón*.

"Nina!"

"Ah, Nina. I wondered when you'd get around to Nina."

"Is she . . . ?"

"She's just fine. *Sano. Sano. Perfecto.*"

That "*perfecto*" passed over my head at the time. I was hearing Nina murmuring with dreamy lust, "Ah, mi garañón! Mi garañón grande!" My big stallion. Who would not rise to such a challenge?

But the word has another connotation. So that when she uses (used!) it on less intimate occasions, in less ardent moods, I could never be sure that she was not calling me a jackass.

On the lips of the Cheshire Cat, the word had no ambiguity. But there were devastating inferences to be drawn, which at the time I was scarce capable of. To whom, and under what circumstances, did she make this intimate disclosure? And *in what mood*?

"She will be interested, your Nina, to hear about your enduring passion for that Martha, don't you think? And about Conchita. The woman, not the cat. And about Maar—now there's a woman—about whom I suspect you've been perhaps a little less than candid."

Well, I wasn't worried on any of those scores. I had a tendency, at times of arousal, to boast of past conquests. Real *and* imaginary. Jealousy but inflamed Nina's ardour. No, what jolted me was the "will". Not would, but *will*.

Reading my thoughts (godlike again) he said, "Do you wish to send her any message?"

"She knows, then?"

"About your being here? All she needs to know. She is anxious that you should be taken care of. Just as you are anxious that she be taken care of. The two things are inter-dependent, don't you see? And both are in my hands. She is *most* anxious for your safety. Gratifyingly anxious, I might say."

"You despicable bastard!" I shouted, blind rage overcoming my cowardice.

"Tut-tut!" he said, laughing. "Tickle him, Rosita."

"Well, I think that's about enough for one day." He turned to the unseen Rosita, who evidently enjoyed her work. "Basta. Basta por hoy."

He began to unfasten the straps. "You've filled in a few gaps for us. And I have filled in a few for you, no? Now that the other canary is dead we must rely more upon you. And since, as you say, you are a coward—since, also, your Nina is so anxious for your well-being and so amenable—I propose to make it easier for you to sing. To sing on paper, as you prefer. Who knows? We may be able to let you have a little more light, even a little variety in your diet. The muse must be coaxed, nurtured, no? We shall see. But should your muse desert you, should your inspiration dry up, well, there's always Rosita."

He summoned the lout to take me back to the cell.

"Hasta luego, profesor."

It was only afterwards, lying here racked of body and sick to my soul, that I realized we had lost track of Martha's child. Dead, anyway, so what could it matter?

XIX

The rest, as they say, is hearsay. Or mostly so. What alarms me is not that, as the Cheshire Cat scornfully suggested, my muse may desert me, my inspiration dry up; but rather that in my distracted state memory may fail me. So much to remember. Day after day Paulo talked, random outpourings triggered by any chance stimulus, sometimes rendered almost incoherent by the firecracker leaps of his thought. Not that my own thoughts are any model of coherence. Nina in the arms of that sadistic bastard! The ghost of Paulo sitting there wearing his granite toque. Ghost in a very real sense, for I smell him yet. And all those other ghosts. Martha dead! Why did that fall upon me like a blow? As if her living presence anywhere in the world had some talismanic power to sustain and shield me. And the child whose existence I never knew of. Ghost of another sort, walking the earth invisible, perhaps passing me on the street, undetectable even by the acute antennae of my enduring love.

It must have been the child who accounted for Martha's sudden departure from her pious relatives' home. She would not have been one to brazen out the shame. How she must have suffered! I lie here nights composing variations on the course of her left-over life, making crazy agreements with God that if ever I get out of here alive I will go and ferret out the truth, follow her steps to the edge of the grave and stand with her, as I stood with her so long ago at the grave of Simon Mallory.

And Paulo? Did he know about the child? His child?

The sequence of events during those last turbulent weeks at Cambridge is confused in my mind. I must rely on others' testimony, as though I were not present. Martha went away. The old stone cottage when I passed in the course of many a sentimental excursion stood empty and forlorn. No dog leapt the wall to greet me. Paulo, too, went away, but whether before or after Martha I cannot be sure. I recall that for a time our friendship went on, superficially at least, as usual. Deep though my hurt was, jealous and bitterly resentful as I felt, I refused to believe that Paulo had done anything worse than catch Martha on the rebound after her estrangement from me. I was foolish enough to think that he had attempted to intercede with her on my behalf and had in the process fallen under her spell. It was easy enough to imagine: first, the potent urge to comfort her in her distress, then the realization that the emotion had passed far beyond mere sympathy. After all, it had happened to me.

And somewhere in the midst of all this personal upheaval, calamity. Calamity for Paulo, that is, but my attachment to him was still so strong that his misfortune added a new dimension to my own anguish.

Ever since he had returned after the death of his uncle Alvaro, Paulo had carried on a voluminous correspondence with his mother, of whom he spoke with a sort of mystical reverence. A framed photograph of her stood on his desk. Sometimes when he was ostensibly studying I would see him gazing at it with intense, faraway eyes. She was indeed a fine, though somewhat ravaged-looking, woman, not unlike Sara Loman in feature but with something of the unworldly, uplifted look I had always associated with Joan of Arc. Paulo awaited her letters with boyish eagerness. I recall that once when there was a disruption of the postal service he fretted like a lover. In fact their relationship struck me as indeed a sort of spiritual love affair. All the inhibited emotion of his mother-deprived youth went into it. On her side, the exaggerated maternal warmth natural to a woman in her situation was intensified by the emotional abandon of someone who had not enjoyed a real human relationship in almost twenty years.

I was privy, especially at first, to much of what passed back and forth in these letters: the business affairs of the hacienda and the other family interests; the new friends his mother was making; the career Tán was making for himself in his own country, despite official disapproval, and his growing influence as expounder of the nation's social conscience; and the direction and progress of Paulo's studies, which had caused her some concern as being possibly "too dilettante". As time went by, however, the passages he skipped over as being "personal" or "not of much interest to you" formed an increasing proportion of the letters' content.

Then, one evening when I returned from a series of lectures at another college, I found him gone. Over his rooms hung a *Marie-Céleste* air of mystery and doom. The door was ajar. An unfinished essay lay on his desk. Some of his things were gone, I found later, but at my first cursory glance after finding his note it appeared that he had simply walked out on everything. A package of Maar's friend's repulsive Turkish cigarettes, with his lighter on top, still lay beside his gold-capped pen.

Scrawled diagonally across the page after the last unfinished sentence of the essay were the words: "Awful news from home. Have to go. Will write."

He never did, though.

When I was at length able to piece it all together from my own parents' letters and from the newspapers they sent me, it became clear why I had not heard from Paulo. The events that engulfed the Hacienda Martínez and sucked Paulo into their vortex could have left little room in his mind for thoughts of me.

According to the official account in the newspapers, the hacienda had been attacked one night by *"una cuadrilla de los ladrones y los bandidos"*. But it was clear even from these specious accounts that the systematic and extensive havoc wrought by the attackers was far beyond the capability and intent of even the most enterprising band of thugs and bandits. Paulo's mother was murdered; but not, subsequent rumour had it, before being cruelly tortured. Several weeks later the charred remains of faithful old Inés, who had been kept on long past the term of her usefulness, were found in the ashes of the house. All the buildings were razed. Except, ironically, the summer-house. Horses perished in their stalls. Cattle in the vicinity of the house were shot. So were the dogs and even a couple of the cats. One dog, however, died with a sizeable piece of blood-soaked khaki twill clamped in its jaws. Tán, who at the time of the attack was away on one of his tours, was able to have this material identified unmistakably as army issue. But anyone, the defence ministry retorted, could come by a pair of army pants. Especially a bandit.

The attackers had gained entry by dynamiting the south gate through which Paulo, in his boyhood, had been wont to watch the old woman and her pig, and to dream upon the distant peak of El Gruñón. Their depredations covered a surprisingly wide area, and were conducted with all the thoroughness and precision of a military manoeuvre.

Many of the details of the disaster remained unknown to me until recently when Paulo, in spite of his professed loathing of sentimentality, would ramble on about "the old days at the hacienda" and then, as though awaking from that pleasant dream, would launch into a passionate diatribe against the army, which through several violent changes of government has remained, in his words, "a bunch of legalized bloody assassins".

One of the facts I sorted out from Paulo's less-than-coherent account was that a certain junior officer of the nearby garrison, who hailed from the local area (and whose family, apparently, had been dispossessed of its land in one of the Martínez expansions), acquired about this time a mysterious wound in the leg. A wound that became badly infected and could not, therefore, be easily concealed. A wound, word went out over the clandestine information network, such as might be inflicted by the bite of a German shepherd dog. Well over a year went by before this officer, now restored to health after almost losing his leg, was knifed in the back on his way home from the *cantina*.

Ramón, soldier himself of another sort by then, claimed credit for this "act of justice", but Paulo was sceptical. Ramón, he said, "did not know how to kill a cockroach until I came back and taught him." Came back, that is, after several years of training and experience in the fine art of killing, applicable in any situation, however you define your cockroaches.

I packed up Paulo's belongings and shipped them to him— at considerable expense, I might add—but I never knew if he received them. If he remembered, he has never mentioned it. It was after all, in the context of both then and now, a matter of small moment.

Another thing that never became clear from his ramblings was how long he remained at the hacienda—sleeping in the summer-house with the ghost of his father—before he awoke from that bad dream. I had the impression that he stayed there for some time; weeks, maybe even months, steeped in a sort of black, impotent madness, from which he emerged hardly knowing who he had been. The dark imago that eventually spread its wings and rose out of the ruins was not a thing of beauty.

During this period Tán and the friends of Paulo's mother "took care of him". They were solicitous of his physical well-being, of course, but they took care of him in a more sinister sense. They were astute enough to realize that although his spirit slept, his subconscious was receptive. One effect of their "caring" was that the lust for revenge, for some immediate, bloody restitution, cooled in him, first to a self-pitying inertia and then to an icy resolve. Urgency gave way to sagacity.

Satisfaction for the wrongs he had suffered became not merely a matter of the visiting of his wrath upon the perpetrators but the preoccupation of a lifetime, his ultimate *raison d'être*. His conception of "the enemy" broadened in time to embrace any person, organization, or institution that might be characterized as oppressive, exploitative, or corrupt. Governments were arch-enemies, but they were sustained by the avarice of the wealthy and they fed upon the tolerance of the masses. Gradually, therefore, this disaffection enlarged to include the whole of complacent humanity, which had to be shocked out of its apathy.

So that instead of taking to the mountains and rallying the ragtag bands of insurgents that chronically—but for the most part ineffectually—plagued the country's successive regimes, Paulo was persuaded to "travel".

"To broaden his mind," Maar, unavoidably confronted in Cambridge several months later, said.

"I thought it was pretty broad already," I said with all the sarcasm I could muster, my eagerness to escape warring with my desire for news of Paulo. She laughed.

"Come on, you can buy me a drink."

I demurred, reluctantly yielded. What harm, anyway?

"What a shocker *that* was."

I sought words to convey my sense of outrage. None came. She leaned back to light a cigarette. Encountering her eyes through the smoke, as I had done that first time I saw her, I experienced again that sense of menace, so disquieting because it had an ingredient of siren-like fascination. In the light of that look I found myself re-examining her words, her tone. "A shocker." A big surprise, no more. Long afterwards, deprived of many delusions concerning honour among thieves, I found myself recalling Maar's manner during that meeting, listening to the echo of her words, and was convinced she knew more of those events at the hacienda than she cared to divulge.

"Fate moves in a mysterious way," she went on to say, watching me with a calculating, bird-like tilt of the head.

"I thought that was God."

"He's reputed to help those who help themselves."

"So Paulo's travelling." How did *she* know? What could be inferred from the fact that she did? Evidently they had re-established their connection, but to what extent? In the hope of picking up a clue I said, "Where, exactly?"

"The where is the Middle East. The exactly I'm afraid I'm not at liberty to say."

Well, the "exactly" was South Yemen, but of course I didn't find that out until very much later, lying here one night with Conchita purring upon my chest, Paulo rhapsodizing over "Wadieh and George" and the blessings they had bestowed upon the world.

"I rather think," Maar continued when I speculated about Paulo's future, "that he will decide to go somewhere to round off his education." The sinister implications of this could not possibly have struck me at the time. There was, all the same, something in her sidelong look as she stubbed out her half-smoked cigarette that would perturb me for a long time, and that would come back to me, causing a small reflexive tremor, when Paulo came out for the first of many times with the words "when I was at P.L." Patrice Lumumba Friendship University, he had to explain, seeing my blank look. Even I knew where that was. But it wasn't so much to fact of his having "rounded off his education" in the Soviet Union that caused my involuntary spasm as the way Paulo's revelation caused the image of Maar to flit across my mind's eye with a faint resurgence of my old sensation of . . . what? Terror? Fascination?

What it was, I suppose, was the recognition that I had been teetering on the edge of submission to her power. I was like a man on the brink of a precipice in the moment of shocking realization that he has leaned out a little too far. And of course as I listened to Paulo all those years later, what came to me with such chilling clarity was that there but for the grace of God spoke I.

Not that I had any clear idea, as I took the hand Maar extended to me across the table, what lay beyond the precipice. Only that the fall would be exhilarating and dangerous. I suppose I imagined that even without the safety net of loyalty to Martha that had saved me on the previous occasion I should somehow come out unscathed, or at least unentrapped. But I didn't really care. In the wretched, depressed state that had possessed me for so many weeks, any change was preferable, any excitement welcome. And Maar was exciting. Perhaps doubly so because of the sense I had of playing with fire. And if I looked beyond that fire, beyond what her fingers were so eloquently promising, I glimpsed an extremely vague future that did not, after all, compare so unfavourably with a lifetime of teaching literature to the Philistine hordes of my native country. At worst I saw myself caught up in a clandestine crusade for the establishment of some sort of universal utopia. I gave no thought to the methods of conducting that crusade. I was, as I have said, naïve, like most members of the public at that time. No doubt it was intended that once Maar had completely ensnared me, I should be packed off to "P.L." to acquire what in the jargon of the trade is called the right "mind-set". The rest would be up to Wadieh and George.

So in this spirit of lustful bravado I indulged in a little passionate dalliance with Maar in a secluded corner of the bar and promised—having learned along the way that Hafiz was in Munich—to visit her that week-end.

On Saturday I ascended the dingy staircase in a horny trance, anticipating an afternoon of prurient abandon. Instead, I spent the afternoon and most of the evening at the police station. Maar's door, when I arrived, stood open. The apartment was in the process of being ransacked by two men attired like comic-book bureaucrats. One of them actually wore a bowler hat. A uniformed constable stood guard at the door.

It was a long ordeal, during which the interrogators (so much more subtle than you, Cheshire Cat, and with no Rosita to assist them) progressed slowly from the belief that I was knowledgeable, cunning, and dangerous to the conclusion that I was ignorant, ingenuous, and harmless. Which, however, did not preclude them from keeping me under surveillance for several weeks thereafter.

Our hero, while awaiting the summons to Moscow, was luxuriating in the hospitality of Dr. George Habash and meeting the élite of half the world's "armies of liberation". This visit, engineered and insisted upon by Maar, was clear evidence of her shrewd assessment of Paulo's character. He was, I had heard him declare, "no bloody Bolshie". He would almost certainly have balked at indoctrination behind the Iron Curtain. But George, who at heart was no bloody Bolshie either, could be relied upon to persuade his new protégé of the benefits to be derived from what he called "friendships of convenience".

Paulo never graduated from "P.L." in the normal sense, but in the profession for which he was destined certificates were of little concern. They could always be forged, anyway. His failure to complete the two-year program of studies may well have been calculated. He was cited, with unconscious irony, as being "a disruptive influence" in an institution dedicated to universal disruption. He passed the rest of his time in the country in "extramural studies".

"A few specialized courses in the fine arts," he said, "and a lot of ideological shit. Brainwashing, to tell the truth. Well, it was useful to learn how their minds work. Most of the people I had to deal with were puppets under their control. It's useful to know what a person's knee-jerk reaction's going to be when your life depends on it. They thought they controlled me, too. Maar pulled the strings for a long time, but she knew very well I would respond only as long as it suited me. There were several occasions when I moved before she pulled. She took the credit, of course. Had to, or admit I was a maverick. Which I was. I think they accepted it, too, in the end. They assigned a Cuban arsehole to bird-dog me. He didn't give me any trouble. His job was to keep an eye on me, to facilitate communication, and, I suppose, to shoot me if I stepped over some predetermined line. Which I did, in the end, but I got my shot in first."

"Fine arts?" I had repeated when he said it. He must have read my lips, because now he came back to it with a grin.

"Fine arts, *claro*. Weapons. Sabotage. Publicity. The psychology of fear. The fine art of orchestrating panic."

He was good at that. An example of how good he was at orchestrating panic was the last occasion when, still under Maar's "guidance", he acted without her pulling his strings.

The superficial facts of the incident—or two related incidents—are well known. They were reported in most of the world's newspapers and have since been speculated upon in several books. The first part of the operation was fairly straightforward from the reporter's point of view. It followed a familiar pattern: the hijacking of a commercial aircraft, hostage-taking, ransom demands, lengthy negotiations, the eventual freeing of the hostages, and the escape of the hijackers to a safe haven in Libya.

Nine of the hostages were NATO negotiators bound for a conference in Rome. They were the real target. After the plane had been diverted, first to Athens and then to Algiers, a deal was struck. All the passengers but the nine NATO men would be freed in exchange for another plane that would fly the nine and their three captors to Tripoli. The other passengers were to remain in the plane until the escape aircraft was well clear. If they attempted to disembark before the appointed time the plane would be blown up by a radio-detonated bomb. The authorities were sceptical about the existence of this bomb. As it turned out, they were wrong. The operation was master-minded by Paulo. Paulo did not bluff. But after two days of terror in the plane, the passengers were only too willing to sit out that extra half-hour. The forces on the ground, however, were so certain that the bomb did not exist that they gambled. They placed sharpshooters at various points to pick off the three terrorists should an opportunity present itself as the group crossed to the smaller plane. Such a chance did come. Two of the snipers were on the point of squeezing their triggers when a panicky voice bellowed through their head-sets, "Hold fire! Hold fire! Hold fire!"

One of the observers watching the twelve men crossing the tarmac had suddenly realized that one of the "terrorists" carrying conspicuously displayed grenades was in fact one of the NATO officials. The hijackers had exchanged clothes with three of the hostages, and with their guns well concealed had forced them to carry the grenades.

This part of the operation was planned by Paulo, as yet still a mysterious figure on the international scene, but he himself was not present. He suffered, in fact, from an almost paranoid aversion to flying that may well have rendered him incapable of the hair-trigger alertness essential in such a situation. But this malady was not the only reason for his absence. He was plotting the sequel. "By day," he told me one evening through a mouthful of beans, "I laid the plans for my little surprise. By night I consoled Maar for the unfortunate absence of Hafiz."

The absence of Hafiz was indeed unfortunate, because he was in a West German jail. He was eventually released, ostensibly for lack of evidence but in truth because a secret deal was struck for the release of a German hostage in Lebanon. During the evenings Paulo and Maar would gloat over the news reports of the negotiations for the release of the NATO hostages and congratulate each other on the success of the operation. When that palled, they would talk idly about "the next job", discussing all manner of far-fetched schemes to "set the world on its ear", Paulo meanwhile smirking inwardly because the next job was already well in train.

"And sometimes, my Gaspar," he said after a long pause, "sometimes we would speak of you."

It seemed unlikely. Several years had elapsed since I had seen either of them.

"Ah, yes, you seem surprised. But Maar really smarted at the thought that you had slipped her hook. She could have made good use of you, she said. I wasn't so sure. You were too deeply flawed with decency, too contaminated with compassion. Maar really liked you, though. It was her greatest weakness. She liked people. You especially. Even talked about you when we were in bed. Had the hots for you, as the kids say nowadays. She fully intended to reel you in one day, even then. Didn't she ever come after you?"

Not to my knowledge. Anyway, she didn't have much chance. Not long after that she was blown up, somewhere in the Pyrenees, along with a carload of Basques, members of Euzkardi Ta Askatasuna.

She did write once, though. The Cheshire Cat produced a copy of her letter, which I had almost forgotten. I don't recall that there was anything in it to indicate that she "had the hots" for me. There were phrases in it like "very special regard" and "treasured memories", but there was always a "we" implicit: Hafiz the falconer lurking in the shadows. They were planning to come to Latin America. "A tour of familiarization," I believe she called it. Another of my providential escapes. But to what end? I recall Paulo saying once, "Here we are, my Gaspar, in the same rat-trap. Innocent and guilty. God knows which is which. Makes you want to blow up the world, doesn't it? The whole stinking world. Well, I made my little gesture. I can rest easy. But you? You're too late. You blew your chance, *amigo*."

As for Paulo's "little surprise", its results are well known and will be long remembered, but the method of its accomplishment has never, until now, come to light. Except perhaps from Paulo under catechism.

When after lengthy negotiation the nine hostages were released, top-secret arrangements were made to fly them to Frankfurt, where they would be met by officials of their various governments and by members of their immediate families. As the plane came in to land and the assembled group pressed forward in anticipation, two masked men (according to the only witness) "appeared from nowhere" and swept the party with machine-gun fire. No one survived. A grisly welcome indeed for the returning hostages.

In the airport chapel lay the remains of a young Frenchwoman who had been killed in a traffic accident. A grieving relative had stayed with the coffin since it was brought to the chapel, and was to accompany it on the flight to Orly some hours later. Not long before the scheduled touch-down of the plane carrying the hostages, a priest arrived to comfort the mourner. An airport cleaner, inadvertently intruding, saw both of them at prayer. He apologized and withdrew, closing the chapel door.

A few minutes later Paulo locked the door and shed his priestly garb, and the two men donned ski masks. They opened the coffin, removed and loaded their weapons, and placed Paulo's vestments inside. Having made sure the passage outside the chapel was clear, they ran down to the arrival gate and burst upon the gathering with their guns blazing. Only one person, a woman selling flight insurance, survived the slaughter. She crouched in terror behind her desk, and so did not see what became of the two killers.

Paulo and his accomplice ran back to the chapel, intending to kill anyone they encountered on the way who might have seen where they went, but the whole area was deserted.

The two men re-emerged, now both attired as priests, and in the midst of the pandemonium were observed offering prayers for the dying and solace to the hostages who had arrived to find their families dead. Their services did not appear to be greatly appreciated by the distraught hostages, but the insurance woman, describing her ordeal on television, concluded by saying that she did not know how she could have endured the frightful experience had not that blessed father, God rest his soul, been there to calm and comfort her. That was Paulo.

Because of the disruption of services, the coffin, the first of many to pass that way, could not be flown out until the next morning. When the bereaved relative passed through the security barrier he turned to wave farewell to the priest who had accompanied him, and to receive his blessing. While he went through this formality, his hand baggage passed through the X-ray machine and the security guard scanned his person. It was not deemed necessary or proper to subject the coffin to the same treatment.

XX

It is not possible, even after listening for untold weeks to his rambling reminiscences, to be precise about the chronology of Paulo's activities during the years following the death of his mother, or to determine with any accuracy the sequence and duration of his sojourns in various parts of Europe and the Middle East. He made reference at different times to numerous acts of terrorism which I remembered reading about long before I had any inkling of the nature of the "career" he had taken up. He spoke for the most part disparagingly of those early operations, in which his part was minor and which were planned—if planned at all—by others. They were crude, often bungled, conceived in blind hatred and executed with very little regard for the possible variety of consequences.

But as Paulo asserted more and more authority the character of the operations changed and their efficacy increased. Where before the terrorists had relied upon the sheer unpredictability and irrationality of their attacks to spread panic and preclude defensive or punitive action, a pattern of careful and ingenious planning now became discernible. Apprehension and terror resulted not from mere randomness but from the growing sense of a fiendish intelligence that rejoiced in the novelty and aptness of its schemes and in the detailed planning of their execution. The very lack of a clear image of this presence magnified the general sense of insecurity, especially among those who saw themselves as potential victims. High-ranking officers were afraid to pick up their telephones after a Spanish diplomat received a call that said, "You are about to die in the glorious cause of Basque independence" and the receiver exploded in his hand. The delay in detonation, long enough for delivery of the message (overheard by the switchboard operator) but not long enough to allow the victim time to react, was one of the many refinements that helped create the myth of The Scourge.

This, one of Paulo's several fanciful aliases over the years, was fed to a sensation-hungry reporter by one of Paulo's women, who phoned and asked in mock innocence if it was true that the assassination was the work of El Azote. Something in the caller's tone suggested that she knew a lot more and was willing to talk, but there were strange sounds on the line and the connection was abruptly broken. This was good for all manner of wild speculation, and within days The Scourge was as real to most people as their next-door neighbour.

The sense of being surrounded by spies and potential— often unwitting—betrayers spread fear and mistrust among the eminent, the rich, and the influential. Paulo had learned a lot from Maar about manipulating people. By the time she was killed he not only had tuned in to her extensive network of social spies and stool-pigeons, but had made many secret connections of his own, which he exploited so effectively that in some European cities no man felt safe with his own servants, and there were some households where members of families eyed one another askance.

Paulo had at one point six women ensconced in different cities. Ostensibly they were mistresses, each secure in her conviction that she was his one and only, but they also provided safe houses for use in emergency and depositories for what

Paulo, reminiscing here in the darkness, in all seriousness referred to as the tools of his trade. *Mis muchachas*, he called these women, "my girls", although one of them was twelve years his senior. They were chosen and cultivated with great care, his *muchachas*. The first prerequisite was that they move in a social milieu capable of being exploited for his purposes, whether as intimates of the great or as ears at their keyholes. The second was that they must be capable of being emotionally enslaved. Paulo by this time was no longer the Adonis of our Cambridge days. A photograph of him found later in one of these love-nests shows a puffy and somewhat debauched-looking face, surprisingly peasant-like in its heaviness, but apparently he could still turn on the charm. From the subsequent statements of a couple of his women to police it is obvious that their relationship with Paulo was at the time the most important thing in their lives. They would do just about anything rather than relinquish it. They were not exactly beauties, these women. To meet the second of his criteria they had to be women to whom romance did not come easily.

"Give a woman what she is beginning to despair of getting," he said, "and you can make of her what you will. She will rise to any challenge or commit any folly."

As witness Rachel, the fortyish private secretary to the millionaire owner of a small but exclusive chain of department stores. Rachel, so far as I can recall from over-enlarged pictures in newspapers, was not unpleasant to look upon, but apparently she lacked the winsomeness of manner that might have compensated for her want of beauty. Love, until the coming of Paulo, had passed her by. Although she was a highly competent secretary, she could not but be painfully aware that she owed her position as much to the well-founded jealousy of her employer's wife as to her professional ability. It was common knowledge that the marriage had come close to collapse as a result of an affair with Rachel's predecessor. The tycoon in question was an avowed Zionist and a vocal critic of the French government's tolerance towards foreign trouble-makers. A prime target for Palestinian hostility and very much aware of it. His name was Myerson or Michaelson or something like that.

Had his attitude to his secretary been different, she would no doubt have been as loyal as she was efficient, but he made it clear in many subtle ways that he resented her, that he found her unalluring and despised her for it. Whenever a pretty woman came into the office, the fulsomeness of his manner, she testified, "fair made her sick". He would frame his flatteries in such a way as to imply pity for his secretary's plainness.

So that when Paulo met her in the Louvre (a favourite haunt, he said, of the unloved) she was "mellow as a peach with untapped passion". He played her gently, however. He had to ensure, before committing himself to a possibly unprofitable relationship, that she satisfied the first of his criteria. She did, eminently. "Heaven sent" he said she was, with no intention of irony.

This affair went on for several months before he saw a way of putting it to practical use. When she had a holiday they went cruising in the Mediterranean on what she laughingly called their honeymoon. She was by now, he boasted, pathetically enamoured of him. Her sexual appetite, so long denied, seemed to feed upon itself, so that in the middle of an afternoon game of deck quoits she would say, "Let's go below," and below they would stay until dinner-time. More than once after she returned to work she called him from the office to say, "I can get away for an hour, if you're free." Her voice would be full of husky urgency.

Paulo skilfully directed their pillow-talk.

"Don't let's think about *him*," she would say, lying in dreamy surfeit, stroking Paulo's thick, black hair. This in response to some disparaging reference to her boss, such as, "Old Shylock doesn't know what he's missing."

The implicit image of "Old Shylock" making love to her would make her shudder. Paulo nurtured this aversion until her mild dislike grew into a lusty and potentially vengeful hatred. The extension of this hatred to embrace what her employer stood for was easy. Rachel was by nature sympathetic to underdogs and victims of oppression. An armchair activist, she deprecatingly styled herself. Paulo could make her weep with compassion for the hungry and exploited of his own country. I wonder if he told her Ana's story? And for the starving hordes of Africa. And, ultimately, for the dispossessed Palestinians whose self-appointed leaders were the sponsors of Paulo's "business".

While secretly contemptuous of Rachel's "maudlin sentimentality," Paulo thought much about how her hatred of Michaelson and her by now blind devotion to himself might be turned to advantage. She wanted to help, she insisted, while having no idea of the magnitude of what she might be expected to help with. And certainly no inkling of the nature and extent of the "business" her lover was involved in.

"I could eventually have psyched her up to plant a bomb in his phone or to poison his coffee," Paulo said, "but I couldn't be completely sure she wouldn't crack up." Besides, that would have been too crude.

In spite of her "don't let's think about *him*," Rachel would turn to him moments later and say, "D'you know what he does?" In this way, Paulo learned not only about Michaelson's business and domestic affairs but also about the elaborate measures he took to protect himself. Paulo wondered with some misgiving for a time if these measures included surveillance of his secretary's private life. She had been very carefully screened before being employed, of course, but after several years of aridly virtuous living she was probably considered beneath suspicion. Rachel was surprisingly well informed about the habits of her employer's friends and business associates. She had, in fact, been well on her way to becoming a nosy old maid. It was all potentially valuable stuff.

"D'you know what the old lech is up to this afternoon?"

It was in the drowsy afterglow of one of their "matinees". Paulo was less attentive than usual, perhaps planning a weekend in London with Cissie or in Munich with Ulrike.

"He's in bed with one of the junior managers, at La Couronne."

It almost passed him by. She was beginning to bore him.

"He has to be damned careful, of course. Madame has a nose for it. But d'you know what he does? He books this room at La Couronne regularly for genuine business meetings. More civilized, he says. Sometimes he takes me along, just to make the whole thing look legitimate. I was *peu disposée* the first time, I can tell you. But I might have been a bedside table for all the attention he paid me."

"A woman?" said Paulo, suddenly alert. "The junior manager, I mean."

"Of course a woman. My God, he's not queer on top of everything else. You weren't listening, were you? Other things on your mind, *n'est-ce pas*?" She snuggled close, only too ready to turn her attention to "other things". Paulo's professional antennae were aquiver, however. He held her off.

"He does this often?"

"Every fortnight or so."

"The same woman?"

"Oh, no. He likes variety."

"Such as? Who are these women?"

"Why, do you want to meet some of them?"

"Be serious, it's important."

She went over in her mind what appeared to be a lengthy list. "Well, people from the company, mostly, I suppose. Anyone who can buy a promotion or exchange a favour. Younger women—junior managers, advertising people, buyers, display designers. But not always. There was a young publisher's rep, I remember. And a lawyer. I forget what she was after, but she probably got it. He's not niggardly in these things. In fact, anyone who comes to the office and happens to take his fancy."

Thus it was that an attractive young woman presented herself at Rachel's desk about three weeks later. A free-lance writer, the visitor said she was, commissioned to do a profile of Mr. Michaelson. When the woman had phoned earlier, Rachel had gone through the pretence of trying to discourage her, since others were listening. Now, having chosen a time when she knew Michaelson would be in and not too busy, Rachel grudgingly agreed to see if he would agree to an interview. The woman had come equipped with a letter of reference and an impressive portfolio of her previous work. She also presented a card bearing a number to be called for verification of her credentials, which Rachel was careful to destroy afterwards. It was the number of a friend's apartment, where "editor" Paulo was awaiting the call.

When she went into the inner office, Rachel took care to leave the door open so that the attractive visitor was clearly visible. Since Michaelson might have been hesitant on account

166

of the slight duskiness of the woman's skin, they had prearranged that as they entered the office she would be casually informing Rachel that her mother was from Haiti, her father a French businessman. She was, in fact, Lebanese.

Michaelson succumbed with surprising alacrity, even for him. "It had been a week or two," Rachel drily commented in her testimony much later. An interview was arranged, at La Couronne, of course, "for the sake of comfort and convenience". The woman took a couple of photographs of Michaelson feigning work at his desk. Then, positively simpering, he escorted her to the elevator.

"I don't think I shall need you, mademoiselle," he said when he went to keep the appointment. It made Rachel so furious that she seriously considered tipping off his wife. That would really have wrecked Paulo's plans. But then, she had no idea of the terminal nature of those plans. She spoke but the truth when she testified that she was *"absolument stupéfiée"* when told that her employer's nude body had been found in the hotel bed.

The body bore no evidence of violence. All the signs pointed to cardiac arrest. Such might well have been the diagnosis without further examination had not the body been draped with a Palestinian flag. The autopsy revealed that Michaelson died from a rare and virulent poison. It had been injected, with an ironic appropriateness that made Paulo chuckle, telling it all those years later, in the end of his penis.

Paulo named the poison. It would, he said, become one of the urban guerrilla's favourite weapons in the future. It was a name I have neither reason nor desire to remember.*

XXI

I have dreamed of that day in the park before, often, but last night it was so real that my waking was like a little death. So real yet so intense in its reality that my senses were taxed to the point of pain. Simply to breathe the burdened

---

*Probably ricin (Ed.)

air was a cruel ecstasy. Every minute detail proclaimed itself, every grass-blade and pebble was pregnant with some life-secret. I could hear sounds: the melody of the droplets falling into the pool, the plaint of a dove, the click of the swing at each reversal. The young girl's hair lifted at one extremity of the arc and settled heavy upon her shoulders at the other. She faintly sang, in time to her rise and fall, one of those skipping-rope rhymes that sound like incantations. Somewhere afar off a runaway clock was telling the hours of eternity.

An Eden-like sense of blessedness reigned; a sense that this was meant to be for ever and that every living creature and every inanimate thing must conspire to make it so, must join together in passionately willing its continuance. A great impotent wisdom informed everything, a tragic knowledge that there could be no higher happiness. The sandal-maker and his client went through their symbolic pantomime in slow motion, the haloed head of the latter nodding and turning mechanically like that of a store window dummy at Christmas, his hand rising as if to exhort some unseen multitude or to drive home the point of a parable. A little light was leaking in under the brim of Clementina's big straw hat, striking soft beams from her moist eyes and delineating the swell of her plump, rouged cheeks. She cast over the scene by the slow sweep of her gaze a promise of pleasure that settled dew-soft upon the dramatis personae of that will-less charade and enmeshed them stickily, like the webs of spiders.

Eliza and her jackal walked without advancing towards the high gate of Heaven, the baby carriage borne up not by wheels but by a pulsing silver ball of light. The jackal's movements were faintly eurhythmic. He was performing a *paso doble* in his mind, the choreography a little comic, constrained by the too-tight crotch of his pants. He was intuitively aware of the big black Labrador with horns pawing and prancing in the distance but he spared it no glance. Eliza herself was enshrined in a circle of red hibiscus flowers, their crimson bleeding out of small white stars of hawthorn. White petals rained down and splashed red upon the baby-carriage casket. Her hand floated white, disembodied, beside the darkness that was her face. Beyond her the swaddled presence on the bench spun a cocoon of secrecy about itself. The thumb of a fingerless hand crooked about a rope that trailed away to nowhere.

I was not there, but my absence was the cynosure of every eye.

It left me prostrate and life-weary, that cordon bleu nightmare. A little joke of Nina's. Rich food always had its revenge of me. Yes, even my own wedding feast, so that I came thrashing and bellowing out of the immense tortilla my mother was folding me into to find myself floundering in the billows of my bride's ample flesh. It tends to make a man abstemious, but who, after enduring beans *ad nauseam* and *in perpetuum*, would dream of scorning *tortilla con picadillo*, even when prepared by a halfwit?

For, yes, the Cheshire Cat has kept his word. The promised amelioration of my lot has at last come to pass. Modest, true, but of immense significance. Food and light. The food would not gladden the heart of Apicius and I am hardly "blasted with excess of light", but far be it from me to look even these spavined hacks in the mouth. The light is outside the grille of the door, out of reach of suicidal impulse. It comes on and goes off at the whim of the lout, but it substantially increases my writing-time.

Where was I, before that enigmatic dream turned my thoughts aside from enigmatic reality? The lout now culls my pages every couple of days, at the same time that he empties the bucket. An unflattering line of thought which I do not care to pursue. He informs me that *el señor doctor* would like to see a little more action and a little less introspection. ("Self-pitying shit" is the way he phrases it.) I wonder idly about *el señor doctor*. About the nature of the thesis that prepared him for his current employment. Before whom did he defend it?

As far as action goes, I have to get Paulo out of Europe and back to this "land of opportunity", as he called it once, only partly with satirical intent. After all, there is no lack of challenge here for a man with an eye to revolution. Or simple disruption. For a man bent on making things worse as a necessary catharsis before which it is idle to speculate upon ways of making them better.

This was one step in Paulo's logic that I could never quite follow. Not that logic was exactly a favourite concept of his. "Logical thinking got the world into this god-awful mess," he used to argue. "Don't you think that a little bit of illogic might help to purge the system? After all, it's the purgation that's important. You hope that afterwards you'll be clear-headed enough to think about the future. Until then, you're too sick to care."

Whatever it was that drove Paulo must have had its roots in abhorrence of the appalling injustices inherent in the economic and social fabric of this country. I can see now that his sense of this iniquity had been gnawing away at the roots of his inbred gentility for years. It was not so much compassion as galling anger that the privileged and not unpleasant life he had been taught to accept as a divine right was founded upon the continuance of that iniquity.

Perhaps it was symptomatic of this unacknowledged inner turmoil that during our Cambridge years he could never be induced to eat honey. It was a foible that had once brought down upon him the wrath of Inés, who stated as a "medical fact" that without the magical properties of honey his hair would fall out before he was twenty-five. She no doubt divined the connection between Paulo's aversion and the girl Ana; his powerful but unexamined conviction that the sweetness of the honey was in some way commensurate with the bitterness of Ana's existence.

In some paradoxical way he was ashamed of this squeamishness. He kept it, the tell-tale honey-hatred, apart, well hidden, and cherished the belief that he would grow out of it, along with other phases which, Uncle Alvaro assured him, everyone went through at that age. Like his misguided concern for the donkey that plodded day after day, year after year, in a small circle to irrigate a remote corner of the estate where there was no electricity.

One of the signal achievements of the series of mentors through whose hands Paulo passed during those post-Cambridge years was to maintain and strengthen the revolutionary impulse arising from these guilty feelings while eradicating the feelings themselves. Although he tended whenever possible to steer clear of lectures or activities aimed at political indoctrination, and was officially censured both at "P.L." and later at training-camps in Lebanon and at Matanzas, the essence of their teachings rubbed off on him through day-to-day contact. He developed "acceptable attitudes"—at least to the extent of being convinced that there was no place for compassion in the "war of liberation".

From there I suppose it was but a small step to the state of mind in which the warfare itself became its own *raison d'être*, carried on with no vision of or desire for ultimate victory, so that when, after his numerous exploits in Europe, he decided—or events dictated—that he should carry the fight to his own country, it was not with any noble desire to redress wrongs, but rather for the greater satisfaction of practising his trade in familiar surroundings. Which betrays an inverted form of the sentiment he so much despised. Here, he could take aim at the shibboleths and bogeymen of his childhood. No doubt despite the exorcistic efforts of Tán and friends there lingered a steely core of resolve to settle the score for his mother. The faces of power had changed but the symbolic enemy would always be there.

In Europe, Paulo, The Scourge of the scare headlines, was getting too well known to the authorities. Those who financed and imagined they controlled him decided it was time to withdraw him from the "outer edge".

"They thought they could turn me into some sort of schoolmarm, teaching hot-headed Irishmen and assorted Arabs how to use a Makarov or an MP5."

He also turned down the offer of an opulent retirement villa in Libya, which, he suggested, would be rather like rewarding Richard the Lion Heart with a caliphate in Mecca.

Paulo's long career as the kingpin of the terror network in Europe demanded some sort of grand finale. Or so he managed to convince his somewhat reluctant sponsors. It was an operation he had been mulling over for some time. Bashir Mabrouk, one of the Palestinians' most valued agents, had been imprisoned in France for several months. They wanted him out. It was not only that his services were missed. The organization badly needed the boost in influence and morale that would accrue from a success of that sort. Haddad's advisers were of the opinion that such a rescue was impossible, that any attempt could only end in disaster. Paulo thought otherwise, and in view of his record he found the Doctor very susceptible to persuasion.

The whole thing was bizarre and from Paulo's point of view unique in that no blood was shed, apart from a pint or so from the head of the tennis umpire, who fell off his perch at the height of the excitement.

"You gave me the idea, my Gaspar."

He gave the nearest thing to a laugh that ever came from him in those last days. My reaction must indeed have been comical. What, I immediately thought, would any listening ear make of that? How would it square with my strenuous protestations of innocence?

Paulo was leafing idly through a magazine one evening while waiting for one of his *muchachas* when he came across an article about an international tennis tournament scheduled to take place near Paris later that summer. There was a picture of the previous year's winner sitting on the lower level of the bleachers at the side of the court. Paulo had already turned the page when he remembered the prank we had played at Cambridge. It was at an inter-varsity rugby match, at which we knew college loyalties would be running high. The spectators always separated into partisan groups. It would be more than a chap's life was worth, one of our friends remarked, to get mixed up with the rival team's supporters. The moment you opened your mouth you'd be jumped on. Well, I said, what if you opened your mouth but weren't there to be jumped on? Our friends ignored this apparently fatuous remark. I had a reputation for being irrelevant, even a little eccentric sometimes. But Paulo silenced them.

My plan was simply to conceal a small loudspeaker somewhere under the seats and from a safe hiding-place cheer on our own team and make provocative comments about the play of our opponents. It worked well, too—almost caused a riot among the spectators who could hear the comments but were too far away to detect the tinny tone—until someone tracked down the source of the sound and traced the wires back to the man with the microphone.

Paulo, however, as he dined with his *muchacha*, was thinking not of loudspeakers but of bombs. What if? What if?

It all came together with surprising ease. A preliminary investigation revealed that security in the weeks preceding the tournament, although superficially sound, would not present much difficulty for the team Paulo was already recruiting in his mind.

On one side of the court where the final match would be played there was a hotel with grounds abutting the court. The hotel had a private viewing-stand from which guests who availed themselves of a special "tennis package" could watch the game. Paulo and his team took advantage of this extortionate deal and moved in several days before the start of the tournament to make their preparations. Each evening they sat at tables in the hotel garden, apparently enjoying a tipsy party. But while they laughed and talked loudly, one or two of them would slip away and carry on their work under the bleachers.

All seemed normal on the day of the match when the finalists emerged from their dressing-rooms and acknowledged the applause of the spectators, Paulo and friends among them. Then, as they took their places on the court, the male voice that had been making the announcements was interrupted by that of a woman. She told the players, officials, and spectators, in a very carefully composed message calculated to preclude a rush for the exits, that they were all, in effect, hostages. If they obeyed instructions no one would be in danger, but anyone attempting to leave or to try any tricks would be shot. Only late in the message did she casually mention the bombs, which, she said, were there only to ensure that the authorities would comply speedily with the group's demands, which she then outlined.

"Lest there should be any doubt of our sincerity," she concluded, "I ask the lady in the red-and-white dress in the third row behind the umpire to kindly look under her seat."

The lady in question did so and screamed: "My God! There *is* a bomb!"

A wave of movement passed over the crowd. For a moment a stampede seemed imminent. But the gun-carrying men who had moved out around the edges of the court had only to point their weapons to quell the impulse. The woman then announced that the game would proceed as planned. If

Mabrouk had not been flown to the appointed destination by the time it was over, "My friend, whom you know as The Scourge, will decide what further measures may be necessary." At this, Paulo, the only member of the team not now masked, could not resist a cheery wave to the crowd. A press photographer laid his life on the line by preserving this gesture of bravado for posterity. And for the files of Interpol.

The players demurred, of course, but needed little persuasion to begin to play. Inevitably the loser claimed later that the result was invalid, but under the circumstances both gave a commendable performance and earned their place in history as their pictures, interspersed with those of the gunmen and those of the plane being prepared to fly Mabrouk out of the country, were broadcast around the world.

At the end of the game, which fortunately went the full five sets and so precluded the need for "further measures," Paulo and his team were driven to the airport and flown to Algiers, together with the two finalists as security. The bombs, the woman said in her final announcement, would be deactivated in about two hours. All went without a hitch, and the two hostages, who flew back to London the same evening, said their captors had treated them with the utmost courtesy, and had invited them to play an exhibition match in Tripoli. Paulo, with faultless documentation and a skilled make-up job, flew back to London in the same plane in the guise of a Carmelite nun, whose arrival attracted little interest. After "setting his affairs in order" and spending a last night or two with his London *muchacha*, he flew out of Heathrow in the same guise, bound for a mission of mercy in several countries of Latin America. Two other nuns and a priest were there to wish him Godspeed.

XXII

In the remote mountain town of La Boquilla the largest building by far is the silver-domed Monasterio del San Clemente. It dwarfs the town hall and the few large houses, which in turn dwarf the sprawling adobe *jacals* of the poor. It dwarfs the squat building that boastfully proclaims itself El Supermercado del Nuevo Mundo. And certainly it belittles the railway station, which consists of several sheets of corrugated iron clinging precariously together like a house of cards. The station is wide open on the side facing the narrow-gauge track, and affords shelter from the sun; but the earth floor is so liberally strewn with the manure of the sheep and goats that seek its shade that most of the human passengers prefer to endure the heat.

The modesty of the station is in keeping with the train itself, which twice weekly, barring washouts in the rainy season, climbs laboriously—and to the unseasoned traveller alarmingly—up nearly three thousand metres elevation from the coast, stands shimmering in its own heat for fifteen minutes while passengers and assorted animals alight and board, then trundles back down in the direction of El Platillo, visible eight kilometres distant and fifteen hundred metres below, nestling in the saucer-like depression from which it takes its name. El Platillo from that elevation, as one of our poets fancifully observed, resembles a piece of fine china hand-painted by God, *"un artista magnifico de cerámica"*. Visiting there a few years ago, conscientious critic that I am—was— I felt moved to comment that although the metaphor is just, provided the "painting" is seen from the optimum viewing distance, which in this case is considerable, El Platillo has apparently not yet finished its firing in the Creator's kiln. Good, it was hot!

El tren, like El Supermercado, smacks of grandiloquence. It consists of but one "carriage," a double-bogied chassis over which an ancient yellow bus body squats like a brooding hen. This comparison gains a fearful cogency as the contraption gathers momentum on the descent. Its fenders flap alarmingly and the launch of its jaundiced carcass out over the abyss seems imminent.

My visit to the region was innocent. Not unobserved, however. The Cheshire Cat was able to remind me of details I had long since forgotten. I was preparing a series of papers, some day, I hoped, to be a book, that would demonstrate how the country's literature evolved out of its very soil, and how the people's inspired choice of place names was a fun-

damental part of that process. The poems of Bernardo Matosas seemed an obvious place to start, and where better than
the mountain scenes of his childhood?

Seen through other eyes, my wanderings may well have
appeared suggestive if not downright suspicious. I find myself
re-examining my conduct during all the years since I came
back from Cambridge, scrutinizing it through the eyes of one
bent on establishing a connection between me and the forces
of anarchy. It is surprising how many burrs and prickles, in
the course of such a reappraisal, cling to one's conscience,
but my interest on the occasion in question was purely
professional.

In El Platillo itself, not yet having seen it from afar, I roved
the streets looking in vain for the artistic hand of God. I went
out of my way to meet the people, "themselves tickled by the
touch of sable" and "possessing chiaroscuro souls". Well, the
touch of sable, in the dark allusive sense, was there all right,
and the chiaroscuro. The eyes were full of dark secrets, the
smiles as enigmatic as they were bright. If I was aware of
being watched, it was not by the forces of "law and order"
but by those who suspected *me* of watching, although I had
no notion what. And it was during this quest for the collective
psyche that I found myself in La Bodega Bomba, an establishment as ominous as its name; which, however, was
assigned to it many years before the proclivities of its clientele
rendered it so eminently suitable. The antique sign outside, in fact, depicts not a bomb but a pump, the original of
which once drew water from "the saucer" and forced it up
to a reservoir to irrigate the tip-tilted meadows where sheep
swarmed like fleas.

The patrons I found to be but mildly interested in the town's
most famous son; in his poetry, not at all. They were, however,
interested in *my* interest. Especially my interest in La Boquilla,
"the little mouth that eats her sons and speaks with fiery
tongue". The towering fissure in the mountain's face to which
this cryptic line refers can be seen, when the sun is south-
easterly, rising like a dark feather out of the monastery's silver
cap, although it is in fact two kilometres distant. As the sun
swings westward, the cleft miraculously vanishes. Or, as
Matosas has it, "La boquilla se cierra." The little mouth closes.

Beyond the opening, inside the little mouth, extends a network of ravines, defiles, gorges, and precipitous gullies that resemble, in recent high-altitude photographs, one of those revolting convoluted funguses prized by the epicure. The region is known as "La Red," the snare, or net. For centuries it has been the refuge of the persecuted, the haunted, the rebellious, the lawless. It defied the might of the Conquistadors and thwarted the best efforts of all oppressors before and since, the present army of El General included. The insurgent forces had always an impregnable fortress into which they could retire and regroup. These were the "sons" who were swallowed up and held secure until it was time once more for the little mouth to speak with fiery tongue.

Most of this was common knowledge, but I felt the need for something more than bare, second-hand facts. Exactly what, I was not sure. The spirit of the place, I suggested somewhat hesitantly to Dámaso after buying him a second beer, the atmosphere. *La alma*, the soul. Whatever it was that had moved Matosas to write one of the greatest poems in the language.

Dámaso was a stocky man with a twisted mouth. I could not determine whether this was the result of injury or merely a physical manifestation of his sardonic nature. A greasy lock of hair hung down over one side of his face. I wanted to brush it aside. It was some time before I discovered that this was not sloppy grooming but a carefully contrived device to conceal a frightful scar surrounding an empty eye-socket, about which, for one of his very evident toughness, he was inordinately sensitive. Our meeting, I began to suspect after a time, was not so casual as it seemed. It reminded me of my first encounter with Hafiz and Maar. My impression, as the day wore on (which Paulo later confirmed), was that Dámaso had attached himself to me in the capacity of something between a watchdog and a ferret.

"We like to look after strangers in these parts," he said, his mouth twisting a little more.

I noticed that another stranger who had alighted from the train was also being "looked after" by one of the regulars, and that the stranger in his turn was taking care of the man's thirst. This stranger, I now assume, was the source of the

Cheshire Cat's detailed knowledge of my doings that day. He had a shiny bald dome of a head with a curly fringe of hair encircling it. He put me in mind of a bust I had once seen of the Emperor Nero. I was to see him again in another guise, in other circumstances, long after he had been "taken care of" in a more sinister sense. But at the time I wasn't much interested in him. I certainly didn't dream that he was interested in me.

Matosas, in the opinion of Dámaso, was more than a little crazy: a dreamer in a land where, in Dámaso's words, "you're either wide awake or dead." Besides, he went on with a wry grin that did strange things to his solitary eye, "He brought a lot of unwelcome attention to the place." I interpreted this as a rebuke, and made penance with another pint of the dark, yeasty *cerveza*.

I came round circumspectly to the monastery. Wasn't it a strange place for so eminent and so holy an institution?

"Well, you know," he said slowly, as though it had never occurred to him before, "it was here first, before the town. And when you think of it, Mother Church also swallows up her sons, no? *El monasterio* was a place where men could escape to when they didn't like what was going on in the world. And women, of course, to *el convento* in the gully behind. Or when they didn't like what the world was doing to them."

Did he mean, I prompted as delicately as I could, that there was, er . . . an understanding between the occupants of the monastery and the denizens of La Red?

He seemed shocked at this irreverent suggestion. But after taking a deep draft of his beer he wiped his moustache on the corner of his sarape and said, "Those who seek God's help go first to *el monasterio*. If God can't help, there's always La Boquilla."

There also appeared, I ventured, pressing my luck more than I knew, to be a very special relationship between the town of La Boquilla and the village of El Platillo. Dámaso when he laughed seemed to have a mouthful of dried maize.

"When you expect unwelcome visitors, it helps to have a squeaky gate."

He left me to work it out for myself. El Platillo was the gate through which everyone—everyone not equipped with mountaineering gear and superhuman courage and endurance—must pass to reach La Boquilla, either by train or in a very rugged road vehicle. There was ample time for the gate to squeak before any prying stranger came near La Boquilla. The train stopped for an hour in El Platillo to refuel and catch its breath after the long haul up from the coast; and, it was rumoured, for the driver to take on a little Dutch courage. Any vehicle coming up the road is seen and heard long before it nears the village. It appears and vanishes a dozen times as the road snakes among the crags and gorges, its progress accurately measurable by the flitting of its echoes from one rocky sounding-board to another. There is ample time for the inhabitants, solicitous always of the safety of travellers, to set up a road-block so that the driver may be warned of a rockfall ahead, which will be cleared in about an hour (during which time the occupants of the vehicle can be fleeced of a few dollars and well scrutinized). In the early days an ingenious variety of visual signals apprised the watchers above of the approach of trouble. This was later refined to include a sophisticated code, predating the ingenious Sam Morse's invention by a decade or more, transmitted by flashing lights. Now of course they use radio, and extremely undesirable snoopers may encounter a real rockfall, or come to grief on an opportunely infirm bridge before they get to the top.

These details I learned very much later, but I never did find out how the watchers in La Boquilla alerted those encamped in the fastnesses of La Red, where radio reception must be at best erratic.

Communicate they obviously did, however, as the muzzle of a Kalashnikov thrust into my ribs two days later would demonstrate.

Dámaso "just happened to be taking the train up" to La Boquilla. He knew a man who had known Matosas personally, and who would be happy to act as my guide for a tour of the literary landscape.

The train left late (despite the ticket agent's boast that it was "en punto, siempre, siempre") because one of the prospective passengers, a formidably horned goat, broke loose. After being pursued for some time through the streets it escaped capture by launching itself from a cliff two hundred metres high. During the journey up to La Boquilla, conversation, difficult at best because of the train's overtaxed engine, was rendered impossible by the loud lamentations of the goat's custodian, whose husband was going to kill her for sure.

So there was little to do but admire the scenery: if "admire" is the word for the fist-clenching fascination with which I, for one, studied the lurching panoramic splendour upon which we gazed from the very edge of oblivion. Little else but that and furtively scrutinizing the other passengers: furtively because there was something disconcerting in the occasional collision of eyes. There were residents returning from their quarterly shopping spree to the city. There was a woman sitting in the back on a crate of chickens; a farmer with a sheepskin and half its former contents, the other half left behind, he had said resentfully as we waited to board, to cover the cost of butchering; and a man clutching two cartwheels, which stood in the aisle and threatened to break loose at every lurch, to the peril of all present. In the front, two nuns sat in placid silence, regarding the abysses that yawned beside them with equanimity, with the comfortable assurance, I supposed, of their total faith in God. Which I envied. I never saw them speak. Was this because they despaired of outshouting the racket or because they had taken a vow of silence? Another possibility was very far from my mind: that one of them, at least, had a deep masculine voice.

"I recognized you all right," the erstwhile nun said much later, easing himself up on his prison bench and farting prodigiously. "Wondered what the hell you were up to. You and that bald-headed nark. You stared pretty hard at me when we got off the train."

Well, who wouldn't? The nun stood head and shoulders above most of us. Her features were rugged. The make-up job had received rather less attention than when it fooled the officials at Heathrow. The hands so busy about their beads were large but shapely—he always had good hands, Paulo—roughened, one could only surmise, by work in the famous gardens of San Clemente. The eyes, however, were cast demurely down upon an expansive bosom and there was nothing to inspire doubt in any but the most suspicious of minds—the nark's, perhaps—concerning the pious sister's gender. But there was, I remember, something faintly suggestive about the face that compelled a second glance. Some vestige perhaps beneath its ravaged lines of the youthful face I had looked into across so many convivial pints at Cambridge; so faint, however, as to belie itself and prompt me to look away at once.

"That was some coincidence. In fact I refused to believe it could be. You had to be up to something. One of the first things I did was to have you thoroughly checked out. And kept under surveillance."

Him and the Cheshire Cat both. How could I have remained so blissfully unaware of all that attention?

"It even crossed my mind that Maar had managed to tame you after all, without my knowledge. She was capable of that. But it seemed unlikely. The other possibility was that you were on the other side. Actively, I mean, as opposed to being one of the guilty complacent multitude. Which in view of your character seemed even more unlikely."

I swallowed my resentment. I had always been mildly—and, I must confess, passively—socialistic, but I considered myself in favour of reform, even tolerant of a certain degree of violence in attaining it.

I digress again. Paulo, as I alighted from that ramshackle train at La Boquilla, could not have been further from my thoughts, even though, as Dámaso walked me to the hotel, we were almost run down by the jeep carrying the two nuns to San Clemente and a blasphemous comment was borne back to us in a bass voice that did not seem to match the puny physique of the driver.

The next morning Dámaso's friend (whose name I have ungraciously forgotten) and I set out on foot to explore the poetic landscape of Bernardo Matosas. At noon we stopped on a wooded knoll overlooking the road to the little mouth, where he could point out places of interest to me while we ate the lunch his wife had provided. He told me tales of the poet's wretched, motherless childhood, when he was bullied by his father, misunderstood and despised by everyone else.

He spoke at length of Bernardo's hopeless passion for Neni, the lame girl who secretly loved him back but was ashamed to confess it, at least until after his death, when his eccentricity came to be acclaimed as genius. She languished now in the cloister, saying daily prayers for his soul. My guide's tone was condemnatory, but it was clear that his own admiration for Matosas was also retrospective.

I asked him about Bernardo's death and the nature of the mysterious malady to which, according to the sketchy biographical notes in his books, he had succumbed.

"Well," he said, "Bernardo used to go off on these long rambles. In search of inspiration, I suppose. One day he was up there" — he gestured vaguely towards the encircling peaks—"where no one but a goat or a madman would go, when he came upon a litter of baby ocelots. He was nuts about animals, as you know. He just sat there on a rock and watched the little fellas tumbling over one another. Didn't even notice mama ocelot watching him from a ledge up above until she snarled and sprang. It wasn't all that bad a bite he got. Managed to fight her off without too much trouble. He headed home, already mumbling the first lines of the poem he was going to write about the experience. I don't suppose he'd have been much worse for the ordeal if the ocelot hadn't been rabid."

It was as we prepared to resume our journey that my friend Nero came sauntering along the rock path below, heading in the direction of the fissure. He looked doubtfully about him, glancing back several times the way he had come; then with sudden resolution he strode towards the narrow base of the opening. My companion made as if to shout to him, but changed his mind, shrugged, and said, "None of my damned business."

He had agreed the night before, with some reluctance, that we might take "just a peek" beyond the opening of La Boquilla at the nearer tortuosities of La Red. I was to stay very close to him and not attempt to penetrate any deeper than he deemed wise, or to stray from the path he chose.

We were three or four hundred metres beyond the opening when a bearded thug stepped from a cleft in the rock, jabbed a rifle into my chest, and quizzed me about my business there.

He kept the muzzle of his gun pressed painfully against my ribs, listening to my replies with the bored, impatient air of one who would as soon shoot me as not. At the time I attached no importance to the fact that my guide addressed this *bandido* as Ramón.

Would *el señor*, he asked my companion, as though it were beneath his dignity to address me directly, perhaps have a few cigarettes to spare? I had a strong impression that a few cigarettes were what my life was worth. I was reaching for them, not with the best of grace, when the sound of an explosion went bouncing from cliff to cliff, sending flocks of vultures screaming into the sky.

Ramón swung about.

"A rat in the trap, by Jesus." He started off in the direction of the bang, but after a dozen paces came back for the cigarettes.

"You'd better get the hell out."

I, for one, needed no urging.

Later, while we were admiring the view from the wretched adobe hut where Matosas had passed most of his life, two men went by carrying a crudely improvised stretcher on which lay the rat who had blundered into the guerrillas' trap. As they retreated downhill in the direction of the *monasterio* I glimpsed the bald head of Nero with its laurel-wreath of curly hair.

"*Los guerreros* must be in a merciful mood today." My guide turned away, apparently not much interested in so trivial an event.

"Merciful, hell," commented Paulo years later, in the days before I gave up wasting my precious paper to quiz him on such matters. "We sent him back to his masters as a warning. Him and his right foot in a paper bag. We didn't get too many snoopers after that."

Nero apparently had set out to follow us, but without my knowledge my guide had taken a roundabout route and given him the slip. He had entered La Red thinking we must be ahead of him. Had I not been guided by Dámaso's friend, I might well have met with the same fate. Or worse. All paths but one through the rocky defile were booby-trapped. That one was guarded by the rifles of Ramón and his comrades. Nero's guardian devil, according to Paulo, must have placed the large rock that deflected the explosion downward, so that it merely severed one foot and crushed the other, which was later amputated. Thus he lived to snoop another day, albeit in a sedentary capacity.

He owed his life to the intervention of Paulo, who had passed through the defile only a few hours ahead of us. It was his first assertion of authority in the three-month-long contention for the leadership of the insurgent forces scattered throughout La Red. The guerrillas, including the self-styled colonel, Guillermo Monteverde de Lorca, gathered around the injured intruder and had decided to shoot him when Paulo pushed aside the gun of Ramón, who was eager for the role of executioner.

"Why waste ammunition? It's hard enough to come by, God knows. Send him back as a present to El Presidente." The logic of this was hard to refute. It was applauded by all but Monteverde, who conceded with ill grace.

The arrival of Nero, footloose, so to speak, his disjoined member wrapped in oilcloth and stuffed into a bag bearing the words OTRA GANGA DEL SUPERMERCADO DEL NUEVO MUNDO,* sent an additional message to President Dominguín which gradually became clear in the ensuing weeks. The armed resistance to his rule would henceforth take a new direction and be prosecuted with escalating ferocity and daring; a process that would culminate, for Dominguín, in the fulmination of the unfortunate Peluche.

It was widely assumed, both here and abroad, that the insurgents would follow up their assassination of the president by forcibly taking over the government, but this had never been their intention. "How can you fight the government if you *are* the government?" philosophized Paulo. "How can you fight tyranny when you are the tyrant?" Or, as a shrewd and knowledgeable British journalist put it: "Assumption of power would presuppose a desire for stability and an intent to bring a preconceived ideology to the process of governing. The insurgents have no such desire, and the only ideology to which they subscribe is the ideology of violent disruption. They seek not to please but to provoke the people; not to achieve good and

---

*Another bargain from the New World Supermarket.

184

just government but to invite repression. They have no vision beyond the violent overthrow of what exists."

Paulo conceded that this lack of ultimate motive or of a sustaining vision, common to violent so-called revolutionary movements around the world, had a microcosmic equivalent in each of the men and women who formed their ranks. Just as most of those organizations began as genuine spontaneous demands for a better life through better government and were led into the quicksands of anarchy and random violence, so did their individual members find that their pursuit of various ideals through violent means degenerated into the pursuit of violence itself. They became, as Paulo himself put it, "good at their business". So good that the requirement for a motive or a justification would cramp their style. The job of a terrorist, asserted Paulo, is to terrorize. You don't have to define your enemy. Your enemy is everyone who tolerates the existing order. Including those you love? Especially those. Christ said to love your enemies but he didn't say you shouldn't blow them all to hell.

XXIII

"Love is a form of cowardice," Paulo said another time. It was a chilling philosophy, but one that he did not hesitate, when the time came, to put into practice, or to impose upon his followers. Ramón, among others. And Tán.

Tán, of course, was not in any sense a follower. He was the guerrillas' foot in the enemy camp. In his capacity as popular hero of professed revolutionary sympathies he lent a certain appearance of legitimacy to their cause. He was tolerated by the authorities, who probably regarded his performances as a sort of safety valve for the harmless release of popular discontent, his ballads as palliative rather than inflammatory. For years they were unaware that his frequent foreign tours afforded opportunities for him to act as "ambassador" for the rebel forces, carrying on clandestine discussions with representatives of terrorist factions in a dozen countries, arranging shipments of arms, enrolling Paulo's recruits at guerrilla training-camps, and planning combined operations.

I'll let Paulo tell that painful story of Tán—and it was painful, I could tell, despite Paulo's vaunted callousness. His words and the occasion of the telling are still very clear in my mind. So clear that as it comes back to me it seems that today's oppressive silence is but a pause in his rambling, vehement outpouring, and that if I turn a little from the light I shall see him sitting there hunched over his forgotten bowl of beans, his gaze following the ghosts of the actors in that bygone drama.

"Cowardice, sí. A denial of hard reality. An attempt to escape, to delude oneself, to create a dream-world of sentiment and complacency. It's a sort of selfish religion. You set up your little god or goddess and evolve your own convenient ethic."

Somewhere outside I heard the halfwit's unmelodious singing: "De quién llora mi niña esta noche?" Who is my girl crying for tonight? I tried not to speculate on that.

"Tán was old enough to know better. Did know better. There was something wilful in the way he threw himself into that affair. He'd had women enough before. I'm not the one to fault him there, God knows. Even though my mother was one of them." He passed over this so quickly, evidently regretting having let it slip out, that I almost missed the note of bitterness. "Hell, I lost count of my own women. It's an indulgence in a way, but it's also part of the business. Couldn't have got anywhere without their insane devotion. In his line of work it was a little different, but it's all part of the legend. A 'great love' can help the legend along provided it's as conditional in private as it is unrestrained in public. Which is what I thought was happening for a time. All that sickening stuff in the glossy magazines. You know: 'Jonatán cancels concert to be with ailing María.' 'María says it's for always: wants her lover's baby.' We chuckled over that, Ramón and I. It was no chuckling matter. She was insanely jealous, for one thing, and demanding as hell."

While he mumbled and blasphemed over this and searched for words to pick at this long-enduring sore there came to me, sudden and inexplicable as the biblical tongues of fire, the certainty that Paulo himself had not been untouched by jealousy, was perhaps even now experiencing its pangs. I laid aside my pencil and looked at him in astonishment. But before I could think of a way of needling him into betraying the existence of that improbable emotion, he spat well wide of the bucket and began again.

"Cancelling a concert was one thing. Missing that meeting with Seibling in Switzerland was something else. It cost us a whole crate of Tokarev revolvers and MP5s and God knows how much ammunition and explosives. Worse than that, it damaged our reputation for dependability. In our business, reliability is everything."

"Honour among thieves," I said, but of course he didn't hear me. He suddenly awoke to the presence of the bowl on his knees and began to eat. I turned away.

"Everything," he repeated, drooling bean juice down his beard. "D'you think I'd be here now if I hadn't been able to depend on others to meet their obligations?"

The irony of this question, considering where "here" was, seemed to escape him.

"More than once my life has depended on finding a gun in a prearranged hiding-place, or a car waiting for me as agreed with some unknown person at the end of a telephone five hundred miles away. I took a team into Israel. Five of us. The whole thing would have been a fiasco and we'd all have been left out in the open, defenceless as clay pigeons, if a girl hadn't happened to be sitting on a certain park bench at a certain time, ready to walk away and leave her shopping-bag for one of us to pick up."

He belched mightily and tossed the bean bowl to the floor. "Tán, the bastard, knew this as well as anyone."

In the vehemence with which he brought out this "bastard" I detected all the anguish of the affair. Tán, in the years following the death of Paulo's mother, had been the one constant in Paulo's life; a mentor at first and subsequently something of an idol, although of course neither of them would have acknowledged such a shameful attachment. But even while they built up the myth of a dispassionate relationship, schooling themselves and each other in its painful exigencies, they were forging an emotional bond far too deep in the bedrock of the heart for reason or casuistry ever to root it out. Tán was, after all, an extension, an enduring influence, of Paulo's mother.

"After all, it's a form of betrayal, isn't it? In Paris I shot a valuable member of my team at the very first hint that he was on the point of selling out. As soon as a person allows something or someone to become more important in his life than the cause he's committed to—or even *as* important— he's too dangerous to have around."

Up to this point Paulo had seemed to be only marginally aware of me, but now he straightened up and jabbed a finger at me as though I were the betrayer.

"That's why you would never have been any good to us. Maar thought otherwise, but I could tell from the start."

Well, thanks, I thought. So that was my best friend's estimate of me. That he had not recruited me for the Cause might have been considered something to be thankful for had I not ended up in the same predicament as him anyway.

All the time Paulo was speaking I was remembering how Jonatán and María had been lionized, their relationship exalted into something mythical, far beyond the emotional range of mere mortals. Together and apart they were hounded by reporters and photographers as though they were royalty. One seldom opened a magazine or a newspaper without coming upon their picture or a headline epitomizing their Olympian lives. At the end of Tán's concerts the crowd would shout "María! María! María!" When she was present, her appearance would be greeted with applause even more thunderous than had been accorded the concert itself. "A song, María!" they would cry, but she always blew them kisses and declined.

Perhaps she thought her sort of music and his would not mix. She was establishing her own reputation as a coloratura. Cynics observed that the rise in popularity of the opera was attributable to the crowd-pleasing performances of Jonatán. This was unfair to María, who had one of those magnificently clear voices that are heard three or four times in a century, and people who had little taste for opera were going to hear her even before the secret of her romance was discovered; to hear especially the incredibly pure and long-sustained high notes that would one day make her, the critic Donato Alvear predicted, "the toast of Europe". When Tán's less sophisticated audience cried, "Sing, María!" it was these notes, which were reputed to have broken three glass shades on the opera-house chandelier, that they wanted to hear. But, "Tán's career is his, and mine's mine," she told reporters. She added mischievously, "If I sing at his concerts he'll start asking for a part in *Tosca*."

All this would have made it impossible for a man less resourceful than Tán to carry on his clandestine activities in support of the insurgents. No doubt it was this in part that persuaded him to keep his affair with María secret as long as possible, although there can be no doubt that despite all the hyperbole their attachment was genuine and deep. That in itself would have been reason enough to maintain the privacy of their relationship. It was a secret less easy to keep, however, than that of his terrorist connection.

After a lengthy interval Paulo took it up again with, it seemed to me, a certain belligerence, as though he had to overcome some obstinate doubt of mine.

"But all that romantic crap aside, I learned in a roundabout way that there was a real possibility that the French authorities were on to him. That was a possibility I wasn't prepared to live with."

"Presumed guilty until proved innocent," I muttered. "Some justice."

He left me to infer that this suspected penetration of Tán's cover, which he had to admit was never confirmed, was in some way attributable to his affair with María.

"Tán wasn't the sort of man you could quietly pack off to a retirement villa in Libya, any more than I was. Besides . . . "

In this unpursued "besides" lay the clear implication that Tán was not merely to be snatched out of harm's way, as was usually the practice in such cases. He had to be "disciplined". That was Paulo's word on an earlier occasion. Tán had to become, I commented unheard, a well-disciplined corpse.

Revenge was called for. Paulo would not admit even to himself that the score to be settled was in any way a personal one. Hatred was an emotion to be despised like any other.

But as he spoke of it here in this cell there was something in his very objectivity that hinted at animosities far deeper than could be explained by Tán's "betrayal" of the Cause through his allegiance to María.

When I remembered the venom with which Paulo had brought out the words "Even though my mother was one of them," it came to me that whatever the cause of his bitterness, he could not bring himself to talk about it without abandoning his cherished pose of heartlessness. But I *knew*. Not of course in any precise factual sense, but as he sat there silent, seeking a way through the minefield of his forsworn emotions, I grasped in essence what he declined to tell me.

Afterwards I realized how hints and promptings that had passed me by, some of them going all the way back to those latter days in Cambridge, now crystallized about the glimpse he had given me of a worm in the apple of his relationship with Tán. Those passages in his mother's letters that had been passed over in more than mere silence. Moods that had come upon him. And of course, more recently, a word dropped here, a sentence half finished there.

I resist, strong though it is, my novelist's temptation to flesh out this intuitive knowledge of mine. What it comes down to is a belief amounting to certainty that during that period between his mother's release from the "sanatorium" and her tragic death a passion flared up between her and Tán the destructive intensity of which could be accounted for only by her long years of emotional privation. In Tán's case, the flare-up was brief. He was fickle and open to frequent temptation. He would remain fickle until the advent of María. But for Elena this was her life's one great love. She would not lightly relinquish it. And truly has it been said that hell hath no fury . . .

All this Paulo must have deduced from his mother's letters, but it would only have been during those last years that he would have grounds to suspect that there had been more to it than that. Seeds sown perhaps by the disgruntled "Colonel" Monteverde. What form Elena's hellish fury took can never be known, but its sting must have been sharp enough to prompt a gesture of retaliation. A gesture whose consequences got out of hand. Even Paulo could not have believed that Tán was in any way actively involved in the attack on the Hacienda

Martínez, but at best he failed to take steps to avert it when he clearly saw it coming; at worst, he set in train by a word in the right place a series of events that he could not control, and that went beyond anything he could possibly in his most vengeful moments have dreamed of. Paulo once let slip that at the time of the attack Tán had not, as he had let it be assumed, been on a professional tour, but was on a hastily arranged "holiday" in Mexico, which suggests, though it does not prove, that he had prior knowledge of the impending raid.

I can picture the scene up there in La Red when Tán's fate was being debated. Ramón, who neither despised nor bridled his emotions, clamouring to be allowed to "go down there and blow the bastard away as soon as he steps off the plane". Monteverde, still resentful at the way Paulo had usurped his leadership but at the same time no less vociferous when it came to matters of strategy, pressing for action equally swift but more spectacular. He had Paulo's sense of drama but not his imagination and finesse. The others, chafing with boredom after a period of inactivity, loudly backing the call for an immediate strike. Tán, with his wealth, his luxurious and apparently safe life, was no hero of theirs. Besides, it was a test of Paulo's own commitment, a challenge. Paulo had made himself more thoroughly a peasant than themselves, while to them Tán was a dilettante, a music-hall revolutionary, all sound and no substance. Not being privy to the full extent of Tán's role and thus being unaware how vital it was to their own, they rejoiced at the prospect of his downfall. The sooner the better.

Paulo, with a greater personal stake in the affair than anyone, was determined to move more slowly. He was well aware that his reluctance might be misconstrued, but he insisted on waiting.

"Since it has to be done, let's consider how it can be done to our greatest advantage." Merely shooting a man was not Paulo's style. Not any more. He had, as Monteverde sourly observed, to make a big production of it.

"Christ, man," said Paulo quietly, addressing Monteverde but turning his back on him, "can't you see that if we handle it right it will look as though *they* did it?"

There was a murmur of admiring assent. Even Ramón nodded agreement. Monteverde maintained a sullen silence. They had not long to wait. As if by the grace of whatever gods ordained the affairs of terrorists, Tán announced that he and María had decided to yield to popular pressure (and no doubt the pressure of his manager) and hold a joint concert. When the applause that greeted this announcement had subsided enough for him to resume, Tán came to the front of the stage and started a near-riot by adding, "And immediately after the concert, María and I will be married."

Since he had no opportunity to say more because of the noise, the details had to await the next morning's papers. As part of the program, Tán would sing a song he had written especially for María. Then they would sing together, giving him, he said, a chance to prove that he had "a real voice". The program would conclude with María, in her wedding-gown, singing her most famous and popular aria. The bride would then be borne on a float "resembling Cleopatra's barge" to the cathedral across the plaza for the marriage ceremony.

It was billed as "The Musical and Social Event of the Century". While the more conservative critics faulted María for "stooping to consort with Philistines", there were others who heralded it as the confluence of two great streams of musical tradition, predicting a potent new renaissance of operatic performance and composition.

As Paulo spoke scathingly of the fanaticism generated by this joint performance, I remembered how excited Nina had been, insistent that we attend. Tickets, which doubled as invitations to the wedding, were sold out as soon as they went on sale. Nina procured two for us through her influential friends, but even their power could not propel us beyond the second row from the back, where we sat wedged between a group of tipsy students and a dozen girls fresh from their shift at the nearby meat-packing factory. "Fresh" is hardly the felicitous word: the odours of their recent employment wafted over us as they leapt up to applaud wildly at the end of every song. In the rare moments of calm they hurled seductive insults at the students.

What Nina called my "stodginess" had placed me firmly on the side of the stick-in-the-muds from the start, and two hours among that undisciplined riff-raff was not calculated to enhance my faith in the confluence of the two great streams of musical tradition. The only renaissance I foresaw was in youthful hooliganism and dark-continent aesthetics. I held my peace, however. My bride was not yet won. And indeed I must shamefully confess that as Tán sang the honeyed words of his paean to his own bride-to-be and Nina's hand crept into mine, I was close to being carried along on the tide of popular sentiment. I even allowed myself to be yanked to my feet to stand there feeling foolish during the long pandemonium of applause.

Tán sang well enough. Alone, that is. María was of course magnificent. Their duets, however, did not seem to me to merit the violent enthusiasm of the audience. Tán's voice, in my inexpert opinion, would never be acclaimed as "real" in the operatic sense. But the obvious depth and sincerity of their feeling for each other tended to mask all imperfections. It was, as the morning papers would observe several inches down from their black banner headlines, "an unforgettable performance".

Unforgettable, indeed.

When María appeared in her wedding-gown for her finale the audience rose as one and there was a sudden silence more powerfully emotional than all the preceding uproar. She stood there resplendent, accepting the homage of that fraught stillness. Tán, standing beside and a little behind her, looked upon her with boyish wonder.

The silence stretched, seeming to congeal about us as the lights dimmed, so that we stood there as though embalmed in it, breathless. In my memory of that scene there is a fearful portent in that total absence of sound. We were all being purged, sucked dry of aural sensation, in readiness to receive the sound to come.

Not, I mean, the pure, soft notes of María, the spotlight finding tears in her eyes as she turned to Tán and began to sing. There were tears in other eyes, too, perhaps even mine. Nina wept without restraint.

Nor the incredibly high note in preparation for which María seemed to reach out and absorb energy and resolve from us all as we stood in thrall. Bouquets showered upon her from the front rows as though sucked prematurely from the hands that held them by the great undercurrent of the common will.

No, not that soaring, tenuous sound but that other, which in retrospect I cannot make myself hear, but of which I receive visual proof in the way the flowers lift and scatter, in the way María's dress for a moment streams in the wind; the wind that even while her pure note lingers as if in defiance of that other satanic sound picks both her and her bridegroom up and flings them, a rag-doll Peter Pan and Wendy, to opposite ends of the stage. Petals fill the sulphurous air and a red rain falls upon the black-tie audience in the stalls.

That scene of horror obtrudes itself from time to time into my remembrance, always forcing upon my attention some grotesque detail not observed at the time: a drum sailing out of the orchestra pit and bouncing up the aisle; a pipe-playing cherub coming adrift from its perch over the proscenium and falling upon the shiny bald head of the conductor; an urn on the low wall beside the performers splitting neatly into two and vanishing, leaving the precise halves of its shape punched, several metres apart, in the gaudy backdrop depicting the bulls of Pamplona.

I close my eyes upon the ensuing pandemonium. This after all is Paulo's story, and from Paulo's point of view the operation was eminently successful. Not only did El General and his rightist thug supporters appear in the popular mind as the perpetrators, despite all protestations and some clear evidence to the contrary, but the resulting bloody demonstrations across the country provoked an inevitable military response and the imposition of the draconian measures that have endured ever since.

"Exactly," said Paulo, ambling over to smite me painfully on the shoulder, "according to the book." His tone was smug, triumphant, like a lawyer's clinching his case with an obscure but telling precedent. The book, I knew from his earlier rambling, was Carlos Marighella's *Mini-Manual for Urban Guerrillas*.

There was, and is, endless speculation concerning the affair. Where was the explosive device concealed? How was it set off? By whom? Paulo, crouching there on his bench (left here in the cell, complete with his unwashed blanket, as if

to afford me the companionship of his garrulous ghost), filled
this dank hole with a staccato clucking sound that could only
have been laughter, mirthless and chilling though it was.

"Soberbio! Perfectisimo!"

By which I took him to mean not only that the plan and
its execution were flawless but that the joy of fooling the
authorities and the newspaper "know-it-alls" was exquisite,
the icing on the cake of his triumph. He was especially tickled
by the theories of two experts, one of whom said the explosives were concealed in one of the bouquets thrown at María,
while the other calculated that the bomb must have weighed
three kilos or more. Whoever threw that weighty tribute,
Paulo commented, would have had to be so close that he
would have risked blowing his own head off. Paulo had
always been contemptuous of that sort of suicidal fanaticism—what he called the lemming mentality—even during
his days in the Middle East, where it was much admired. I
had heard him ridicule it years before in discussions with Maar
and Hafiz, when it all seemed remote and highly theoretical.
It was crude, he had insisted, the resort of the unimaginative.
A sort of inverted bullying. It was doing by blundering, blind
force what should be done with subtlety and finesse.

To none of the experts and amateur theorists did it occur
that for a voice that could shatter glass lampshades, the tripping of an acoustic detonator would be, as Paulo put it, reaching back to the public-bar slang of sixties Cambridge, "a piece
of cake".

XXIV

I fear that I may be falling victim to what my colleague Juan
Moreno used to call the Magic Mountain syndrome, that
phenomenon by which one becomes so inured to one's situation, however wretched, that any prospect of change is
contemplated with alarm, even terror. Men long incarcerated
have been known to commit crimes simply to regain the security of the prison routine to which they have been conditioned.
Juan used the expression satirically in reference to his galling

state of wedlock, which, despite the threats and blandishments of a younger, more compatible mistress, he could not bring himself to renounce.

Not, of course, that I am confronted with any choice, or that I would opt to stay here if I were, but the unvarying routine of write, eat, sleep, write, eat, sleep has accreted around me a sort of shell that accepts perfectly the painfully sensitive, etiolated organism that I have become.

Recalling how in the unremitting press of academic and social activity I used to joke about fleeing to some remote island that would furnish only the bare essentials for my serenity—food, shelter, and writing materials—I now realize that it was a joke only because such a decisive measure was beyond me. And that having "enjoyed" those basic necessities for what must now be months, a fearful lethargy, a near-paralysis of the will, has descended upon me, and I have caught myself more than once in the delusion that my continued presence here is in some convoluted way the result of my own procrastination. No, that's not quite it. That I am procrastinating about *wanting* to be free. A state of mind I snap myself out of by recalling that the Cheshire Cat may at any moment summon me for catechism.

The condition I am trying to define is the mental equivalent of the atrophying of an unused limb or the deterioration of a neglected skill, a state in which it becomes increasingly comfortable to accept the limitation even as one dreams of transcending it.

For of course I dream. I dream of mountains and rivers and fleecy-clouded skies. I dream of fields and browsing cattle and the steamy, extravagant splendour at the fringes of the rain forest, from which my father made his fortune (and so was able to send me to Cambridge to meet Paulo). I dream of market-day in Mezlán, a kaleidoscopic scene of swarming colour, rebozos and sarapes and multicoloured merchandise. I dream of children at play in the Recreo García, lovers whispering beneath the big umbrellas of the cafés along the Avenida de la Independencia, kites flying over the treetops of the city park.

I dream of Nina. In happier times. Happier, I mean, in terms of the sanctity of our relationship. If, indeed, we can still be said to have one. I think of her now as though I were dead, dreaming as perhaps the dead dream of the blessings enjoyed while living. Except that she knows I'm not dead. In a nice moral dilemma, is she not? She betrays me for my own salvation. And probably seals my miserable fate in the process.

But when it comes to fidelity, who am I to be so censorious? I who dreamed—and dream—so fondly of Eliza? True, my lusting after her had about it a certain redeeming aura of sanctity, as though her being young enough to be my daughter elevated it into a thing of the spirit only. My thoughts of her were reverent, manifested as an exquisite ache of the heart, but perhaps this means that I was not more chaste in my yearning, only more romantic.

Well, at least I now know the secret of her irresistible appeal.

I slept with my pencil in hand, dreaming of her, when the door clanged and the Cheshire Cat came to stand over me. He picked up my fallen pages and read them with evident amusement, sitting on Paulo's bench, sniffing fastidiously at the lingering stench.

"A harsh word, betrayal, to apply to one who is so solicitous of your welfare, is it not?"

I made no reply. Instead I fought off the image of him bouncing and grunting upon the fervid billows of Nina's flesh.

"*Pues bien.* There is much chaff with your grain, *mi amigo*, but that is the way of you scribblers; prone to self-indulgence, all of you. But little by little the truth comes out. After years of theorizing, the great Murder at the Opera mystery is solved and El General is cleared of all blame. A matter of no small moment. So that although you try our patience we are going to indulge you a little longer. Rosita grows restive, of course. She is bored. But her sort of persuasion does not always elicit the kind of information you trot out in the course of your rambling. To catechize, as you so wittily call it, one has to know the right questions. Names, for example. We'd like you to name more names. Recent names, I mean. But that we can safely leave to Rosita. For the present, let's put our conversation on a more civilized footing."

I cast an ironic glance over our "civilized" surroundings.

197

"Ah, yes, I should have invited you to my office. But then, perhaps you would not have been at ease out of your shell. Besides, offices have windows. Windows can be seen through, and although you may not be readily recognizable under all that hair . . . I mean, after we've denied all knowledge of you, how could it be explained? You see my difficulty?"

I saw his difficulty all right. And while he rambled on in that vein I began to see the extent of my own. If they had never acknowledged my existence, how could they ever let me go? My mind was so numbed by this—it was like a doctor's corroboration of some dire condition one has long been concealing from oneself—that I missed the start of something new he had begun to say.

What brought me back was the word *Eliza*.

". . . surprised," he was saying, sitting there hunched over, looking, on the hazy periphery of my vision, uncannily like Paulo come back to haunt me, "during our last little tête-à-tête, to find you knew so little about her. In view, I mean, of your extravagant professions of . . . " he cast about for a word to characterize my absurd infatuation and abandoned it with a shrug. "Your Nina finds it hilarious."

While I sat there thinking *you bastard, you don't need any help from Rosita*, he rose and went to stand under the window, so that I had him in fiery-fringed silhouette. "Especially in view of your obsession with her mother."

He watched me intently. It took a long time to sink in.

"*Mother?*" I said idiotically.

"By God, you really didn't know, did you?"

No, but I didn't need him to tell me now. I sat there astonished at my own blindness, seeing the faces side by side. Eliza and Martha. No spitting image but the evidence was irrefutably there. In the eyes, mainly. In the way the light fell sometimes on the tawny hair, a hint that tended to be obscured by contrast between the free-flowing abundance of Martha's and the severe straightness of Eliza's. Even in a certain way they stood, but to detect it you would need to take the skinny shape of Eliza bending down to comfort the General's baby, sketch in ample breasts where none are perceptible, enlarge with deft strokes the almost pathetically thin waist, and there you would have Martha bending that day over her dough and salting it with tears for dead Uncle Simon.

"Which of course is why she came here, to this country."

I looked at him, uncomprehending. The sun had shifted a little, tipping his aura askew. Under the dark plunge of hair one eye glowed as from a tunnel, faintly but with enough expression to suggest that he was enjoying this.

"Well, she was brought up on stories of this wonderful man, this legendary lover, this Gaspar, whom by now her mother had convinced herself she had cruelly wronged. The mother, apparently, was as obsessed with the memory of you as you were—are—with the memory of her. She no doubt laid it on a little thick to assuage her guilt at the way she treated you. And perhaps as an antidote to the memory of what happened after."

I wondered once again how he knew all this. Futile to ask. "We have ways," he would say. "You'd be surprised." I wouldn't, though. I wondered also why he was telling me, and made bold to say so. He dismissed it, however, with a small gesture of deferral.

"So it was natural, wasn't it, that the girl should make it a sort of pilgrimage, to come out here in search of her father."

I leapt up in astonishment. I do believe that in the turmoil of my emotions there was a fleeting surge of something resembling elation, as though by some latter-day virgin birth Martha could possibly have borne my child. And before I had fully come to grips with the absurdity of this there came a thought—no, a feeling merely—*but if Eliza was my daughter, what of my fantasy of becoming her lover?*

"But that's crazy," I said at last.

He turned to me so that the sun lit up his laughter.

"It is, isn't it? At least, if what you've written is true."

"It's true." Even after all those years I felt the pain of its truth.

"A natural enough mistake, though, for the girl to make, given her mother's continual singing of your praises and her silence about what happened later. Maybe in the circumstances the mother was not averse to letting the girl draw that conclusion. What harm could it possibly do? How could she have foreseen . . . ?"

But why had Eliza never avowed it? Why, even with her painful shyness, had she not ventured some word, given some sign? Was I such an ogre, after all? I began to think back over the all-too-few opportunities she had had. That evening at Doña Sofía's, for example. But as if I had posed all these questions aloud, the Cheshire Cat went on before I could find any clue.

"Still, there would surely have been an element of doubt in the girl's mind. Her mother had never come out point-blank and said it. If the subject of paternity came up—and you have to remember that the girl was still quite young—her mother would probably prevaricate, and then after a time she would begin to talk about you. So that, while she made the natural assumption, the girl must have been left with a sense of something tragic in her mother's life, something that was always obtrusively there but never spoken of.

"Anyway, she was not the sort of girl who would go up to a virtual stranger and say, 'Are you by any chance my father?' "

I conceded the point, but I had given Eliza credit for being resourceful enough to overcome that difficulty. I began to wonder where all this was leading.

It was leading, of course, to Paulo. The Cheshire Cat was investing this information, so to speak, in the hope that it would yield a return; that whatever I might be prompted to say or write by these new insights would contain some nuggets of truth which no amount of torture would elicit.

The Cheshire Cat began to pace. Six small steps to the door, six back, the narrowing band of sunlight slicing his neck at each passing like an executioner's sword.

"What she needed was a go-between. Or at least someone to advise her, and perhaps prepare the way a little."

She thought of confiding in Doña Sofía, he said. The old lady took a lively interest in the affairs of her protégées. Too lively. She would have been only too eager to take the matter in hand. But Eliza, so naïve in so many ways, was shrewd when it came to the assessment of character. Doña Sofía was a manipulator. If she took on Eliza as her current cause, the poor girl would relinquish all control of her own destiny. Besides, Doña Sofía was a gossip, and God knows what scandal might ensue if the affair went awry. If I, for example, denied everything, Eliza's inclination would be to let the matter drop. Doña Sofía, however, would be hell-bent on litigation.

During all this, Doña Sofía began to emerge in my mind as one of the Cheshire Cat's "ways of knowing", not only about Eliza but about me, about Paulo. She had doted on Nina for years; was, in fact her godmother. She knew my parents also, having been one of my father's most valued customers, or patrons as he preferred to call them. And how could she have failed, at the meridian of her social career, to be intimate with La Familia Martínez?

There was, the Cheshire Cat went on to say, one last hope for Eliza. Somewhere at the remotest edge of memory lingered a name: Paulo. It had for a long time little or no meaning for her. Then one evening, rummaging through the ancient Gladstone bag that contained the pitiful remnants of her mother's life—letters, clippings, some of Uncle Simon's poems— she came upon a photograph of me. There were others, of course, larger and more distinct. But what drew her attention to this one, passed over so often before, was that it had been cut down the centre, leaving an extraneous hand perched on my shoulder like an epaulette. A little gruesome, she remembered, to a six-year-old girl. On the back, in the writing she remembered so well, the ink now much faded, she could decipher:

My darli
and frie
Paulo
Martíne

Although the by now legendary Azote was not much referred to by his own name, even Eliza must have known who Paulo Martínez was. And at this point, as a preposterous resolve began to grow and harden in her mind, she must have blessed her stars that she had not taken Doña Sofía too far into her confidence, because this was the time when, thanks in part to the waning but still considerable influence of her *patrona*, she was being considered for the position of nanny to the General's infant son.

It was by now becoming clear to me that Eliza must have had another confidante. Although much of what the Cheshire Cat told me may well have emerged during Paulo's catechism, I found myself wondering, when I was at last alone, where Nina figured in all this. I shall not likely have another opportunity to ask. The two and two I put together may be making more than four, but is it not possible, I now ask myself, that in spite of—or even because of—her jealousy of Eliza, Nina cultivated her acquaintance, perhaps became intimate enough to elicit that sort of confidence? There would have been ample opportunity. Nina at that period spent several hours a week helping Doña Sofía sort through the material for her memoirs (which, I suspect, I was later to be pressured into writing).

At first I rejected the idea of collusion between Eliza and Nina out of hand. Surely it was inconceivable, first that Eliza would broach *that* subject with my bride of a month or so; and second that, having been told, Nina would be able to refrain from taxing me with it. But as my mind teased at it during interminable sleepless hours I amassed enough evidence in memory to satisfy me that Nina could wheedle anything out of anybody, especially a girl like Eliza. Probably when she took the first step along the confessional path, confiding that she had come to this country primarily to find her father, Eliza did not know of my relationship with Nina. And having seized hold of that one thread, Nina would pull and coax until the whole story unravelled. As for Nina's silence, two conclusions suggested themselves; one generous and the other, although unfortunately more credible, not.

The generous conclusion was that Eliza, realizing what she had blundered into, would have emphasized the lingering element of doubt, and Nina would have reserved judgement—held her fire was the metaphor that occurred to me—until that doubt was resolved. Nina would thus have had an incentive to encourage and assist Eliza in her quest for the truth. The other possibility was that, without formulating it even to herself, Nina saw my imagined guilty secret as ammunition to be stored away for future use. Distressing as those possibilities are, they could at least in part account for the Cheshire Cat's apparent insights into Eliza's secret thoughts, which, although not likely to emerge from Paulo under

Rosita's ministrations, might well be extorted by means of the sweet torture of the bedchamber.

Nina, despite her aristocratic birth and upbringing, professes to a certain qualified sympathy with the insurgent cause. She abhors violence, but if pressed will say reluctantly that desperate circumstances demand desperate measures. She usually adds that much of the violence attributed to the guerrillas is really perpetrated by reactionaries. She was fully persuaded of this in the case of the explosion that killed Tán and María. Her support for the revolutionaries is more theoretical than real, however, a thing of the drawing-room rather than the public forum. She prizes the good things of life which the status quo enables her to enjoy, seeing nothing anomalous in her enjoyment, which she would not lightly do anything to jeopardize.

If, therefore, it was she who pulled the strings, those strings must have been long indeed, and the mechanism they set in motion complicated and impenetrable. But she is good at that sort of thing. Her scheming would culminate in a meeting between Paulo and Eliza in a back room in some obscure corner of the city. Or perhaps Eliza joined the small bands of tourists who could not bear to return home without boasting that they had experienced the roller-coaster thrill of the train journey to El Platillo, where the rendezvous might take place upstairs at La Bodega Bomba. Or again, Eliza being of a somewhat pious turn, they may even have met in the privacy and security of the *monasterio*, with, of course, the blessing of the Superior.

It is not easy to imagine that meeting. Paulo, no doubt, would have relished it. Why he never boasted of it to me seemed strange and highly uncharacteristic at first. What opportunities it would have given him to gloat over and torment me. But it has to be borne in mind that he was well aware of my cowardice. He was not about to trust me with information that even Rosita had not been able to extort. Not that in all probability it would have counted for much in the ultimate weighing of his guilt or innocence, had the General deemed it politic to stage some farcical parody of justice.

Yes, Paulo would have enjoyed it: this naïve, diffident girl with the big delicate question she did not know how to ask, her eyes wide with incredulity and fear at finding herself face to face with the notorious Azote. That he was plainly repulsive to her would only add spice to his enjoyment. For her it must have been like being shut in a cage with some loathsome and potentially ferocious animal.

And as her reason for being there began to emerge, Paulo must have anticipated with malicious pleasure the sport he saw impending. "Gaspar!" I hear him shouting when she mentioned my name in oblique reference to the subject at hand. "Gaspar? You surely don't think . . . ?" I see him slap his fat thigh. "You surely don't think Gaspar got María in the family way?" For of course he would get the name wrong to convey the impression that it could not possibly be of any importance to him. "Gaspar your daddy? Why, he never even got into her bed. Told me so himself. Seemed proud of it. Can you imagine that? Honour, reverence for her chastity, all that romantic trash. No, my dear, you may rest assured he never laid your mother."

He would probably have couched it in far coarser terms, which my penchant for "romantic trash" inhibits me from using, even in the imagined presence of one so innocent as Eliza. And while she was mastering her revulsion, trying to assess the validity of his assault on her most cherished fantasy, he would drop the bombshell.

"*I* did, though."

No! No! her whole being must have cried out in anguished contradiction. She may even have said, it, the words forced out of her by a violent spasm of repugnance. "No! No!"

He would sit back, then, big hands entwined upon his belly, bushy eyebrows arched in mock surprise, a satirical twist to the lips that had once been sensual but were now gross in their fullness. He would sit there like that and let her come to it of her own accord. Like a lawyer declaring with smug nonchalance, "I rest my case," leaving the jury floundering in a sea of speculation about all the things he had so pointedly left unsaid, that he scorned to say. And around Paulo's silence as Eliza sat there in appalling confusion and distress would swarm the memories of all those other silences, all those prevarications and transparent white lies, all those conversational quicksands to be pussyfooted around for the sake of domestic peace and harmony.

It may have been during this period of—for her—agonizing reappraisal that Paulo himself underwent a change of mind. (Of heart, I almost absurdly said.) Well, of intention, at least. Perhaps in that moment the shade of Maar rose to admonish him, for the one thing he never ceased to admire about Maar was her almost clairvoyant sense of the potential usefulness of people. I gained, God knows, enough insight into the convolutions of Paulo's character to be sure he would delight in gloating to Eliza, as he had so often to me, of his conquest of Martha. In disgusting detail. But before he had indulged this sadistic impulse too far and perhaps driven her sobbing from the room vowing never to have anything to do with him again, he must have experienced that small tremor of prescience to which he ascribed his more spectacular triumphs of terror.

So he would soften to her, talk instead in reminiscent vein of Martha, of the times they had had together, recalling scenes and inventing memories. Or stealing mine. Forgetting that a few moments before he had been unable to remember her name.

He couldn't have progressed far in what he called his business if he hadn't been an actor of sorts. As witness his masquerade through Heathrow customs as a nun. No sudden transformation on this occasion of course, but by the time Eliza left he would have given her a sufficient glimpse of himself as long-lost father not to preclude the possibility of future encounters, should there appear to be any profit in it.

XXV

Eliza was probably not much in Paulo's mind during the days that followed. Nor in mine, it pains me to confess. Our preoccupations were very different, however, Paulo's and mine. I was on a trip with Nina, a sort of phase-two honeymoon, the first having been cut short by a death in her family. We went by sea to Buenos Aires and then to Rio, where we stayed for two weeks and did with sybaritic gusto all the things appropriate to a honeymoon. And more. Nina is like that. Her lust for life, and for the delights of Hymen in particular, afforded me little opportunity for errant thought. Or even errant glances. But a new bride of possessive tendency might well imagine errant thoughts and glances where there are none. And she did. In fact, such a suspicion on her part was the occasion of our first spat, and by one of those ironies apparent only in retrospect, Paulo was the cause of it.

We are lying sardine-close in the midst of a swarm of sun-worshipping humanity on the warm sands of Copacabana. Near by, a girl is softly strumming a guitar and crooning a tear-jerker ballad, accompanied off-key by a gull circling expectantly over a small boy with a bag of popcorn. The sea when I sit up is painful to look upon. Nina's hand steals out to rest provocatively upon my burning belly.

"I'd just *love* an ice cream."

Now you have to hear Nina say something like that to appreciate the incredible wealth of connotation in it, the cajoling note of promise, the augury of infinite and bountiful gratitude, and not least the flattery; you cannot leap to her service with alacrity enough, so privileged she makes you feel. Only an ice cream, her circling hand says, will cool her ardour long enough to get back to the bedroom.

I'm coming back with a cone in each hand, stepping gingerly over the baking bodies, when I'm arrested by a headline, five or six centimetres high, as scare headlines always are in this sensation-loving country: EL AZOTE ATTACKS AIRFIELD.

I'm so gripped by this and by the photograph of what looks like a building in flames that as God is my witness I do not even notice the body of the woman whose face the newspaper shades from the sun. (I see it now, of course, here in my privation: the superb breasts adorned with scraps of silk no bigger than the nipples they purport to hide, the slim waist, the smooth, soft arms alluringly sugared with sand . . .) I bend over to read the large bold type of the opening paragraph. Something about helicopters. Then the ice-cream cones, too long in the sun, drip on the glowing flesh beneath, the owner of which leaps up with a shriek, scattering the day's news, which lifts and sails out to sea on the first sportive breeze of the tide-turn.

I pass over, gladly, the ensuing hours, except to say that the ice cream, which the intonation of that word *love* had suggested was an indulgence without which Nina could no longer confront life, was dumped unceremoniously in the sand; and to say also that to escape the miasma of resentment that lay so thick and suffocating in our hotel room I stalked out to buy all the newspapers I could find, and went to a bar to read them and get petulantly drunk.

What I read, and later hazily speculated upon, was that a band of guerrillas had attacked not the airport but a nearby warehouse. For some time the army had spied upon and harassed the insurgents in La Red, using two ancient helicopters. These, however, had been out of service for several months awaiting delivery of spare parts from the United States. The helicopters themselves were well guarded, but when Paulo learned that the needed parts were being shipped it occurred to him that at some point they might be more vulnerable. This of course I learned much later. The shipment had been kept under observation by Paulo's people throughout the journey, but there had been no opportunity to act with any assurance of success. The warehouse therefore offered their last chance.

The newspaper reports were voluminous, but all I could refine from the low-grade ore of their verbiage was that "A gang of leftist thugs" had somehow gained entry to the building. ("Gang, my arse!" Paulo commented later. "There were only two of us.") Witnesses testified that there was a huge explosion and a fire, although there was some disagreement about which came first. The fire gutted the warehouse and severely damaged the buildings on either side. Later editions reported that a man with his clothing on fire had been seen to come out of the warehouse, but no one could say what had become of him.

There would be nothing to make this attack more worth my while to record than a dozen such related by Paulo during our imprisonment had it not been for the identity of the man who, according to an eye-witness, "shot out of the door burning like a Roman candle". That man was Ramón.

Paulo, musing about Ramón's fate, showed little remorse. Ramón, he said, was prone to fall over his own feet. "He knew the rules of the game. We went over and over the operation. Timed it to the split second. But Ramón, well, he could never resist the opportunity to do a little free-lancing."

Ramón survived to tell his side of the story.

Paulo's side was that they waylaid a security guard on his way to work at the warehouse, stripped him of his uniform, and dumped his body down a manhole of the city sewer. Ramón, wearing the uniform, entered the building first and disposed of the guard waiting to be relieved. He then let Paulo in through a back door and the two of them set about planting the explosives. Paulo left first. He was to go to their car, parked in a cul-de-sac nearby, wait thirty seconds, then drive to the side door of the warehouse, by which time Ramón, having set the detonator, should be ready to be picked up. They were to drive to a safe house, change clothes, and escape to their mountain retreat.

Ramón didn't show.

"I gave the bastard twenty seconds' grace. Ten seconds to the scheduled time of the bang. I hadn't gone fifty metres when she blew." He sat there, beard splayed over up-drawn knees. His eyes glowed fanatically in the last of the sunlight, seeing her blow. "Well, that was a relief, anyway. At least he hadn't screwed *that* up."

He stayed like that for a long time, the reminiscent glow fading with the light until his eyes grew dark, dark, as if repudiating that last lingering sliver of light from the world without. Then at last he said, "As I drove away I thought, 'Well, I suppose that's the way he'd have wanted to go.' "

It wasn't though. In fact Ramón didn't "go" at all. He's still alive, or was when last I had a way of knowing such things. Even during my last days of freedom I remember seeing him begging on the corner by the *panadería*. Not that I had any idea, then, who he was. There was nothing to connect this cruelly disfigured one-legged man with the bearded thug who had bruised my ribs with the barrel of his gun the day I ventured into La Red; even less to relate him to the handsome uniformed *chófer* who had procured for Paulo's father and taken his percentage on the side. I had seen him often, this pathetic travesty of a man, but he was only one of a hundred such to be seen about the city, beggars who sometimes moved me to acts of extravagant charity by the very lack of expectancy in their outstretched palms and downcast eyes. This one was memorable only for being more repulsive than the rest. I had no reason to be curious about him, or to inquire into the cause of his evil fortune.

Paulo was not able to get to the bottom of it for several months, when Ramón had won his long, excruciating battle for life and had groped his way back to something resembling sanity. He didn't, even then, want to talk about it. It was almost as if talking about it would bring it all back, not in memory merely but as a physical recurrence: the trapped-animal terror, the flames biting into his body, the long hell-fire of his delirium.

"He shrank away from me, away from my questions. You'd think the very words were white-hot needles I was bent on stabbing him with. But I got it all out of him in the end."

After Paulo left the warehouse, Ramón measured out the requisite number of seconds on his stop-watch before setting the timer. It was during this tense interval that he noticed, in a corner by the corridor through which he was to make his escape, several small drums marked PELIGRO: GASOLINA. On an impulse, as a sort of insurance against failure of the bomb, he said, when he had set the detonator he stabbed a small hole in one of the drums with the spike of his pocket-knife. He ignited a piece of paper and dropped it in the path of the slowly spreading stain on the concrete floor.

Ramón had still comfortable time to get away. In fact he stood there for a second or two to make sure the creeping stain of gasoline would reach the flame. Then off he ran down the corridor.

"If he'd just set the fuse as he was supposed to and got the hell out, he'd still have got clear with no problem, even though there was an unforeseen snag."

The unforeseen snag was an additional guard who had been put on duty that day, and it was during those few crucial seconds that he entered by the very door that Ramón was supposed to go out of. This guard must have been away in another part of the building, because he didn't seem particularly alert, or aware that anything was amiss. Until he saw Ramón. At the sight of the guard, Ramón panicked and ran. He could still get out by the small door Paulo had left by only a minute before. But just as he reached it the flame came blasting down the corridor, according to his own account, "like a bloody great blowtorch".

"He turned pale as a corpse and broke out into a sweat when he came to that part. He had nightmares, he said, every night and sometimes in the middle of the day when he was wide awake, about how the flame came curling out for him like the tongue of an enormous fire-breathing frog, intent on licking him into its inferno of a belly."

He got outside, though, and ran. No idea where. Just away. Away from that tongue of fire he was convinced was pursuing him. He ran slap into a woman with a bucket of slops. It was filthy, unspeakably foul, but it was liquid, more or less. It didn't extinguish him entirely but the woman flapped at him with her *rebozo* and got him out somehow, just as the roof of the warehouse opened up and shot a tree of fire and debris into the sky.

There was a sequel to this story that Paulo didn't tell me for a long time, wouldn't have told me at all if I hadn't rescued him from a nightmare of his own, if I hadn't literally beaten the demon out of him with my fists and shaken him into a state of semi-wakefulness. Not that nightmares were any rare occurrence for Paulo. Or me, for that matter. Usually I plugged my ears against his moans and mutterings and left him to sweat it out. But about this particular nightmare—about its physical manifestation, I mean—there was something unutterably harrowing. As well leave him writhing there in its toils as ignore the cries of a drowning child.

I couldn't make much sense of what he said at the time. It was only by returning to the attack again and again later, until he crumpled up the note I had thrust under his nose, seized me by the shoulders, and shouted, "For Christ's sake, man, leave me alone," that I was able to piece it all together. But now he was wide awake, defensive, secure behind the façade he had been a lifetime building. It was only in the first minutes of his waking, while the terror still had him by the throat, that he betrayed the sensibilities, and, it almost seemed, spoke with the voice, of the boy who had seen his own initials carved on the cross by the roadside, and had looked beyond it, down, down, into the beckoning chasm of the *barranca*.

It never became clear to me exactly who the woman was who came so timely to Ramón's rescue. Paulo at some point let fall the name Maruja, and later, Marujita, suggesting a degree of familiarity, more likely on Ramón's part than on Paulo's. She may well have been one of the peasants who had migrated to the city from the uplands around the former Hacienda Martínez after it was seized by the military and made into some sort of country club for senior officers and sycophantic politicians. She was probably too young to have been one of the *queridas* Ramón had scattered over the landscape to be visited when his rut and El Amo's did not happen to coincide. More likely the child or younger sister of one of these "sweethearts", perhaps bribed with a piece of Inés's home-made toffee to stay outside and play. My novelist's fancy suggests that she may even have been one of the ragged urchins he had seen flicking and prodding at that small boy's genitals the day Ramón had "a little business to look after"; the day Paulo had seen the old woman crapping over the cliff and heard screams coming from one of the hovels teetering on the brink. Ramón liked to talk of his "girlfriends," sometimes at tiresome length, Paulo had told me once. They must have known of one another's existence, the way gossip travelled in those parts, but he managed to make each feel that she was very special, and so was welcomed into a dozen households like a member of the family. A great favourite of the kids, he claimed. He must have spoken so much about the mother or big sister of this Maruja that even Paulo came to know the child by the diminutive. The only clue to this former intimacy that emerged from Paulo's piecemeal revelation was his reference to Ramón's last words to her before he foundered in the fiery sea of his long torment, which had become a sort of myth among the peasantry.

"God bless you, *chiquilina*. I always said you were a little angel, didn't I?"

This was followed by a sound so frightful, half moan, half scream, that it was, according to the legend, "as though he felt himself falling into hell".

Whatever Maruja's history, she must have been tuned in to what Paulo all those years ago at Cambridge had called the *telégrafo subterráneo* of that mountainous region around the Hacienda Martínez, which evidently reached out to its urban expatriates. Another thing she must have carried with her to the city was her peasant's hatred of the ruling regime. She was moved by pure compassion to get Ramón indoors and to offer what minimal comfort she could, but it must have occurred to her very quickly that a man who had emerged from a building which then blew up was, regardless of political allegiance, too hot to have around. (No tasteless pun intended.) It was a matter of urgency to determine on which side of the political fence the injured man belonged. If he was "one of them", his presence had to be reported immediately; if "one of us", then it was only a matter of time before "they" came looking for him. So, "Soldado?" she asked, made cautious perhaps by some charred vestige of his stolen uniform.

Ramón was in agony but he had not yet passed beyond reach, not yet plunged into that scalding black abyss that would engulf him with the onset of shock. His words probably came out half smothered by his moaning, but they must have been the right words, because by the time the soldiers came looking for him, Maruja was sitting quietly at her sewing and the stench of Ramón's burnt flesh had been exorcised by fumes from an enormous pot of chili.

What went on during the long hiatus Ramón had only by hearsay. He awoke—surfaced, rather, for he insisted that he found himself in another world, trapped in an alien self from which he wanted passionately to escape—in a house in the mountains, little more than a peasant *jacal* but, he would notice in time, clean and lovingly cared for, with ornaments on the shelves and pictures on the walls.

The face of the young girl looking down at him from one of the pictures would eventually penetrate the clouds of his abstraction as being vaguely familiar, but he was not for a long time in any condition to notice such things. He felt as though he had been skinned alive, and he seemed to be drowning in a nauseous odour that arose, he would discover, from his gangrenous leg, which despite the heat was covered to keep away the flies.

This was one aspect of the affair that had come back to torture Paulo in his sleep, to haunt him as not even the ministrations of Rosita had haunted him. As he tossed and fretted there upon his bench the stink of Ramón's bloated leg swirled about him like a contagion, crept into his blood and permeated his flesh until he felt like a giant slug writhing in its own slime. His dream had no clear chronology. He was there with Ramón and his smell of putrefaction even as he crept among the rocks of La Red in pursuit of the interloper. Doing, in fact, Ramón's job. A dark figure standing between him and the sun personified, somehow, the galloping corruption of his own flesh, which in the dream was Ramón's also. Some dread power emanated from the object in the hand of the stranger who was not a stranger. Paulo brought his rifle up. His flesh turned soft and spongy upon his bones and he left a meandering trail of mucus where he moved. God in the guise of Señorita Smith, thunderous of voice among the mountains, berated him, filling him with shame and self-disgust. She derided him for inhaling the assuaging smell of the stranger, who was dead but not dead. When he drew near the dead mouth opened. "Hola!" it said, over and over again, "Hola!" The dead hands seized him by the shoulders and shook him until the last fragments of flesh fell from his bones, and from the dark sockets of his skull he saw a long-ago face swooping down from the sky with predatory intent. Mine.

"For Christ's sake wake up, you crazy bastard!"

The women who had ministered to Ramón were as efficient and solicitous as Maruja had been. They were mere shapes at first, ghosts flitting in and out of his peripheral awareness, but as they gradually assumed substance he noticed that despite their kindness and concern there was a distance, a constraint. And about the place itself there was an air of gloom, even though the mountain sunlight streamed through the door and the days were loud with birdsong. Sometimes the women would weep as they went about their work. They wept in a way that made him burn with guilt and want to get away. One of them, the one with the long Indian-style braids that were always in her way—dipping into the water she brought to wash him, tangling with the yarn when she sat spinning in the corner—would stop in the midst of whatever she was about and say in an aggrieved tone, "I don't understand why she did it. I don't."

The other woman understood, though. She was the mother of whoever had done whatever Indian-braids didn't understand. Ramón knew this but he didn't know how he knew. No one had said anything about it, at least while he was conscious. The knowledge had stolen into his mind during the delirium, along with the certainty that there had sometimes been a third woman present, the one who had done the inexplicable thing. Ramón wouldn't have remembered her presence at all had it not been for this continual questioning of her motive for doing whatever she had done, and for the responsive silence of the mother which said so clearly that she understood all right but that it would be a waste of time to try to explain. When she was saying all this with her silence, her face would be ravaged by a look of afflicted love that made Ramón think of a long-forgotten picture of Mary at the foot of the cross.

It was not until after the doctor had been and cut off Ramón's leg that the older woman, whose name was Estela, warmed to him and began to talk, as though his guilt had been lodged in that diseased member and had been buried with it and covered with a huge rock to stop the goats digging it up. And perhaps to keep down the demon.

Whenever Estela was talking, the woman with the braids would loiter near by, and sometimes as if for emphasis Estela would turn upon her and interject, "Believe me, Rosa María, believe me." But after a time she appeared to forget both Ramón and Rosa María and would seem to be talking to a third person they could not see.

The "she" whose conduct was so puzzling to Rosa María was the subject of the small and somewhat faded sketch that hung on the wall and appeared to be watching Ramón all the time. One day, when she saw him returning the picture's stare, which had some sort of challenge in it, Estela reached up as if to take the picture down from the wall, changed her mind, and said, "That's her. My little girl. My daughter. *Mi pobrecita*."

"Poor little thing!" retorted Rosa María. "She's a sight bigger'n me. Was. Fatter, too."

Estela ignored this, her hands still raised to the picture as if in supplication.

"Not that fat's so bad. A man needs something to bounce on, my Pancho used to say. Something soft to wallow in."

Estela gave her a look that seemed to say that Pancho had done more than his share of bouncing and wallowing.

"Well," she said. "No one bounced on my Anita." She turned to the window, looking as though she would weep again. "Not since . . . "

She went outside to compose herself. But almost immediately she came back, announcing as if to a large gathering, "Never had nothing to do with men. And can you blame her? That was a shocking thing happened to her when she was young. Little more than a kid."

"Jesus Christ!" Ramón involuntarily sat up, howled with pain, and sank back on the bed. The two women rushed to his side, fearing some dire relapse. But he lay with closed eyes, murmuring as though once again in the grip of delirium, "That's it! That's it! The little honey girl!" And he was seeing her as he had seen her last. He had seen her and never said a word to a soul: seen her leaving that day before he found El Amo bloated and stiff in his bed, leaving not by the main gate but scaling the unused south gate, handing down her candle basket and honey bucket to the old crone who always grazed her pig along the walls of the hacienda.

"You'd better rest," Estela said with the finality of a parent evading an untimely question. She shooed Rosa María out the door and followed.

It was not until Rosa María had gone off on some errand next day that Ramón managed to get Estela talking again.

"She was a good girl, that little Ana," he offered by way of bait.

"So they all said." She seemed a little suspicious, wondering what he knew. As if it could make any difference now, after all those years.

215

"Nobody blamed her."

Her eyes were dark, appalled, as though by an indiscreet word she might open all the wounds anew, might be required to go through all that fear and foreboding again.

"It was me that found him. Puffed up like a bladder, he was."

She made a small flinching movement and turned away.

"Nobody blamed her. He had it coming, the bastard. Felt like doing him in myself once or twice."

"What a horrible thing! Ana was beside herself. Crazy she was, for weeks and weeks. She never got over it. Never. Never the same again. And the rest of us going about in terror all the time, looking over our shoulders, expecting the *polizonte* to come for her every minute. That's when my hair turned grey."

"Your hair is beautiful," he said, aware of the words' irrelevance but with a sudden pang of pity at the thought that probably no one had said such a thing to her for thirty years. It was true, too. Her hair curled in white wisps about her dark, ravaged face, pathetically childlike.

"Flowers grow well in the dung."

"Yes," he said, embarrassed by this. "Well, I found him, like I said. I found something else, too."

He waited. It was a long time before she turned back to him.

"What, then?"

"Her hair ribbon."

She came close then and stood over him, letting him see the slow fall of her tears.

"You're a good man."

"Not many think so. I'm a *terrorista*."

"One person's *terrorista* is another's *salvador*."

"Yes, well. She had a baby, I understand, our little Ana."

"Her blessing and her curse, he was. She loved him for what he was and hated him for what he would not let her forget. She doted on him, spoiled him. Went hungry herself to feed him. And then he grew up and . . . " She brushed aside the memory as though it had been a fly. "And she always said he looked like *him*. No, no, not that monster, that animal, but the little boy. The one she was sweet on."

"Paulo. Yes, I remember now. He was moony over her, too. We used to laugh about it, Inés and I."

"It sounds silly, I know, but . . . " She bent close, her eyes big with earnestness, wanting her words to belie their silly sound. "She carried the torch for him all those years, that little Paulo. 'Forget that rich brat,' I used to say. 'They're all the same.' And she'd stamp her foot like a child and say, 'He's not! He's not! He's different.' "

"And she lived to say 'I told you so.' "

"She didn't need to. He's like a god around here. An avenging god. They'd do anything for him."

"Like take care of me."

"We're honoured to do that." He watched the play of thought over her face, waited, sensing something distressing that had come to her mind. Her mind was far away in search of words.

"The ways of God are strange."

"If there is a God."

This disconcerted her. He hated himself for saying it.

"Well, perhaps it was the Devil's work. I mean, that the bad blood passed down not to Paulo but to Ana's Felipe. Little Felipe of whom she expected so much, such great things."

Ana fired him with ambition, this Felipe. He was wayward but he was willing and energetic, so that for a few years when he was old enough to work they prospered by his industry. Even Ana found a sort of grim contentment during her hours of waking, although for a long time her nights were filled with terrors. But as he approached manhood he changed. As Estela put it, you can nurture and tend the tree, but God determines whether its fruit will be sweet or sour. Where Felipe had once been proud, he became arrogant, domineering. The Martínez blood ran thick in his veins. He despised the peasants among whom he found himself, and antagonized them by saying their state of poverty was the result of their own laziness and stupidity. They were fools to think that a few malcontents skulking in the mountains could ever accomplish anything, or that things would change for the better if they did.

So no one was surprised when, as soon as he was old enough, he became a soldier. Good riddance to him, they said. His mother was distraught. Heartbroken. They parted with a bitter quarrel, not by any means the first. It had been impossible, of course, to keep the knowledge of his paternity from him. He refused to see any shame in it. During that last quarrel, when in her anguish she said, "You're cruel and heartless. Just like him," the neighbours heard him shout back, "and you're a hypocrite. It's not my fault you were a whore. You got what you deserved. And what you wanted, if you'd only be honest. Good for him, I say. At least I've got more than llama's piss in my veins." He strode out of the house and never came back.

"What became of him, then?" Ramón asked when Estela had regained her composure.

"He did well in the army. They made him an officer, even though he had no education other than what he got from her. And she was proud of him in spite of everything, even though she hated what the army stood for." She sat shaking her head, her lips quivering like a child's with the imminence of tears. "Such a waste of a young life."

"You mean he . . . ?"

"Died, yes. Killed. They said it was revenge, but I don't know. Maybe it was just one of those tricks of fate."

"Revenge?"

"Yes. Well, you must remember how they murdered that poor woman? That Señora de Martínez? And how they set fire to everything and killed just about every living thing on the place? Well, he was in charge of that. They were just supposed to kill her and rob the place and make it look like the work of bandits. But he suddenly went berserk. Or so they say. Ordered his men to destroy the whole place. Went about shooting animals, even cats. Made them put the torch to all the buildings. All except one." She paused, frowning, trying to command the facts that would make sense of it all.

"You see, he had this crazy idea, ever since he was a boy, that he was going to be some sort of saviour. A leader who would make this country great. He would have, too. It was an obsession with him."

A rat scurried across the floor. She went after it with a twig broom. She came back to the bed and stood holding the broom like a soldier with rifle at the order.

"Juana Castillo, she told us about it. She was a nurse. She looked after him and some of his men who got burned. And she told how they said he wouldn't let them burn that one building. How it would be a sort of shrine one day because he was conceived there. Only that wasn't quite the way they put it, Juana said. You know the way soldiers talk, she said. Shrine! Can you imagine it?"

He had a sense of history, evidently, this Felipe. A sense of destiny. But in the end it's God that disposes, Estela said. He sometimes sticks out his toe to trip up the proud ones. She told him that while Felipe was going about shooting animals, one of the big dogs came up behind him and took a sizeable lump out of his leg.

"Went bad on him," she said. "Just like yours. Only they managed to save his, in the end. And then when he was able to go back to duty, one day . . . "

But Ramón wasn't listening any more. He knew more about that "one day" than she did. Because he, too, had a sense of destiny. Ever since the attack on the Hacienda Martínez. He was going to get the bastard who did it. It wasn't so much the Señora, martyr though she was in the eyes of the freedom fighters. It wasn't so much the buildings and the crops and the animals needlessly slaughtered. It was poor old Inés, who'd been like a big sister.

So that by the time Estela said, little above a whisper, "And one night they found his body in the bushes near the barracks," Ramón had lived again through that two-hour wait in the shadows opposite the canteen, when he had almost botched the whole thing by following the wrong man. He had come back and eventually seen his man emerge to stand boasting loudly to another man who addressed him deferentially as Señor Teniente and had seemed disposed to talk all night. But at last they separated and Ramón, by this time a bundle of nerves, crept along the far side of the street until they reached the place where, as he had planned, he could cut across the corner of the cemetery and spring out from the bushes just as the lieutenant passed. The victim stopped, in fact, at the exact chosen spot to light a cigarette, so completely unaware of the knife poised in the air behind him that Ramón thought for one dread moment that he wasn't going to be able to do it.

And now all he could think of to say as Estela finished speaking and set about preparing their soup was, "So *that* was Ana's little *penitencia*! One of God's little jokes."

She gave him a long, puzzled look, but he left it at that.

They consumed the soup in silence, except for Estela's involuntary murmurings. Then he said, "She took it hard, no?"

She considered this for a long time, wiping her mouth on the back of her hand.

"Who knows? She shrank into herself. She did her work: cooked, cleaned, looked after the bees, went to market. She never said much. She spoke about *him* sometimes, that Martínez boy, the one she always called "the little master" when she was a girl. Sometimes it was as though she was telling a story she had learnt a long time ago. At other times you'd swear from her crazy ramblings that she thought he was still there at the hacienda, still a boy waiting for her to come with the honey. But then almost in the same breath she would speak of him as El Azote instead of El Dueño Poco. Her eyes, her whole face, would glow, like it used to as a girl when she received the blessed sacrament. As though a Scourge was a wonderful thing to be. Some sort of saint, you'd think he was, for all the innocent blood on his hands."

Ramón bridled at this. He started to say that those who are not with us, etc., and therefore no blood is innocent, but she went on unheeding.

"And I remember that she got this idea into her head that she was letting him down, that he needed her. You'd think they were two young lovers. You'd swear he was pining away for want of her, not able to keep his mind on the great work of . . . of . . . " The word eluded her. "Rosa María nudged me and giggled. I hated her for it but it did make me see Ana the way she really was, and how ridiculous it was to think of anyone pining away for the likes of her, the pitiful blighted creature. Life is cruel, what it does to us.

"But Ana jumped up from her chair and snatched her *rebozo* down from the nail as if she would rush off to find him that very minute. Then just as suddenly she sat down again and stared at the wall and seemed to forget all about it."

Ramón, exhausted, was hearing this in a semi-dream, seeing the two Anas, the pretty young Ana of her own imagining encased like some exotic fruit in the aspic of the obese, middle-aged reality. He was drifting deeper into fantasy when she said abruptly, "Until you came."

There was sufficient stress on the "you" to imply accusation. He was suddenly wide awake.

"Until I . . . ?"

"Well, she became obsessed with the idea that someone should let him know. We all did, I suppose. There is a way of doing these things but they take time. But she saw it as the call she had been waiting for. Her special mission. She shone with it.

"Madness, of course. We told her so. Refused to let her go. Watched her day and night. But she was cunning. The crazy are always cunning. And desperate. We were tired to death, watching over you, watching, watching, one of us always awake. And then one night to my eternal shame I fell asleep, and like a shot she was gone."

Ramón could not find words to frame the question. She answered it anyway.

"A couple of weeks later a young man came here. A well-spoken man from the city. Looked to me like a priest in the making. A stranger paid him, he said, to come and tell us Ana was dead." She covered her face and turned away. Through her convulsive sobbing she said, "And he handed me a package and said, 'The man who sent me said this will be proof enough.' " She took one wet hand from her face to point up at the wall.

"That was in it."

Above the sketch of Ana hung an ebony crucifix inlaid with mother-of-pearl.

"It hung over her bed all those years. I never even knew she had taken it."

The crucifix leaned out a little from the wall, as if expecting something of him. He had a fleeting image of Señora Martínez, seen from the lips up in the rear-view mirror of the limousine, her eyes, flinty-hard with rebellious determination, compelling his. And when El Amo had got out, as Ramón leaned in to assist the Señora, she hissed through her teeth, "Under the seat. Give it to Paulo." He stood at attention until, with her husband clutching her arm, she vanished through the forbidding portal of the asylum. Then he turned and brought down his fist with all his strength on the roof of the car.

Gazing up at the cruicifix, he had a long-forgotten urge to cross himself, which he resisted.

Paulo's account was reluctant, fragmented, studiously dispassionate. He was squatting on the bucket one day, bound tight and prodigally flatulent from underdone beans. I retreated to the window, but the day was still, offering no relief.

"Some of the others I couldn't trust, but Ramón with all his faults was a good watchdog. So after we lost him I took to scouting around occasionally myself to keep them on their toes. And that day I had a hunch. One of my *hormigueos*, as Inés used to call them. Going along the spine of the ridge I heard rocks falling. There was no call for anyone to be where there were loose rocks, and anyway my men were drilled to move like Indians. They wouldn't dislodge so much as a pebble. They'd deserve to get shot if they did. So I went to investigate, and there, blundering up the scree, making enough noise for a regiment, was this, well, this man. Fat, sloppy, obviously out of condition. We saw each other at the same time. There was a gun in his hand, so I shot first. Got him right in the left tit."

He looked at me quizzically, then left it there while he devoted himself with loud grunts to the business at hand. I waited.

"Yes," he went on at last, "Tit. Because when I got down there my man was a woman, wearing a peasant's cap, the sort they call a *boina*, and a pair of corduroy pants. And the gun was a goddamn crucifix. My mother's. She thrust it at me with what I suppose was meant to be a smile and said, 'Hola, Dueño Poco!' That's when I twigged who she was, when she called me 'Little Master'. Then she started to say 'Adios', but a great gout of blood came out with the word and she died."

I turned away and waited till he had finished at the bucket. When I faced him again he was wearing a specious grin.

"Almost like one of your sloppy novels, my Gaspar. Except I suppose you'd have contrived a happier ending. What a hope! Fat old bitch like that. Grey hair, half a dozen chins, smelling like cat's piss."

"Not exactly a sachet of roses yourself, were you? Not an Apollo either, for that matter."

The taunt was wasted, of course.

And that was his story. Or so I might have assumed had I not seen him writhing in torment on his sweaty pillow and heard her name wrung out of him again and again as if in response to some new triumph of sadistic ingenuity by Rosita.

Over the next few days I wasted a lot of paper plying him with questions, provocative statements, and calculated guesses, finding my replies not only in his reluctant words but in the nature of his silences and in the sort of things that aroused his anger.

Thus, little by little, I extorted from him the details of the story he had heard from Ramón and the horrors of the dream with which that story became interwoven. And little by little I became convinced beyond any possibility of doubt that in spite of the casualness of his account of it, the death of Ana at his hand had so deeply penetrated the shell of his vaunted indifference as to call the whole tenor of his life into question.

"So why," I wrote and passed to him to show that I saw through his pretence, "if it was a matter of so little importance, did you trouble to send the crucifix back to her mother?"

He gave that same derisive smile. "I just didn't want that damned fetish around. I was going to bury it with her." And then he went on a little too hastily, realizing the shameful sentiment implicit in this admission, "Besides, I wanted them to know what would happen to anyone else who came snooping around there."

He did at least give her a decent burial, then?

"Sure." He narrowed his eyes and made plain that this would be his final word. "I packed her off to the *monasterio*. They relish such absurdities." He gave me a last ambiguous look before turning away. Away from all that.

"And of course I sent flowers."

XXVI

"One last little talk, my Gaspar."

It is not, however, the voice of Paulo but the suave, insinuating tones of the Cheshire Cat. He stands looking down at me while the lout cinches up the straps. He might be a doctor making his rounds, a little bored by my humdrum case.

"What time is it, Rosita?"

Her voice is husky: might, under other circumstances, sound seductive. "Nearly four o'clock."

I have seen her before, I think, this Rosita. A woman surprisingly small of frame to accommodate a nature of such immense and joyful cruelty. Blonde hair in small, meticulous curls, metallic, like a brazen chain encircling her head. Plump cheeks and purplish lips. Not the thin lips that bespeak cruelty but pert, with a pronounced Cupid's bow. Wide, somewhat bird-like eyes, watching me now, making me feel very much the edible worm. A tip-tilted nose that gives a little rabbit-twitch at the smell of me. Yes, she is vaguely familiar. An extra from some scene in the faded drama of my past life. Hat-check girl? Waitress? Student in some long-ago class?

I indulge these pointless speculations while the Cheshire Cat stands over me, cracking his knuckles. So unnerved am I at the prospect of the ordeal to come that the ominous possibilities of his first words escape me. Only later when it is all over and the residual waves of agony are slowly subsiding as I lie alone in the darkness will the word *last* boomerang back upon my mind's ear.

"No time to waste, then. You ordered my car for five?"

"Sí, Señor." The lout seems disposed to linger for the fun, but Rosita banishes him.

"Well, now. You haven't been very forthcoming, have you? One must admire the stubbornness with which you maintain your innocence. So many common factors. So many crossings of your path with his. All coincidental, you say. You did nothing to incriminate yourself, observed nothing that might help us. Well, yes, we did take your tip and pick up that scarecrow Ramón. What a sorry mess of a man! A dubious gift you made us there. Becomes a babbling idiot if Rosita so much as shines a light in his eyes. But enough idle chatter. Rosita."

Oh Christ, the agony! In whatever sense this "little talk" is the last, I thank God for the finality. This pain is past enduring. Death, rather.

And yet, deep down, a cowardly voice demurs, posits a sickly hope.

"You know, Rosita, I'm beginning to believe him. About his innocence, I mean. What a deplorable thing! No, no, Rosita, don't be alarmed. I won't deprive you of your pleasure.

"No, Gaspar. Innocence or guilt is not our concern. Information is our business. Now, let's take it from the beginning, and see if perhaps with the aid of Rosita's little memory-jogger we can shed a little new light on . . .

"You are standing on the bridge in the park, feeding the ducks. No, before that. Why are you in the park? How did you get there? Rosita."

It works, Rosita's time machine. All my nerves are humming like enraged bees. My muscles are the strings of some instrument tightened until they twang with the imminence of breaking. I am conscious of the shape of my bones. And I soar beyond myself, laved in light, every cell of my flesh caressed by the warm cessation of pain.

I'm walking jauntily along the Calle Linterna. Actually there! I am feeling the scorch of sun, inhaling the tantalizing waft of roasting coffee from the Café Lucero, seeing ahead of me a snaking column of schoolgirls in white hats and blue uniforms being swallowed up by the dark granite maw of the Museo Nacional. Even, yes, *hearing* the faint sound of the their chatter as the big-bosomed *maestra* gestures impatiently from the top of the steps as though spooning them into the doorway.

Where are you coming from?

From Alejandro's, where I've left Nina's bicycle behind, sprocket still unfixed. I see the bicycle, its saddle set at a strange angle to accommodate Nina's ample *trasero*. Enough sunlight strays in to catch the reflectors on the pedals that go up and down eerily in the dark as she speeds away, kissed for the first time—by me, that is—and calls back . . .

He wanders, Rosita.

Blackness.

You are at Alejandro's.

Yes, an earlier time. His back is to me. I notice details. They seem forced upon my attention, as though Señora Calleja de Velasco stood again before me in kindergarten, pointing them out with her sawn-off billiard cue, demanding, "And here, Gaspar *el soñador*, what have we?" Gaspar the dreamer sees a tattoo on Alejandro's arm, just below the elbow. A nude woman with angel's wings. And to the left of that a greasy red cloth where a moment before there was no cloth, where there was . . . ? There was, before the swift magician's movement of Alejandro's hand, a flat contraption that might have been a box of big cigars, but with wires, gadgetry. Alejandro appears not to have noticed me but he is now holding a wheel, which he raises to the light and spins. I see him framed in a small mirror, not observed before, one eye closed, ostensibly checking the wheel but watching me watching him. And when I move towards the baby carriage he swings about and says, almost shouts, "Qué desea?"

What do I want? At this moment I want only to examine the luxuriously appointed interior of the carriage, fit for a prince. But why, I have time to wonder before Alejandro captures my attention, has it been necessary to strip out the bottom of the carriage in order to straighten the wheel? The padded bottom board, pale blue as befits the gender of *el nene real*, lies beside it on a newspaper on the bench.

Alejandro bemoans his forced absence from the races and deplores at length his reluctant ungodliness. But now, as if by another one of his feats of conjuring, the carriage is no longer there and with a flick of his oily finger he has spun the hands of time. It is several days later and I walk away disgruntled, sans bicycle but preternaturally observant still. I see, for example, the monstrously disfigured beggar— Ramón, but this knowledge comes to me in some mysterious manner from the future—sitting on a crate at the corner by the bakery where he often waits in hope that a stale bun or two may come his way but where today, to judge from his jumpy alertness, he sits with some secondary purpose in mind. With a minimal turn of his head he can encompass the wide, shady walk up from the river, the corner of the plaza where

Clementina presents to him a profile calculated to inflame desires such as no doubt still exist in him although beyond hope of gratification, and the wide central avenue of the park, including part of the playground. I note as I pause before him that three pairs of legs swoop at random intervals into his frame of vision and recede, one of them thrusting stamen-like from a pink flowering of skirt. To my left, the river path is empty save for a man with a dog walking swiftly towards me. Clementina, I notice, holds up a mirror, which she looks into and lowers. She turns to glance in my direction, having I suppose seen my reflection. A prospective client. I drop a coin in the box beside the beggar's foot without looking down at his pitiful approximation of a face. During the minute or so that I stand there, pretending to study the pastries in the bakery window but in truth weighing the chances of seeing Eliza if I dally in the park instead of taking the Calle San Fernando, I notice that the beggar cranes to look around me several times as though watching the progress of the man with the dog.

He's just babbling, isn't he?

Maybe, Rosita. Maybe not. No, not yet. Wait.

As I move on, the legs of the youthful swingers in the playground are eclipsed first by a yellow parasol, then by the dark bulk of the body beneath. This figure enters the park gate, pauses, turns to look back along the Calle Linterna, then walks on slowly up the avenue. The sandal-maker looks hopefully in my direction as I pass. So does Clementina. Still vacillating, I turn into San Fernando, walk swiftly along beside the park fence, stop. With sudden resolve, the image of Eliza rising compellingly before me, I duck (literally because of the arching mass of bougainvillea) into the small side gate and head for the bridge, which affords elevation enough for me to see her coming. If she does.

By the time I get there the yellow parasol blooms over one of the benches by the playing-field. I look idly around as I delve in my pocket for the remains of my lunch (Nina having been, as always, over-generous. I don't eat enough, she says). A quacking commotion as the ducks converge. Beyond the gate, a bearded, scholarly-looking man emerges from the Museo, driven out perhaps by the invasion of schoolgirls. He lingers on the steps to light a cigarette. I watch him sauntering on, unwary fly, or so I think, towards the sandal-maker's web of blandishment. I turn my attention to the ducks.

Looking again moments—minutes?—later, starting from a reverie, I see the scholar entrapped, yielding up his foot. The beggar down the block, on the far side of the street, takes a red handkerchief from his pocket, shakes it out, and mops his brow. Clementina consults her mirror again, takes off her hat, examines it critically, and puts it back on. I take out my pocket radio and place it beside me on the parapet.

Ah, yes, the radio. I noticed. Just an ordinary radio, pro*fesor, or one capable of performing other functions? Why, at that precise moment, a radio?*

I intend to tune in to the news. Today they are to announce the winner of the Nobel prize. But my watch is slow. I am too late. And in any case I catch a glimpse of—something, conceivably a baby carriage, between the bushes, on the river path. I am about to switch on the radio anyway, but my attention is caught by the melodious drip of water from the rocks into the pond and for a moment I stand there guilty beside the wedding-gowned ghost of Nina.

The man with the dog has circled the park and now stands gazing up at the towers of the *palacio.* The frump on the bench is seized by a fit of deep-throated coughing and turns to spit copiously on the grass. The beggar down the block stands and swings away on his crude home-made crutches.

Eliza comes, slowly, lingering in the shade of the moss-draped oak trees. She nods her head as she passes the yellow parasol. Her white-gloved hand rises an inch or two in diffident greeting and falls back upon the carriage handle. There is no perceptible response. The jackal follows, his eyes darting hither and yon beneath the brim of his beat-up sombrero. He saunters along, evincing interest in everything except the true object of his vigilance. He bends down one of the big hibiscus blooms and peers into it, perhaps surprising a bee at work, for he steps back suddenly and turns his attention to the playground, where a small girl, her pink dress ballooning as she swings, watches with disdain as her two companions leap down with ready fists to repel a would-be invader in a sailor suit. The yellow parasol tilts a little at the jackal's approach, further obscuring the veiled face below. Something about this person attracts the attention of the jackal, who passes, stops, turns to look back. Downright rude, I think, the way he stands and stares, taking the dowdy apparition in from the soles of the once-white shoes to the tip of the jaunty parasol.

With good reason, eh, profesor? *You know now who was concealed in that frightful get-up, of course.*

As I relive this moment, the burden of subsequent knowledge does indeed cast shadows over the scene, so that there is something agonizingly bitter-sweet in the sight of Eliza when, after watching Paulo in his ridiculous garb stump across to the door marked DAMAS, I look back to see her bending to peer in at the baby. I find even greater poignancy in the skinny, alluring shape of her.

The point is, Gaspar, did you know then?

I hear, without relinquishing the scene, without letting go of Eliza, the words of my vehement denial, shouted, it seems, from far away. I am aware of my tormentor probing around my psyche like a dentist seeking the vulnerable spot in a tooth.

No, no. El Azote is far, far from my mind as my heart goes out to Eliza. It is just that there is something . . .

Something, profesor?

Well, a strange feeling about that scruffy overdressed figure emerging now from the *servicio*. A feeling I can't account for except that as the door swings shut and a hand goes up to twitch the veil properly into place there is a darkness where one might expect the pallor of flesh. As though there is an emptiness behind that curtain of black lace.

Or a beard?

I surface briefly to consider this point, this insinuation that not only did I see and recognize a beard behind the veil but that it was no surprise. The Cheshire Cat is leaning down to look more closely at me, clearly wondering whether a little tickling from Rosita might improve my memory's eyesight.

But no. At this point, I protest, back in the hell of the present, I did not know that Paulo had grown a beard. The occasional newspaper photographs one saw of him were all of a much earlier period. And in any case nothing, no one, could have been further from my mind. I was totally, blissfully, unaware of all this furtive activity going on around me.

All? What else, then, were you unaware of?

Clearly a devious question, calculated to get me enmeshed in the confusion of my own sketchy recollections with the details I subsequently gathered from Paulo's rambling talk. But I plunge in, terrified of affording Rosita the least excuse.

I had peripherally observed, for example, the flourishing of the beggar's red handkerchief and the removal of Clementina's hat, but as I stood there idly casting my bread upon the waters I attached no importance to these two trivial acts. I had no inkling that they might have any connection with the other event that a moment or two later would engage all my attention: the advent of Eliza at the far end of the river path, presaged for me by a fleeting blue motion and a glint of chromium beyond the border of shrubbery.

It all took on a Euclidian simplicity when one knew why Paulo was sitting there got up like a bag lady. Eliza could be seen as soon as she appeared by Ramón, but not by Clementina. Paulo could see Clementina but not Ramón. Clementina could observe Ramón by means of her mirror. And so by this rather involved system of signals the complicated angles of the intersection could be monitored and the news of Eliza's coming transmitted to Paulo very much as the beacons on the hills of Britain announced the coming of the Armada.

"Clementina! Well!"

The Cheshire Cat is silent, thoughtful, trying perhaps to recollect past indiscretions, careless words uttered in the heat of passion. Rosita takes advantage of his abstraction to give me a gratuitous jolt. When the raging darkness ebbs, he is half turned away.

She greeted him, then, this Eliza. She recognized him, then? Knew who it was? Why he was there?

No, no, no. No kamikaze, our Eliza. She is clearly relaxed, contented, innocent as she saunters along, pushing her carriage. Her jackal is the jumpy one, receiving, one could swear, some malign emanation from the frowzy figure on the bench. Eliza walks on unconcerned while the jackal lingers, watches, waits with the solicitude of a lover while in the privacy of the ladies' toilet Paulo takes from his voluminous handbag and fiddles with the device that activates Alejandro's ingenious cigar-box bomb. The jackal, he of the darting eyes and the droopy moustache, the tight pants and the outrageous codpiece, gives up and reluctantly follows Eliza. What, after all, can he do, on the basis of a mere frisson?

Eliza bends over the baby carriage to peer in at the General's son and heir, wondering perhaps whether to pick him up. This gives me a retrospective frisson of my own. But instead she sits down, rocks the carriage gently. In her pale-blue dress she is decidedly skinny but I find her lovely. Her loveliness is an incurable ache within me. I watch Eliza. The jackal watches me.

I fall into a reverie, an enchantment. All the beauties of nature around me seem to emanate from the small blue figure of Eliza, rising now and walking slowly on, leaning a little to her work as the path slopes up to the gates of the *palacio* and the dark tunnel of the trees beyond. The shadows of the smaller trees she passes mould themselves caressingly about her body, relinquish her with reluctance. The imperfect carriage wheel sends forth its stream of fiery darts. The black dog comes frisking, fails with its lifted leg to quench the fire. Its owner lifts a penitent hand, shouts, "Lo siento mucho." More sorrow in it, it seems to me, than so trivial an offence appears to warrant: my painful hindsight endows his words with prescience—soon there will be occasion for sorrow.

Eliza enters the gates. Her white-gloved hand flutters acknowledgement as the sentry salutes. Her jackal follows. They are both received into the shadows. Above, the windows dazzle and flare. The flag hangs limp, and in memory there is a great portentous stillness. I linger for a moment only, noting as I turn and hurry away that the dowdy figure on the bench has vanished.

Crowded from my mind as I hasten away, late and ill-prepared for my afternoon lecture, is the image of Eliza leaning over the carriage to lift out the baby for the General, his father: one of the recurring domestic rituals against which a man of the General's vulnerability should be on constant guard. A cat, a baby: fatal chinks in the armour of inhumanity. Only today he is lucky. An importunate foreign consul delays him a little. The baby, too, is importunate, and Eliza bends to lift him out.

I am almost at the university gate when I hear the explosion.
I pause for a moment, wondering, and exchange glances with
the drowsy *vigilante*, who yawns and shrugs hugely. Such a
sound is no big thing. I shrug likewise and hurry off to
expound on the genius of Gabriel García Marquez.

XXVII

Several suns have swept a finger over the walls of the cell,
traversing slowly from the corner still fraught with reminders
of Paulo to the empty socket of Tit Rock. The rock they have
taken away, imagining perhaps that I might contrive to crush
my own skull with it. I wait and wonder. Sometimes with
fleeting, desperate hope. More often in craven terror. Hope,
only because I am yet alive. Terror because I hear, over and
over to the point of madness, the Cheshire Cat's last words.

After he had said, "I guess that's all we'll get from him,
Rosita," he called in the lout, gave me a last sardonic, unde-
cipherable look, and said, "Take care of him." Then rushed
out, his thoughts already on whatever business or pleasure
awaited him.

EPILOGUE

I came upon the pages on which the foregoing narrative was written while conducting a preliminary archaeological survey in the Herradura Valley, some fifty kilometres south-east of Leñogalpa. At the southern spur of the valley there was a deserted army outpost built over the foundation of an ancient fortress which seemed a promising place for an experimental dig. The outpost appeared to have been very hastily abandoned, presumably during the coup of last September. There was every indication that the place had been evacuated in great panic, although there was no sign of any attack. No one, apparently, had entered the buildings in the interval, and although I encountered a scene of great disorder, everything seemed to be exactly as it had been left. Some effort appeared to have been made to obliterate evidence that the place had been used for torturing prisoners, but whoever carried out these hasty measures forgot, or was unaware, that these pages contain repeated references to torture, and the apparatus described by Gaspar Sánchez was, in fact, later found.

It is probable that the officer in charge of the outpost was— perhaps by design—absent at the time of this precipitate evacuation. Among those arrested and later executed was a certain Colonel Tomás Prieto of the Policía Secreta, who, so far as I could judge from the fuzzy newspaper photographs and the somewhat sketchy descriptions in the manuscript, may well have been the man Sánchez refers to as the Cheshire Cat.

I found parts of the manuscript in several different places. I am not at all sure that I found it all, and since the pages were not numbered a great deal of guesswork and deduction went into the editing of them.

The last few pages I did not find until my second visit, when with some of my colleagues I carried out a more detailed examination of the old foundations. We were about to quit for the day when, seeing a rat emerge from a hole in the rock wall, I went idly over and shone my flashlight into the opening. At first I could see nothing but a few sheets of paper scattered about the floor. But to one side there was something white and spherical which after a time I realized with dismay was a human skull.

It took us some time to find the way down to that frightful, evil-smelling place. There we found two rude benches with mouldering, rat-gnawed mattresses on them. On one of these lay all that remained of Gaspar Sánchez. Beside him were the pages describing his last "catechism".

Several other pages lay about the floor, but they had been rendered virtually illegible by the damp they had soaked up from the earth. All I could determine from the very few decipherable words was that as he lay there, failing at last from hunger and the debilitating effects of the recent torture, he wondered about the ominous silence and the absence of the men he called the lout and the halfwit.

But what shocked me so much that my wife had to wake me to stop me shouting like the damned in the middle of the night was that all the doors leading to that foul dungeon were unlocked.

Tito Bernat Ferrer
Leñogalpa, August 1988